Praise for Denny S. [Bryce]

Wild Women and the Blues

"The music practically pours out of the pages of Denny S. Bryce's historical novel, set among the artists and dreamers of the 1920s."
—Oprah Daily

"Perfect for fans of *The Seven Husbands of Evelyn Hugo* . . . a dazzling depiction of passion, prohibition, and murder set in the nightclub scene of 1925 Chicago." —*Shelf Awareness*

"This is the best kind of historical novel: immersive, mysterious, and evocative; factual in its history and nuanced in its creativity and connection to the present." —*Ms.* magazine

"Perfect . . . Denny S. Bryce is a superstar!" —Julia Quinn, *New York Times* bestselling author of the Bridgerton series

"Travel back in time to the Jazz Age this summer with this time-hopping read. It follows two stories of a chorus girl in the 1920s and a modern-day film student, past meeting present in a book about loss, forgiveness, and joy."
—*The Pioneer Woman*, Best Books of Summer

"Evocative and entertaining!"
—Laura Kamoie, *New York Times* bestselling author

"*Wild Women and the Blues* deftly delivers what historical fiction has been missing."
—Farrah Rochon, *USA Today* bestselling author

"Immersive and exciting, Denny S. Bryce's *Wild Women and the Blues* [is] a vibrant novel that gathers elements of Chicago's jazz past together." —*Foreword Reviews*

"An ambitious and stunning debut novel . . . With a sparkling cocktail of evocative detail, world-wise characters, and heartfelt prose, Bryce celebrates the glam, danger, and promise of Chicago during the Jazz Age, giving readers an intricate, multigenerational story." —Stephanie Dray, *New York Times* bestselling author

"The author deftly weaves fiction with reality and paints a vibrant picture of the sparkling yet seedy era. . . . Perfect for fans of light historical fiction led by a complex heroine."
—*Kirkus Reviews*

"Denny S. Bryce paints a vibrant picture of the 1920s Jazz Age in this alluring and well-researched novel. Ritzy dance clubs, bootleg whiskey, chorus girls, gangsters, celebrities, secrets, and murder, *Wild Women and the Blues* has it all! A highly entertaining read!"
—Ellen Marie Wiseman, *New York Times* bestselling author of *The Orphan Collector*

"A scintillating debut that whisks you away on a gritty yet glamorous ride through Chicago's Bronzeville district during the Jazz Age . . . a highly intriguing and entertaining story."
—Jamie Beck, *Wall Street Journal* and *USA Today* bestselling author

In the Face of the Sun

"Bryce excels at placing readers in a glamorous time and place. Her 1928 LA is riveting and vibrant. Recommended for historical fiction readers who like to get lost in a time and place."
—*Booklist*

"The scenes are cinematically vivid, the language fresh and vibrant, the characters complicated and real."
—Historical Novel Society

"The author of *Wild Women and the Blues* is back with another historical fiction novel to dazzle and amaze." —*BookRiot*

"An engrossing family saga filled with heartbreak and love, victory, forgiveness, and loss, and a wonderful character study of several unforgettable women." —*All About Romance*

"Denny S. Bryce's page-turning novel opens with a murder that transports readers from Black Hollywood in the 1920s to an unforgettable road trip across the US during the 1960s. Bryce weaves the two timelines together in a fascinating story arc that leaves readers marveling at the connections between characters as the echoes of the past shape the present."
—Chanel Cleeton, *New York Times* bestselling author

"Hollywood scandal lovers, this one's for you."
—*BookRiot*, "11 Books to Read After *The Seven Husbands of Evelyn Hugo*"

THE TRIAL OF
MRS. RHINELANDER

Kensington books by Denny S. Bryce

Wild Women and the Blues
In the Face of the Sun
The Trial of Mrs. Rhinelander

Also by Denny S. Bryce

The Other Princess: A Novel of Queen Victoria's Goddaughter

Can't We Be Friends: A Novel of Ella Fitzgerald and Marilyn Monroe
(with Eliza Knight)

THE TRIAL OF MRS. RHINELANDER

DENNY S. BRYCE

KENSINGTON
PUBLISHING CORP.

www.kensingtonbooks.com

KENSINGTON BOOKS are published by
Kensington Publishing Corp.
900 Third Avenue
New York, NY 10022

All Kensington titles, imprints, and distributed lines are available at special quantity discounts for bulk purchases for sales promotion, premiums,
fund-raising, educational, or institutional use.

This book is a work of fiction. Names, characters, businesses, organizations, places, events, and incidents either are the product of the author's
imagination or are used fictitiously. Any resemblance to actual persons,
living or dead, events, or locales is entirely coincidental.

To the extent that the image or images on the cover of this book depict
a person or persons, such person or persons are merely models, and are
not intended to portray any character or characters featured in the book.

Special book excerpts or customized printings can also be created to fit
specific needs. For details, write or phone the office of the Kensington Sales
Manager: Kensington Publishing Corp., 900 Third Avenue, New York,
NY 10022. Attn. Sales Department. Phone: 1-800-221-2647.

Kensington and the K logo Reg. U.S. Pat. & TM Off.

ISBN: 978-1-4967-3788-5 (ebook)

ISBN: 978-1-4967-3787-8

First Kensington Trade Paperback Printing: August 2024

10 9 8 7 6 5 4 3 2 1

Printed in the United States of America

For Sharon Shackelford Campbell,
my dearest friend

PROLOGUE

ALICE BEATRICE JONES

1943

I grew up around rich people. So I knew how ornery they could be and how poorly they treated those who weren't them. The wealthy believed that what they wanted, thought, and said was what everyone should want, think, or say.

Nothing mattered to New York's café society but the four hundred, those illustrious members of the *Social Register*, the acclaimed list of New York's wealthiest and most elite.

I'd learned a lot about the rich by sixteen, working in most of the mansions, estates, and summer homes in Westchester County. I cared for their children, cleaned their kitchens, scrubbed their bathroom bowls, and mopped their floors on my hands and knees.

I could tell the difference between old money, like the Huguenots, and new money (seemingly everyone else), or the robber barons, the gangsters and politicians, who corralled bucketloads of ill-gotten gains.

Domestic. Maid. Servant. Everything they asked me to do— paid me pennies to do—I did with my head down and my lips sealed, other than to mumble, "Yes, ma'am" or "Yes, sir." So, how come in the summer of 1921, when I was twenty-two years old and feeling like a spinster, I lost the ability to see what was in front of me?

That summer, I worked at the Orchard School in Stamford, Connecticut, a private live-in clinic for young people from wealthy New York families. The students—or patients, as some of the staff (including me) called them—were a particular lot. Their parents had shipped them away from their fancy New York homes because they had trouble learning things like controlling their tempers, overeating or not eating, or getting a sentence out of their mouths without stammering.

I first met Leonard "Kip" Rhinelander in the school's cafeteria. I was clearing his food tray when I stopped doing my job to stare at him.

He wasn't the most handsome fella I'd ever seen, more Charlie Chaplin than Douglas Fairbanks. Although he wasn't short, his shoulders and hands belonged to a tall man. Still, his nose was too broad, his chin wobbly as Jell-O, and his eyes, though I couldn't get a good look with his head down, appeared too close together like those of one of those hoodlums from Hell's Kitchen my father hated.

But he was a spiffy dresser, decked out like Joe Brooks, the consummate Fifth Avenue New Yorker in his waistcoat, sack suit, and wing-tip lace-up oxfords. Pretending to pick up a dropped fork or knife, I peeked at his shoes under the table.

He also wore a Swarovski gold collar bar and a Cartier Santos-Dumont wristwatch, which every stylish man wore, and the icing on the showing-off-my-wealth cake.

I lifted another student's tray but kept an eye on Rhinelander. I liked his hair. He wore it like Rudolph Valentino—with a side part and slicked back away from his face.

Ab-So-lute-ly. He was one of them.

He must've felt my unabated gaze, for he raised his head, looked directly at me, and smiled. Just the ordinary run-of-the-mill smile and not like he was cock of the walk. He grinned at me with the friendliest expression.

Usually, while working for rich people, if our eyes met, I'd quickly lower my gaze or turn away, but this time, I couldn't. I was frozen.

The smile was dazzling, but it was the eyes that had my feet stuck on the floor. They were a shade of blue I'd never seen. Like the sky over the Hudson on a clear day. But no. More beautiful than that, more stunning than sky.

The Star of Bombay—that was it. The violet-blue sapphire Douglas Fairbanks gave as a gift to his wife Mary Pickford. I'd never seen the 182-carat gemstone, but from how it was described in the newspaper, I imagined it to be the same color as Mr. Rhinelander's eyes—which sparkled like scattered pieces of cut glass caught in the moonlight.

I couldn't stop staring, not at all the behavior of a proper cleanup girl.

Then, *bang! Crash.* An explosion of dishes smashed and broke into pieces on the hardwood floor.

Someone had dropped a tray, but it wasn't me. Thank God. I had hung on to mine. But the noise—that loud, startling noise—broke the spell. I blinked, and—hallelujah—my feet weren't glued to the floor anymore. I was free to walk away.

I didn't speak to him that day. Nor did he speak to me. But his easy smile. The friendly nod. And for a few seconds, I had that strange feeling of being on equal footing with a young, wealthy man. I wasn't a servant, born to wait on him hand and foot, and it caught me off guard. I didn't like surprises.

It was 1921, and I had a future. I was the middle child, born in America, of immigrant parents. The only home I knew was in New Rochelle, New York, Westchester County.

I came from sturdy English stock, and I'd fulfill my parents' dreams and never fail them or myself. And by God, it would take more than a rich boy with pretty eyes and a kind smile to flip my lid.

You could bet your bottom dollar on that.

And I had—*once upon a time.*

PART 1

—◆—

MY AUNT ALICE

The New York Times

March 18, 1940

MAJ. RHINELANDER DIES IN LONG BEACH:
Member of One of This City's Oldest Families Stricken
at 74 After Operation LARGE OWNER OF REALTY
A Veteran of the Old Seventh Regiment—An Ancestor
Came as Exile in 1686.

CHAPTER 1

———◆———

ROBERTA

1940

Ida B. Wells. Nellie Bly. Marvel Cunningham. Pioneers of investigative journalism. Women who cut a path in the newspaper industry—a path I plan to rip wide open one day.

Who am I?

I'm Roberta Brooks. And I have talent. I don't mean to boast, but some people (my mother mostly) call it a gift.

I find the truth, the heart, the center, the why and how of a thing. The story behind the story is the only story I want to tell.

I know it's pretty bold for a twenty-year-old to say such things, but it's as if truth has set up shop in my bones. I am full of conviction, righteousness, persistence, and a firm hatred of injustice and deceit; my enemies are lies, liars, and deception. And I am proud of my stubborn belief in myself.

It's 1940, and women shouldn't turn a timid cheek to oppression, especially us Negro gals. We must stand tall and be even more resilient, which is precisely what I do. Usually.

However, this morning, I was not as courageous as my mother raised me to be.

I've been sitting in this office on the third floor of the *New York Amsterdam News* for thirty minutes, waiting for the proverbial shoe to drop—although it may be an anvil rather than a strappy leather pump.

Holden Richards, the weekly newspaper's city editor, the golden boy of Negro news (he wrote something courageous a decade or so ago), summoned me to his office late yesterday to set up a nine o'clock meeting for no reason I can think of . . . other than to fire me.

By the way, this would be a tragedy magnified by the fact that I have no idea why he'd do such a thing. Or why he'd make me wait thirty minutes to do it.

So I sit with a gulp in my throat, my hands in my lap, and my knees pressed together like a child waiting for a spanking. *Obediently silent. Obediently still. Obediently invisible.*

A sudden change of position on the other side of the desk, and my spine snaps to attention. I'm about to be seen, perhaps even spoken to.

As my thoughts race, I brace myself for disaster: What do I say to "You are fired"? Say thank you and then get up and leave? No. I can't give up. I'll fight for my job and give him a piece of my mind, too. He's losing one of the stars of female journalism (potentially), and he needs to know it.

I am ready to wage war, but anticipation dissolves when nothing happens other than a man reaching for his coffee cup (which must be cold by now) and then turning the pages of another newspaper.

Doesn't he remember that I am here?

The moment passes. Mr. Richards pushes his glasses up on his nose. He's not going to speak to me. Not yet, and all I can do is stare at the top of his head.

I've seen his face a thousand times before and will recognize him if he ever looks up. The strong nose, flirtatious brow, chiseled jawline, and perfectly trimmed mustache cause some to say Holden Richards is the most handsome man in Harlem. But I don't care about rumors. I want to find out why I'm in his office before I upchuck on the floor.

I hate being ignored. I want to yell at him to stop riffling through the papers on his desk, lift his head, and look at me. *Come on. You can do it. What do you say, Mr. Richards? Are you going to fire me or not?*

I close my eyes and take a deep breath, allowing some semblance of logic to enter my thoughts. As I do, a calmness comes over me, and I ask myself: *Why would the city editor of the* Amsterdam News *fire me?*

I'm girl Friday to Ann Petry, writer of "The Lighter Side" column, a society gossip rag. A tell-all on the happenings in Sugar Hill among the Negro rich and powerful. I'm not a reporter yet. I'm just another busy assistant racing about, trying her best to keep up with the workload.

Now, if Ms. Petry was to stroll into Mr. Richards's office, I'd panic. But it's Tuesday, and she took the day off.

"Ms. Brooks."

Did someone say something? I think I'm dreaming when I hear my name. That explains why the next time it is spoken it's so loud I nearly leap out of my chair.

"Ms. Brooks!"

"Yes, sir." I swallow the squeal in my throat.

"Sorry to make you wait, but I was checking the newspaper reports, making sure there was no conflicting information on a certain subject. As a weekly, we must scour the dailies. Sometimes we get story leads from them, but sometimes they can lead us astray."

I manage to grimace a smile, but he doesn't return it.

I am doomed.

He clears his throat. "I was surprised to learn that you've been keeping secrets from us."

"Secrets?" I am confused. "I don't have any secrets."

His gaze drills into me. "How about your relationship with Alice Beatrice Jones? She's your aunt, isn't she?"

My stomach drops. Why is he asking about her? Perhaps I didn't hear him correctly. My aunt Alice is not someone I talk about and, surely, not someone who fills my heart with pride. More like I'm ashamed to be related to her and, frankly, would never utter her name unless . . .

Damn. "Yes, she's my mother's sister. But that's not a secret." The lie slips from my mouth as if slathered in grease. "I just don't talk about her at work." I smile, praying for an end to the discussion of my aunt.

The infamous Alice Jones spent years with her name on the front page of newspapers across the country, telling lies about who she was and what she wanted. Lies that hurt my parents and me. Unforgivable lies. Denying her race and her ambitions. A woman I haven't seen in two years but haven't spoken to in ten years. Which is as long as I've blamed her for every bad day my mother and father have lived through.

I slump in the seat. It's my fault. Mr. Richards learning about my aunt and me is because I mentioned my secret last Friday while having drinks with my coworkers Gabby and Crystal. They're the only ones that could've told him. *Damn them to hell.*

That's what I get for trying to fit in, running my mouth about my infamous aunt. I swore them to silence, but what was I thinking? Newspapers aren't a place for secrets.

"Your aunt has agreed to see you on Thursday."

"Excuse me?" Another round of panic I can feel in my scalp and at the back of my eyeballs, and it's spreading to every bone and muscle in my body. "See me for what?"

"Don't worry, Ms. Brooks. This is good news. Ann Petry has told me you are a talented young woman who will make a fine reporter one day. So we thought this little project and your connection to Ms. Jones would be the perfect outing for you. Right up your alley."

How dare he grin as he reaches for his coffee. I hope it's bitter cold by now, and when he sips and frowns, I feel a small jolt of satisfaction as he places the cup back in the saucer.

"I did have to swear to Ann that the city desk wouldn't

need you for more than a day or so. And I'm sure that's all you'll need."

"You want me to meet with my aunt?" I am still stuck. "Why? I mean, what could I possibly talk to her about?"

"Not so much talk but encourage, Roberta. May I call you Roberta?"

My nod is a reaction more than consent. "Of course, but why? I mean, she hasn't been in the news in a decade. Has something happened?"

"Smart. Yes. Something has occurred. We want her re-action to the death of Commodore Philip Rhinelander." He reaches for a pack of Chesterfields and shakes out a smoke. "You know her history with the Rhinelander brood." He smirks. "Fifteen years ago, the entire family was part of the most riveting news stories in New York history." He smiles and lights his Chesterfield. "Think of this as a way to test your chops. For one day, I want you to think of yourself as a full-time reporter. And if you are successful, and your aunt agrees to an interview, who knows what might be next for you." His chuckle is meant to be encouraging, but his eyes are hidden behind cigarette smoke and the only things that stick in my head from his spiel are the ifs, ands, and the silent buts.

"Do you think anyone cares what she has to say after fif-teen years?," I ask, my frustration boiling over. "Other than an article a few years back when she was fined for speed-ing and supposedly driving drunk. But it wasn't front-page news, but a half dozen local papers, including the *Amster-dam News*, carried it."

"Uh-huh. You are aware of the news stories about your aunt."

"Not really," I say, striving to sound indifferent and regret-ting my outburst. "My mother keeps a scrapbook. I stumbled upon it a while back."

"I sense reluctance. Do you not wish to help us with this? Is there a problem between you and your aunt?"

Just like a newspaperman. Digging. Digging. Digging. Fishing and threatening all at once. I'm not sure I like Mr. Richards. I don't have to be a brain surgeon to figure out there will be consequences if I refuse.

"No, sir. There is no problem. Just want to make sure I understand the assignment. That's all."

"Excellent. I am thrilled to have you on board."

I smile weakly. "Yes, sir. Of course, sir."

"You had me worried there for a few moments. We were up a creek without a paddle without you." He takes another puff of his cigarette before stubbing it out in the ashtray. "Rhinelander died on Saturday, and the newspaper reached out to Alice, I mean, your aunt, for a comment, but it was a fast and flat no. Frankly, I was surprised."

He lights another cigarette. "She had refused our request, but then I mentioned that you worked here and perhaps you could convince her to be interviewed—and well, she agreed."

"Does she know I'm not a reporter?"

He laughs. "Yes, she knows. All I want you to do is talk to her and see if you can convince her to talk to one of the reporters or me. I'll do the interview. Tell her that."

My chin twitches. Every ounce of me wants to say no.

"Now, are you sure you're in?" he asks with a broad smile.

I want to yell, *Hell no*, but— "Of course, I'm in."

"Very good." He leans forward, elbows on the desk, fingers intertwined. "Now, if she feels like talking to you about the commodore's death—just take notes. If the opportunity to do a preliminary interview presents itself, be ready. We'll use them as a guide."

"I don't know anything about Commodore Rhinelander, Mr. Richards."

"That's okay. I'll give you tomorrow morning off to do some research. Thumb through the *Amsterdam News* archives. Go to the library and review old dailies. You were a child when this story broke, but you're a newspaperwoman now. And that means you never go into a situation ignorant of what is common knowledge." His grin is like a dirty glass covered with dark smudges and fingerprints.

"You mean if I get her talking, I should interview her?" I don't like what I am about to say, but I say it. "If that's the case, I should dig into the Rhinelanders before I meet with her."

He pounds the table triumphantly. "That's exactly what I mean, Roberta." Reclining in his chair, he folds his arms across his chest. "I knew you'd help us out."

I don't respond. The reality of what is happening has landed on my back, and I need to get out of Mr. Richards's office, which I think is his thought, too.

He picks up the telephone receiver and pushes a button. A woman answers—his secretary, Mrs. Moore. He presses another button. "Was there anything else?" he says to me.

I shrug.

"Okay, then. We're done here."

I rise and backpedal toward the door. "Thank you, sir. Thank you very much."

CHAPTER 2

I hurry out of the fourth-floor office and do my best to strut through the hallway as if I don't have a care in the world. But when I reach the stairwell, I'm hopping down steps two at a time as if my pumps are on fire.

How did this happen to me? How did I go from barely thinking about my aunt Alice (without my stomach churning) to being tasked with persuading her to talk about something I don't want to talk about?

There is only one flight of stairs to go, but I'm moving too quickly—my heel slips. I grab hold of the railing before I tumble headfirst down the last few steps and have the entire newsroom witness my shame.

Thankfully, uninjured, I stand erect, straighten my skirt, and gather my wits. I can't walk into a newsroom discombobulated.

I fill my lungs with as much air as possible, open the door, and step into the sun-streaked first floor of the *Amsterdam News*.

I avoid eye contact and don't greet a single soul. But as I stride across the room, no one gives me as much as a glance, which is strange and disappointing after putting so much effort into not causing a scene.

Damn.

Someone, please explain why I behave this way. Is it the voice in my ear? Constantly repeating the same three commands: *Tell them who you are, Roberta. Tell them what you want. Tell them why you matter.*

Was it my contrary ego that drove me to tell Crystal and Gabby about my aunt?

I'm a few feet from my desk, but everyone I pass by is overly animated. Some are even shouting. Slowly, awareness settles in.

It's Tuesday. This week's edition of the *Amsterdam News* will hit newsstands on Wednesday, so reporters, stringers, and typesetters are circling editorial desks like wolves on the prowl. The newsroom is a madhouse and will remain so until tomorrow's issue is put to bed.

I blame Mr. Richards for my forgetfulness and march toward the far corner of the newsroom, where my desk is hidden behind a row of metal file cabinets. Although, I can't help but glance at Crystal and Gabby. Then I proceed to walk by them without a word.

I finally reach my desk, my thoughts racing. Did I agree to meet with my aunt, the woman whose lies and selfishness destroyed her family's and my parents' lives? I swore I'd never see her again, but now, before the end of the week, I will. What should I do? Study the story in the newspaper as Mr. Richards suggested. Or deal with the pain in my heart?

I grab a sheet of carbon and paper and stuff them into the typewriter carriage. My fingers hover over the keyboard as I contemplate beginning my letter of resignation, but quickly I change my mind. Quitting is foolhardy.

I've wanted to be a reporter as long as I can remember. Digging for answers is in my blood. I should look at this from another angle a conversation with a woman as notorious as my aunt Alice could speed up the clock on my career.

I snatch the carbon out of the carriage.

Now what? Should I sit here all day and pretend I'm working? I stare at the telephone. I could call my mother and tell her about my new assignment for the newspaper. But that would open a can of worms the size of alligators. I refuse to hurt her any more than she has been by bringing up her sister.

Then I'll have to lie to my mother. Or perhaps, a white lie of omission. I just won't mention the planned visit to Aunt Alice. Sounds like a good idea. But what if Aunt Alice contacts her big sister, Emily, after all these years?

The Jones sisters—my mother, Emily; Aunt Alice; and Aunt Gracie—haven't seen one another or spoken in two years, since my grandmother's funeral, where they barely looked at one another. I know because I kept eagle eyes on them that day. They would not have a chance to upset my mother with their pettiness and lies.

But it wouldn't be easy keeping this from my mother. She and I have talked about everything since I was a little girl, as young as six. How can I not tell her?

Truth runs through my veins, and I hate lies and liars, but I may have met my match in my aunt Alice.

Sitting at my desk, I block out the noise surrounding me and bury myself in a memory, but not one about my aunt Alice. It's about my mother and a redheaded boy.

It happened at the Baylor Castle in Westchester County, where Momma was a lady's maid and Papa worked as the family's chauffeur and butler. One day, Momma scolded me in front of the entire household (or that's how it felt) for hiding in a shed in the backyard.

She reprimanded me often (I was a handful), but never as she did that day. When I got older, I understood better why she had to show white folks that her child wasn't a trouble-maker. My mother might've been as light-skinned as a white woman, but I was almost as brown as my father. My mother had to prove she could handle her Negro baby girl—prove she was a disciplinarian and that the Baylor family shouldn't fear me. Momma would make sure I acted right.

The public talking-to humiliated me, but it didn't stop me from hiding in that shed again. I had a good reason. The Baylor's oldest son, Teddy, a year my senior, had the fowl habit of lifting my skirt to see my undergarments.

The following day, my mother found me in that same shed, but my punishment wasn't a verbal spanking. She asked Papa to break off a tree branch and make a switch, and on that day, Momma gave me my first whupping. It stung awful badly, but I refused to allow one tear to fall from my eyes. Except, I must admit, no one would've noticed if it had, for I kept my head down, unable to look at anyone. Shame was a cross on my back, but I had learned a lesson.

I stopped hiding from Teddy. The next time he asked to see my bloomers, I showed them to him and then punched him in the nose. That was the last time I was welcome at the Baylor estate. From then on, I stayed with my father's mother or her neighbor who lived across the hall. There were even times when Aunt Alice watched over me.

When I told my mother why I'd struck Teddy, her eyes filled with tears; hitting was wrong, she explained, but she added, "I'm proud you stood up for yourself and defended your dignity." She kissed me on the cheek. "You've got a good head on your shoulders, Betty." (That's what my family used to call me when I was a child.) "You are the best of us and don't forget it. But next time, let me know when someone bothers you. If you're in trouble, I'll always be there to help."

Something possessed me at that moment. "And when you're in trouble, I expect you'll do the same with me."

She hugged me to her bosom, and I wrapped my arms around her. We made a pact that day. One we kept for the longest time.

I decided. There is nothing to tell Momma until after I meet with Aunt Alice. My trip to New Rochelle might be uneventful. My mother need not ever know.

Aunt Alice won't call her to discuss a visit from her estranged niece. Momma won't telephone Aunt Alice on a whim to catch up.

Now, I'll do as Mr. Richards suggested and focus on Commodore Rhinelander.

I could visit the archives at the *Amsterdam News*, which would have a lot of information. But, I'm not interested in having more people at work know about my relationship with Alice Jones.

I pick up the telephone receiver and dial Ethel Ray Campbell, a high school friend who was a senior when I was in my first year. She is a librarian. If anyone can help me beef up on Commodore Philip Rhinelander, she's the one.

CHAPTER 3

I leave the apartment I share with my mother before the sun can make its mark on the horizon. It is a cold, windy morning as I slog my way to the Lenox Avenue subway station, but I can't dawdle. I hate cold weather. My body detests it. I am happiest in warm sunshine and sniffing spring flowers but hateful when smothered by icy breezes rolling off the Hudson River.

Walking briskly, I am at least prepared for the cold with layers of wool—a brown tweed Chanel suit, a knitted cardigan with an embroidered blue butterfly on the breast pocket, and a thick wool coat with a fake-fur collar buttoned to the throat. I also slipped on my favorite pair of kid gloves, a cream-colored soft leather in the gauntlet style. Just in case a brutal breeze tries to run up my coat sleeves.

My Dutch beret has ear flaps tied snuggly beneath my chin. It might be the most unattractive outer garment I own. My pin-curled victory rolls hairstyle will suffer, but sacrifices must be made.

Chased by gusts of frozen wind, I reach the subway entrance and race down the long flight of stairs to the platform, arriving as my train to 135th Street pulls in. Miraculously, there is an open seat, and I collapse on the bench and remove my Dutch beret, but only to check my curls. I have to hurry.

My destination is the street branch of the New York Public Library, the home of the Division of Negro History, Literature and Prints. A seemingly unlikely branch for what I'm looking for, but my friend works there. She'll find what I need.

When I exit the subway, I break into a run.

Ethel Ray is meeting me at the employee entrance in the library's loading dock. As I turn the corner, she is holding the door open with one hand and waving me in with the other.

"Are you all right?"

I'm panting and feel as if I have an icicle dangling from the edge of my beret. I can't reply until I catch my breath and we're inside out of the cold.

"Since the day we met, you've had trouble with chilly days." She shuts the door behind me.

I smile stiffly. "I feel as if I walked naked from the subway."

She laughs. "You'll warm up soon enough, dear." She takes my gloved hand and leads me into a hallway.

"Thank you for doing this," I say.

"You're welcome, but I'm not sure what I'm doing other than providing you with some information about Philip Rhinelander. I've gathered a few artifacts, old newspapers, and academic journals for you to peruse."

She walks ahead briskly, her long legs outpacing my shorter ones. I skip to keep up.

"You know he died," I say, trotting behind her.

"I read that. Passed away on Saturday, leaving only one living direct descendant, his daughter, Adelaide."

"The only one?"

She stops in front of a door with a sign that reads: STAFF LOUNGE. "I set up a room for you. Let's get settled, have a cup of joe, and then we'll dive in."

She removes a set of keys from her suit pocket, jiggles the lock, opens the door, and enters. I linger in the archway. The room is a perfect square with no windows or shelves, but a sparkly chandelier hangs from an obscenely high ceiling. A rolling cart piled with newspapers and books is pushed against a wall. Two mahogany desks are stacked with manila folders and cardboard boxes, large enough to hold more folders and smaller boxes.

I step inside but don't travel too far. Despite the height of the ceiling, the room is tiny, chilly, crowded, and airless, and the smell of linseed oil is so thick it wrinkles my nose.

"The cleaning people are overzealous," Ethel Ray says, noticing my hesitation and assuming the smell has me glued to the entrance. She gestures for me to take a seat, which I do. "I'm curious. Why is an editorial assistant to a society columnist who writes about the Negro elite in Sugar Hill interested in Commodore Rhinelander? What's the connection?"

I had hoped she wouldn't ask that question. "It's a reporter's job to ask questions," I say, smiling. "Isn't it?"

Ethel Ray turns toward the table with the coffeepot and a plate of pastries. "If you don't wish to answer me, just say so."

"Oh, come on. That's not it."

"Uh-huh." Ethel Ray pours two cups of coffee. "Sugar and cream? Danish?"

"You didn't have to go to all this trouble," I say. "Black is fine."

She places the coffee and sweets in front of me. "Spending time with you is never trouble unless you hide something from me." Her gaze is deadly serious. She's been a trusted friend for years. Someone I rely on. Someone with whom I can discuss things I can't with my parents, like politics, women's rights, civil rights, jazz, and poetry, or my aunt Alice.

My leg shakes under the table.

She sits across from me, hands wrapped around her coffee cup. I owe her the whole story. "Okay, here's the deal. Holden Richards, the city editor at *Amsterdam News*, gave me the morning off to do this research."

"I know Holden," she says.

I nearly knock over my coffee cup. "You're not close friends or, heaven forbid, dating him, are you?"

"Lord, no." She chuckles. "Every librarian in the city knows him or someone at the *Amsterdam News*. Reporters love to research, including Holden Richards."

I lick the dryness from my lips. "Well, he arranged for me to meet with my aunt Alice tomorrow."

Ethel Ray's eyes widen. "Your famous aunt Alice." She blinks. "Oh, I see. That's why the interest in the commodore. It's the only reason the *Amsterdam News* would be interested in the real estate king of New York."

"Did they call him that?"

"He was one of them. But that doesn't matter. I want to hear more about this meeting." She pushes her coffee cup and Danish aside and rests her elbows on the table. Her gaze is intense. "Are you going to do it?"

"The newspaper had approached Aunt Alice for an interview about Philip Rhinelander's death, but she refused. Then Mr. Richards told her I'd be the one to visit her and chat, and she agreed." I sit back in my chair and wait for her reaction to what I've said so far. But Ethel Ray is speechless. She twists her mouth from one side to the other.

"So, what do you think?" I ask, my voice shaking slightly.

"What's important is what you think and what you decide. And I ask again. Are you going to do it?" Ethel Ray's gaze drills into me.

I swallow. "Yes, I'm going to Pelham Road to see my aunt tomorrow."

"Wow." She shrugs. "I'm not surprised she wants to see you, but I bet she won't talk about Philip Rhinelander."

I sigh. "Maybe. But if she does talk to me about him, Mr. Richards implied that I could run with it."

"And interview her yourself on behalf of the newspaper?" Ethel Ray leans back in her chair. "If that happens, you need to be ready. Start reading." She points at the rolling cart and the stack of documents on the desk. "Newspaper articles and books about the man and his family are there. The particulars about the trial are here." She pats a stack of newspapers. "Her relationship with the commodore, you'll have to get from the horse's mouth."

I notice the tension in her voice. "This bothers you. That's why I hesitated to tell you everything."

"I worry about you, Roberta, not Holden Richards or your aunt Alice. You're the one who burst into tears whenever our friends mentioned their fathers in high school. And that was when he and your mother had been separated for five years. And I'm not sure anything has changed with you since then. You're still hoping they'll reunite and give you back your fairy tale of a home life again. But you're twenty years old." Her fingers drum on the tabletop. "Then again, God only knows. Maybe sitting down with your aunt will be good for you."

"That's not why I'm doing this. There's not one damn word she can say about my parents that will change what happened—or who she is. What matters is getting her to agree to an interview with the *Amsterdam News* or letting me interview her about Rhinelander."

Ethel Ray downs her coffee and smacks her lips. "Then you need to get to it. There's a lot to riffle through about the Rhinelanders." She nods at boxes and newspapers stacked throughout the small room. "You'll find plenty to munch on in these stacks. It'll help you, and I quote, 'dig for the story in the story.' The story behind the headlines."

I chuckle. "Do you remember every word I've ever said?"

"Only the important words."

CHAPTER 4

Pelham Road is an uncluttered block, different from what I remember. I pause halfway to the house, looking for what has changed from what remains the same.

A beautiful cone-shaped red maple tree has always been where it is, but the hedges dividing the yards are sparse, and not because of the season. They are simply unkempt.

It is deathly quiet, too—no sounds of children's laughter or gossiping women. No people. No traffic and only a few parked cars.

This street had never been so empty and lifeless before.

When I was young, people, photographers, and newspaper reporters hid in bushes, sat on stoops, or stood in front of the Joneses' house, waiting for the comings and goings of the family that lived at 763 Pelham Road. Not that they could see much from certain angles. The residence was behind a grocery store, a small shop run by the Mitchell sisters. Two elderly women who smelled of allspice, cinnamon, and clove, the flavor of the Wrigley's chewing gum they loved to munch on. I don't know why I remember them, perhaps because they were friendly gray-haired women and immigrants, like my mother's parents, my grandparents.

As if stepping out of a dream, I suddenly am on the front porch of Aunt Alice's house on Pelham Road.

The unpleasant taste at the back of my throat fluctuates between sour and bitter. My fingers curl into a fist, and I lift my arm, poised to knock, until I spot a doorbell. But before I reach for it, the door creaks open, seemingly of its own will.

"Roberta. I've been waiting for you." The voice is husky but soft; the murmured words are barely audible. But it's her. No one else is left in the house but her.

"Aunt Alice?"

Footsteps echo, fading as she moves deeper into the house. She's left the door ajar, which is likely as much of an invitation to enter as I'll receive. I push it open but don't move. The foyer is too dark. But it's not a cloudy day. The sun is shining brightly in the midmorning sky. Aunt Alice must have closed her venetian blinds tightly and hung heavy curtains over the windows.

"Are you coming in or staying out?" she rasps. "Whatever you choose, hurry up. You're letting the heat out, standing there with the door open."

I peer into the darkness but am drawn toward the sunlit walkway. I am reluctant to let go of the daylight. "It's difficult to know where to plant my foot," I say. "Would you mind switching on a light?" I don't want to give orders, but how can she see anything?

Then a match flame flickers, and a cigarette's fiery tip blazes. "Give it a minute," she says. "Your eyes will adjust."

I close the door, and she is right. My vision clears slightly.

Aunt Alice is on the opposite end of the living room. Only a hint of her profile is visible, but I can tell from her posture, the tilt of her head, and the length of her neck that she is as attractive as the newspaper articles boasted fifteen years ago. Slender but not too thin. Tall but not gangly. The tallest of the three sisters, she is statuesque and damn fashionable, too, in an expensive suit I swear I saw on the cover of last month's *Vogue* magazine.

"Are you going to stand there all day?" She gestures over

her shoulder, and I wonder if she has eyes in the back of her head.

I feel my way to the edge of the living room in fits and starts.

"Now, don't diddle dawdle."

"Yes, ma'am. Of course, ma'am." I scamper forward, tripping over my feet. Embarrassed, I consider apologizing. But why? She can't see me with her back turned.

I was in this house many times as a child, my parents holding on to me tight as if I'd vanish if they loosened their grip.

Once upon a time, the family enjoyed each other's company. Thanksgiving. Christmas. Easter Sunday. The smell of pastries baking. Boiled ham and potatoes on the stove. We were a close family, a loving family.

I take another step forward. I can see her better now.

Her hair is a mid-length feathered bob, curling prettily below her earlobes and brushing the sides of her neck. The color is auburn, a bold choice. Almost the same color as mine if I didn't dye it black, the color of midnight, my mother says: *Like a starless sky, stark but eye-catching against your light brown skin.*

Aunt Alice's reddish-brown hair looks vibrant against her almost white skin, but I prefer her natural black hair. It was black at her mother's funeral; a few strands escaped the veil she wore.

"Thank you for allowing me to visit you," I say. "I thought you might change your mind."

"I did. Every time I received a telegram or telephone call from the *Amsterdam News*, I said no."

I was referring to me. "But you changed your mind this time?"

"I haven't changed my mind about anything. I agreed to a visit from my niece. That's all."

I take off my wool coat, gloves, and Dutch beret, place

them on the coatrack in the entryway, and move forward on stiff legs.

The living room is smaller than I remember, and the furniture has changed. Two lounge chairs, a mahogany-trimmed Georgian sofa, and a two-tier coffee table—different from my grandparents' furniture—overwhelm the room, leaving little space to move about. However, Aunt Alice lives alone and probably doesn't have guests often, if at all. At the funeral, Aunt Gracie called her a recluse.

But I wonder. For someone who prefers to be alone, she's dressed up mighty fancy. Why bother owning *Vogue* fashions when there's no one to see her?

Unless she dressed up for me.

"Stop lingering."

Her sharp tone jars me into the present, but I don't sit. I stroll over to the unlit fireplace.

"How is your mother? Is she well?"

The question makes me feel like a ton of bricks are tied to my chest. She could call her if she wanted to know about my mother's well-being, but they don't talk on the telephone. "She was fine when I left the apartment this morning."

"And you? How are you? A City College graduate, top of your class. Congratulations. First in the family to attend college. I didn't get to finish high school. Daddy insisted I start working. The only job I could get was cleaning up after rich people—never something I wanted. Who would want to do such a thing?"

"My mother. She's worked as a maid all her life."

Aunt Alice smacks her lips. "Oh, that's right. I forgot she still cleans up after people for a living."

Damn it. What was that remark about? How dare she judge anyone in my family, especially my mother.

My chest is heaving. We're not long-lost relatives playing catch-up. We haven't seen each other, except at a funeral, because I can't stand being in the same room with her. My face feels hot. Poor little me. I will fizzle if I can't control my temper.

I backpedal from the fireplace. "City College was great." I must focus on the reason I'm here. "Major Rhinelander died."

"I know. Holden told me when he called, and I told him I don't give a fuck."

I gasp. It's not the word she used but the intensity in her tone, as if she wanted to wield the sword that slayed him.

"You sound bitter."

She lifts the edge of one of the window curtains. A thin stream of light slips into the room for a brief moment. "I'm not bitter. I'm telling the truth."

"Is that why you refused to do an interview? You didn't want to speak unkindly of the dead?"

She's so jittery, as if she's missing her cigarette smoke.

"Aren't you a clever girl, Roberta? Asking ridiculous questions to get a rise out of me. Don't bother. Nothing upsets me anymore."

I wet my lips, taking her words as a challenge. "I wouldn't think so after all you've been through." I ease toward the sofa, sit, and cross my legs. "The commodore was like a dictator, from what I read. Ruled over his children with an iron hand."

Her hard laugh has no rhythm. "That's also true. But I am not interested in talking about him, remember? Your cleverness aside." She puts out what's left of her cigarette and opens the curtains and blinds. It is like seeing her for the first time.

"You look like Hedy Lamarr."

"Oh, I do? Who is that? Is she pretty?"

"Very pretty. She's beautiful." I am immediately embarrassed. Why would I blurt out such a thing? "She's a Hollywood film actress."

"Oh, so she's white?"

"She is."

Aunt Alice suddenly closes the curtains and the blinds, strolls to the coffee table, and picks up a gold cigarette case. She snaps it open, removes a cig, and saunters to the window.

She doesn't say anything. I don't say anything. The silence is deafening. Why did I mention Hedy Lamarr? We remain quiet for as long as I can take it.

"I realize you don't wish to talk about the commodore, but I've done some research. How about you just listen? You can raise your hand if I've got anything wrong."

"I don't like that idea."

"Come on," I coax her. "I'm asking you to listen. That's all. You married a wealthy white man in 1924 and were front-page news a month after the wedding. Then you were in court with lawyers, his and yours, refusing to take the witness stand—"

"Stop it. Stop talking," she snaps, her chin quivering. "Do you want to be a reporter that badly? I told you I don't want to discuss Philip Rhinelander, which means the entire family. None of them. And if you can't do that, get out."

The rage inside me has grown since I walked into the house, devouring my resolve to keep our conversation professional. Suddenly, I am on my feet. "How dare you talk to me that way. How dare you." My voice trembles. "Not after what you've done. Not after how you and the Rhinelanders destroyed my parents' lives?"

She steps back, bumping her leg on the coffee table and wincing as she moves toward the fireplace.

"Is that what your mother says? I didn't do anything to her or her husband."

"What? How can you stand there and lie to me? My father walked out on us because you made my mother choose—her Negro husband or you, passing for a white woman you could never be. You disrespected our race and shamed my parents. But what did you care? You got what you wanted: fame and

Rhinelander money." I wave my hand at the room. "But look at you now. What do you have? A lonely, pitiful life. Where are your friends? You dress up in the latest fashions, but for what? You don't have any place to go. No one cares about Alice Beatrice Jones."

"Get out." Her voice is low and deadly. "Get out of my house!"

I grab my coat and hat from the hall rack. Within seconds, I am out the door and halfway down the block before it hits me—what did I accomplish? Did she agree to be interviewed? Did she talk about the commodore? I accomplished absolutely nothing and may have lost my job to boot.

What in the hell is wrong with me?

A stupid question, but an easy one to answer: Alice Beatrice Jones. She's what's wrong with me—her and her damn lies.

PART 2

LENNY

CHAPTER 5

―・◆・―

ALICE

1921

A golden monarch landed on the black-eyed center of a white lion daisy. The tapestry of colors was languid and lovely, like the slow flap of a bald eagle's wings over open water in winter.

It reminded me of when our father would take us girls fishing. As we sat in the small boat, waiting for the brook trout to bite, he'd point up and say, "Beauty is all around us, but never forget the sky or the color of butterfly wings."

He was such a romantic, such a dreamer.

It was a Thursday afternoon during my lunch break from the Orchards. As I strolled through West Park in downtown Stamford, my heart pounded with delight. My joy wasn't so much about my memories of fishing with my father and sisters, the flight of butterflies, or the sweet scent of the poppies, which I loved. I was busy counting my lucky stars.

My dream was coming true.

Applications were being accepted at Saks & Company and Lord & Taylor for salesgirls in women's clothing, and Daddy had said it was okay. I could apply.

The timing was perfect, too. The end of the summer marked the last days of my stint at the Orchard School. By fall, I could be taking a train to work, to a new job, carrying a clutch purse and a lunch box, and wearing lipstick and eyeliner.

I'd stand behind a lavish makeup counter or in the women's department selling silks, dress goods, shawls, upholstery, lace and embroideries, gloves, and hosiery. I knew everything about everything. I read *Harper's Bazaar* and the Franklin Simon fashion catalog as if God's angels wrote them. How could I not be hired?

Joy flowed through my fingertips and toes. I danced, sang, laughed, and shed a tear. I was in my own world, loving every moment of freedom and my future. Then I looked up.

Standing in the middle of the gravel pathway was Lenny. (I called him Lenny because Leonard or Kip was too Fifth Avenue and Newport.) And he and his sapphire eyes were staring at me.

I fought the urge to turn tail and run. How long had he watched me skipping like a child and grinning like a Cheshire cat?

But there he was—a wooden bench to his right and a cannon, a monument to the Revolutionary War, in the grass to his left.

Having read too many of my mother's British romance novels, I couldn't stop the next thought that entered my mind—had I come across a prince, a general, or a member of the royal family? It could've been all the above. Either way, with no witnesses to scold me, I approached him, smiling broadly, my heart fluttering as if made of butterfly wings.

"What's your f-favorite motion p-picture?" he asked instead of saying hello. "I like s-swashbucklers."

I pretended not to notice his stutter as I introduced myself and him to me, but I already knew who he was. After seeing each other in the cafeteria days before, I'd asked around.

"I'm Alice. Alice Jones, and I adore Mary Pickford and Douglas Fairbanks."

"Did you see Fairbanks in *The Mark of Zorro?*"

"I did."

"How about *When the Clouds Roll By?*"

"I loved him in that, too."

"He and Mary Pickford are Hollywood r-royalty. Don't you—you think?"

"Absolutely, positively," I said eagerly. "I bet they both win an Oscar this year."

He went on and on about Fairbanks and Pickford, Fatty Arbuckle, Charlie Chaplin, and many more. He surprised me, too. He talked a blue streak about Hollywood, his stutter barely slowing him down. It was like he'd memorized a year's worth of *Photoplay* magazines. I was mighty impressed.

"I predict a young a-actress named Mae West will be a h-huge s-star." His face turned as red as the poppies.

"You must have a crush on her. Your cheeks are the color of fire." I pointed at him teasingly. Or that's what I meant to do.

He didn't make eye contact, but I didn't miss his shy smile. "I l-like older women."

I wished for a witty reply but came up empty. We stood in the middle of the gravel pathway in awkward silence until a clap of thunder drew a loud gasp from my throat. An army of rain clouds had darkened the sky.

"Oh no." I covered my hair with my hands, fending off the first raindrops. "It was nice talking to you, Lenny. But I've got to get back. My lunch break is almost over." I dashed back the way I'd come.

But then, I stopped and turned, remembering something I wanted to tell him. "Did you notice you barely stuttered the whole time we were talking?"

He stood on the gravel path, his head cocked, and smiled. "N-nope. Didn't notice one b-bit."

Lenny and I didn't always talk about Hollywood. The day before my last day at the Orchard School, we met in the park again, except this time, the subject was comic strips—*Gasoline Alley* and *Winnie Winkle.*

Lenny didn't like Winnie, and I hated everything about everyone who lived in *Gasoline Alley* (except the babies Hazel and Emily). Walt, Avery, Doc, Slim, and Bill got on my nerves.

"They're so fancy with their automobiles, iceboxes, and new this and that," I grumbled as we strolled through West Park. "Does anyone in that town have a job?"

"How can you have a beef with the idle middle class of *Gasoline Alley* but not with Winnie? She's the family breadwinner whose choices p-place a t-terrific burden on the women in her family, and she does the same to women readers, too. Y'all don't need to work outside the home unless forced to. And it takes a lot to force them. I would think." He flicked the tip of his nose. "Frankly, the comic is too farfetched for my taste."

"Women who aren't rich work, Lenny. Look at me. What do you think I'm doing? Visiting this place because I like the food and—"

"The c-company," he interrupted with a smile.

Even though I was heated, I returned his smile. It was okay to have a different opinion, and we laughed about our little quarrel for a minute or so. Then, our easygoing chat hardened between the poppy field and the tall grass.

"My father says New York is getting too crowded." Lenny sat on the bench across from the war monument. "Between the European immigrants and Negroes from the South filling up Harlem—the city's real estate values could plummet."

My jaw dropped. Had I heard him correctly? Of course I had. He was one of them: old money, the wealthy who hated anyone who didn't come to America on the *Mayflower.*

"My parents are immigrants." I squared my shoulders and faced him, my blood boiling.

He started to say something, but I raised my hand. "I'm

not finished. My family and I don't live in New York City. So we won't be adding to the overcrowding. We aren't rich like the Rhinelander or Rockefeller families, but we aren't beggars. We work hard, and my parents are proud of how they raised my sisters and me and what we're making of our lives." I placed my hands on my hips, indignant. "You disappoint me, Lenny. I thought you were different."

He looked stricken, skin the color of ash, lips slightly blue, eyes wide and sad. "I didn't m-mean you, Alice. Or your family." He brought his fist to his lips and pounded them twice as if trying to take back his words. "I don't know w-why I s-said it. It's s-something my father would say. Please accept my a-apology. I wasn't thinking."

"Is that something you do regularly? Randomly recite your father's hatefulness?" I rubbed my fingers across my forehead. "I'd rather hear you talk about how you feel. I'd rather know what you think, not him."

He cocked his head, but the sadness in his eyes was all I could see.

"What is it?" I asked gruffly, angry at feeling bad for upsetting him. "Why do you look that way?"

"Most people don't."

"Don't what?"

"Want to know what I think." His Adam's apple looked like a knot had stuck in his throat. "I said I was sorry. Y-you were b-born in America. You aren't a f-foreigner."

"You didn't answer my question. What do you think?"

"I'm not the same as my f-father."

"How would I know? I'm not one of those rich people in the *Social Register*."

"How'd you know we're in the *Social Register*?" Lenny's expression changed from apologetic to suspicious. "Did you get a copy and check to see if you'd find me there?"

"I don't give a nickel about the *Social Register* and who is or isn't in it."

He smiled suddenly as if my agitation amused him.

"What's so funny?" I shot back.

The grin split his cheeks. "I was joking. I don't care where people come from or when they came to America. I care about people who are kind and smart." He looked down, struck by a sudden fit of shyness. "Or like you—the pretty ones."

"Oh, so you think I'm pretty."

"Come on, Alice. You know you are."

I smiled shyly. "If you say so."

"I do."

As I left the park that day, I was sad. Summer was over, like my job at the Orchard School. My conversations with Lenny—sometimes friendly, sometimes too earnest, and our gentle flirting—were over. Would I ever see Lenny again? Hard to believe that I cared whether I did or not, but I wanted to see him again.

And until I reached Pelham Road, I swear I'd forgotten the one thing I should never forget.

He was one of them.

And I was me.

CHAPTER 6

A daughter is a gift from the gods, Daddy liked to say, but Mummy always reminded him that he had three daughters.

"Are they all gifts?" Mummy asked with a challenging smile.

Daddy winked and replied, "My girls are better than gifts; they are my little treasures and the angels of my life."

Hearing this, Gracie and I clapped and giggled. Emily hugged him around the neck. For the remainder of the day, we'd play checkers or the Uncle Wiggily board game and snack on Pep-O-Mint candies or Mummy's ginger nut biscuits. Little did I know that those days, those words, that laughter and love had a warranty—the price we paid for growing up.

My parents, George and Elizabeth Jones, immigrants from England, were kindhearted, good neighbors, regular churchgoers, and hardworking. Daddy bought the house on Pelham Road after Emily was born in 1894. He purchased his first taxicab shortly after I was born in '99. Mummy laughed a lot and gave us kisses while Daddy snarled and scolded. But we never took Daddy's gruffness to heart. How could we? He treated his girls like angels.

Every evening, he had a book in his hand and, with his daughters surrounding him, read us stories, Bible verses, fairy tales, comics, and whatever was written on the *New York Tribune* or *Daily News* sports pages. By age eight, I knew more about the New York Yankees than most men.

My mother fussed at him. "You're gonna turn my girls into tomboys with all that sports talk."

I agreed with Mummy. Tomboys sounded like bad people, and I was a good girl. But Emily didn't mind being compared to a boy. She was Daddy's favorite, no matter what she did.

They talked for hours about baseball, checkers, fishing, carpentry, and driving automobiles. They played catch in the backyard. He taught her card games Gracie and I weren't allowed to learn. They read the sports pages together. And when her limbs were long enough, he taught her how to drive. I wanted to know, too, but Emily was five years older than me. And Gracie said her husband would drive her wherever she needed to go.

Mummy teased Daddy often, saying he didn't need a son—he had Emily.

One Sunday evening, a few years later, after Emily had taken a job as a live-in maid at a manor in Manhattan, my father, Gracie, and I sat at the kitchen table, waiting for Mummy to serve dinner: beef and kidney pudding with treacle tart and jam for dessert.

Just as we finished the blessing, there was a knock on the door, and Daddy scowled. He didn't like to have his meal interrupted, especially when he was already on edge. Then we heard the door creak open and Emily's voice, "Hello. It's me."

Yes, it was her. She usually joined us on Sundays if she could unless her employer had other plans for her. If that was the case, she was supposed to call. This Sunday, we hadn't heard from her.

So when she bounced into the kitchen, Daddy's face was dark with irritation.

But Emily hadn't even removed her coat and hat. She stood in the archway with excitement oozing from her body and joy beaming from her eyes.

"Daddy, Mummy, I have a surprise I didn't know how to tell you before, but I can't wait any longer. And please don't be angry with me. I hope you'll understand."

I looked from my father to my mother, wondering if they knew what she was talking about. But from my father's hardened jawline and Mummy's open mouth, they were as clueless as I.

Gracie was twelve years old and had barely raised her head, more interested in the food on her plate than the drama surrounding her.

"Say what you came to say," Daddy said, his eyes as hard as the muscles in his jaw. "But it better be bloody good. Interrupting our Sunday supper like this." Daddy was a stickler for eating meals on time, and everyone had to be seated at the table five minutes before him.

Emily cleared her throat. "I wanted you to know I've met a boy."

Mummy put down her knife and fork, freeing her fingertips to cling to the edge of the table. Under the table, Gracie kicked me, but I kicked her back. I saw the giggle in her eyes and gave her a sharp shake of the head and a mumbled, "Don't you dare."

"What boy?" Daddy asked.

It wasn't that Daddy didn't allow us to date, but there was a proper way a young lady introduced a prospective beau. First, Daddy had to meet him. But Emily had entered the house alone. I craned my neck to see if he was standing in the hallway. But I saw nothing but her.

Emily stood panting, her eyes too bright and shiny, her voice quaked somewhere between excitement and nausea.

"He's a chauffeur at the manor where I work and, sometimes, a butler, too. I've known him since the day I started the job, but we didn't, well, you know, we didn't start seeing each other as boyfriend and girlfriend until much later. And, of course, we haven't done anything you would object to. Still, I felt it important that since we are talking seriously about . . ." She paused, eyeing Daddy briefly, before turning to Mummy. "But you see, he's a good man. The best, but there's something about him that might upset you."

It was the longest speech Emily had ever made to my recollection.

Daddy slammed his fist down on the table. "Stop beating about the bush. What is it you want to say about this boy?"

"Daddy, he's dark-skinned."

My father leaned back in his seat. His long chin lengthened; his dark brows knitted. "Is he Jamaican born? A mulatto?"

Emily whispered something I couldn't hear, and neither did our father.

"If you don't speak up, I'm gonna get mad!" Daddy said, but he was already furious. The veins in his neck looked like twisted rope.

Emily swallowed, then coughed. A bucket of dust must've been stuck in her throat, but she was the one who had walked into the house that Sunday covered in determination and a good heap of fear.

And now I was about to find out why.

"His name is Robert Brooks," she said softly. "And he's a Negro."

"A Negro? Oh my Lord." The words raced out of my mouth.

My mother's gasp sounded like a car horn and poor Gracie dropped a forkful of beef and kidney pudding on the floor, making a mess.

But Daddy, he was on his feet. The fingers of both his hands had closed into fists. He leaned forward glaring at Emily, pressing his knuckles into the table. "You better be telling me a goddamn lie. No daughter of mine is gonna be gallivanting around with a Negro."

"I'm not lying, Daddy. Robert and I are in love and plan to marry." Now she trembled badly, and her eyes were wet with unshed tears. "I knew this would trouble you. That's why I was afraid to tell you, but I couldn't keep the secret any longer." Tears flowed down Emily's cheeks. "We will be married this summer."

Daddy threw his dinner plate to the floor. "Get out."

"George," Mummy said softly. "Don't do this."

"Keep quiet, Elizabeth." Daddy's tone chilled the air. "I promise you this, Emily Jones, if you marry a Negro, you will never set foot in this house again."

"Mummy?" I cried with a frightened glance at my older sister. "Daddy doesn't mean that, does he? She can come home without the colored man. Can't she?"

"Shush," Mummy said wiping tears from her eyes. "This is your father's house. We don't question his decisions, dear."

No one spoke for several minutes. Gracie slipped into my lap and wrapped her arms around my neck. We didn't know what to do other than to cling to each other.

Emily wiped away the last of her tears. "I should've told you sooner, but what happened here is what I expected and feared." She exhaled. "I'm going to marry him. And I hope you will be at my wedding."

Then Emily walked out of the house.

It was the worst Sunday dinner I'd ever experienced.

A few months later, after church, a woman with shabby clothes and a dent in her chin was talking loudly with some members of the congregation. I held my mother's hand as we walked toward them, but we didn't need to get close to hear what they said about my sister.

"Emily Jones went and married a Negro, but that's not the worst of it; on her marriage license, she cited her race as Negro."

The groans continued to echo through the pews the following week. I had taken Gracie to church on my own. But if my parents had been with us, they would've joined the congregation with the loudest protests. Instead, they were home, discussing where they went wrong raising Emily.

Their problem with the marriage was plain as day. Mummy was a white woman, and we were white children. It was on our birth certificates, and when she filled out the census, that's what she wrote for race. At certain times, Daddy's skin appeared somewhat tanned, but that didn't mean anything as far as his girls were concerned. We were white like Mummy. Now and then, we'd be asked if we were colored, but only if we went out with Daddy. With Mummy, there was never a question about our race. Why would there be? We were white girls with or without Daddy.

He changed quite a bit after Emily's wedding, and Gracie and I had to take Daddy's gruffness seriously. What else was there to do? He didn't smile like he used to and stopped reading to us in the evening. So much had changed, and it seemed overnight.

Emily Jones had married Robert Brooks in August 1915. It took five years for Daddy to invite her and her Negro husband into our house on Pelham Road. And that only occurred after Mummy pleaded with him. In 1920, Emily gave birth to a baby girl, Roberta Brooks, and Mummy wanted to know her grandchild.

"You can hardly tell she has Negro blood," Mummy had boasted. "With her reddish-brown hair and hazel eyes, Roberta is a beautiful child. A lovely baby girl, and only the slightest hint of brown in her skin." Mummy smiled at Emily. "Which I'm sure she'll grow out of—just like you did."

* * *

By the fall of 1921, the world had changed dramatically from the decade before. Prohibition. Flappers. Suffragettes. Women voters. Jazz. Rudolph Valentino. Doublemint chewing gum.

At twenty-two, girls my age had their own apartment or shared a flat with a couple of friends. They didn't live at home with their parents. They applied for jobs at Saks and Company, like I had planned to. Except on that day, Gracie had asthma and needed watching until her breathing improved. With Emily married off, I was the eldest sister, and it was up to me to do my part. Of course Mummy helped, but Gracie begged me to stay with her, pleading with me not to leave her.

So I stayed. She was sick for a week, and I stayed and cried myself to sleep every night. Mummy tried to lift my spirits. I could apply again in a few months, she'd said. I shouldn't despair. Department stores were always hiring and firing girls. I'd have another chance.

Gracie had recovered from one of her latest bouts with asthma and announced at dinner that she wasn't going to let the Roaring Twenties pass her by. I frowned, for it struck me as a strange statement to make. Why bother? She wasn't going anywhere. Daddy wouldn't allow it. He pitched a fit when we brought up moving away from home and getting an apartment together. "Two girls who work as servants to the wealthy should live at home until married."

"How come?" Gracie whined.

"Because I said so," he replied stoutly.

Daddy's retort crushed Gracie. I wasn't as keen on hooch, roadsters, and dance halls as my eighteen-year-old sister.

Since Emily had married Robert Brooks, Daddy had become horribly old-fashioned. But at least he didn't quibble about us going to the motion picture house on a weekend night. Those were the nights I lived for.

One Saturday evening, after grocery shopping, I was anxious to finish in the kitchen, change my clothes, and hurry off to the cinema.

The Three Musketeers with Douglas Fairbanks was playing at the new Pelham Picture House on Wolfs Lane. Gracie and I would have to hurry to arrive before the overture began.

I dressed quickly in a brown cotton gingham dress with a white lace collar, a pair of lisle black stockings, my only color, and a gray cardigan my mother knitted for me. I smashed a cloche over my head and stood impatiently in the bedroom doorway, waiting on Gracie.

As usual, she was slow as molasses. She had finished with her makeup, mascara, and rouge and had brushed her short bobbed hair into place. But she had changed her outfit three times.

I was fit to be tied but didn't want to fuss. Douglas Fairbanks was waiting.

"We're just going to the cinema," I reminded her.

She faced me and twirled, her full skirt billowing. "What do you think? Do you like this better than the green?"

"If you don't get a move on, I swear I'll leave you behind." It was a threat of frustration.

"You won't do that."

"You don't think so?"

"No, because Daddy won't let you go out unless I'm with you."

I plopped down on the edge of the bed. She was right, but I wasn't going to admit it. "Then neither of us will go."

"You're giving up, just like that. Why? All the time, you quit. That's why you haven't had a date or made new friends in a year. No male friends. It makes me wonder."

"Wonder what?" I asked angrily.

"Do you enjoy being a spinster?"

"I'm not a spinster."

"You're twenty-two and not only unhitched but with no prospects."

"And you have prospects?"

"As soon as I find the right one, I'm taking him off the market." She flipped the edges of her hair saucily. "Since the Great War ended and the soldier boys returned home, every season is prime for finding a man. But you spend every Saturday night at the cinema with your kid sister."

"Shut up, Gracie. That's not true."

"Which part?" She strolled over to the bed, nostrils flared. "All you and I do is go to the cinema or play jazz records on your bloody Victrola. The world is changing around us, Alice. You can't keep sitting on the front stoop, watching it pass you by."

She had made it to the bed and sat next to me. Legs crossed, she circled her ankle, eyeing her strappy red pump. "All the time, we hear that we can't do this. Can't do that." She gave me a conspiratorial wink. "We should tell Daddy we're going to the motion picture, but instead go to a speakeasy or dance hall where we can meet boys. We deserve a night out."

"Are you encouraging your sister to lie to me, Gracie?" The deep voice from the bedroom doorway belonged to our father, who was shaking mad.

"Daddy." My back stiffened. "She wasn't serious."

Lips puckered, he looked around the room, pausing at the family photos on the wall beside our vanity. "She was serious. Damn serious."

Gracie was silent, but I had to say something.

"Daddy, please—"

"Damn jazz music and Prohibition are giving young people a license to misbehave," he barked. "Everywhere you go, y'all drinking hooch, dancing in saloons, necking in the rumble seat of automobiles. The 1920s are dangerous times." He hit the wall with his fist. "You will stay here until hell freezes."

He left, muttering as he stomped toward the den.

Palms pressed into the mattress, I pushed off the bed and planted my feet on the floor. "I'll be back."

"Where are you going?" Gracie demanded but then rolled her eyes. "Don't tell me. I already know."

"He's upset. I want to make sure he's okay."

"Good idea, seeing that you're his darling girl."

Her sarcasm rang in my ears as I trotted down the hallway toward the den. His "darling" daughter lived in Harlem with her husband and child, but I did my best to fill the void. Although unappreciated, which was Gracie's cruel point.

When I entered the room, Daddy's attention was on the *New York Tribune*'s evening edition and the sports pages. I sat on the stool beside his chair.

"Did the Yankees win?" I asked, treading lightly.

He huffed in reply. "What do you think?"

I smiled. "A silly question. I should know better." Daddy frequently said that the New York Yankees losing a game was as "likely as a blue moon."

"So they are well on their way to winning another pennant," I added.

I had learned about baseball and a few of Daddy's other favorite things after Emily married, which I used to cheer him up, especially when he was angry.

He looked up from the newspaper.

"You're mad about what you heard," I said. "But I promise we will go to the cinema and come straight home after— Scout's honor—Gracie was upset because I'd threatened to leave her behind. And she'll say most anything when she's got a bee in her bonnet."

He shut one eye and squinted at me with the other. "You can go to the cinema but keep her away from those boys. Understood?"

I smiled a thank you but wished that once in a while, he

expected me to be the one chasing after the boys. But I was a good girl.

"Yes, Daddy. I swear. You don't have to worry. We'll come straight home." I kissed him on the cheek and sped back to my bedroom.

My sister and I were out the front door a few minutes later, hightailing it to the cinema and Douglas Fairbanks.

CHAPTER 7

The Pelham Picture House on Wolfs Lane in Pelham, the next village from New Rochelle, was less than a two-mile walk from home. But I had on high-heeled pumps and a dress with a tight skirt and couldn't walk quickly. Especially while dragging my sister by the arm. Worried about causing the slightest hint of sweat on her brow, she never ran, walked fast, or moved with even the tiniest bit of urgency.

"Damn it," she suddenly declared.

She had stopped in the middle of the sidewalk, shaken free of my grip and leaned against a lamppost. But we were still a several blocks from the cinema.

"What are you doing?" I exclaimed.

She lifted her leg and examined her foot. "Horsefeathers!"

"What's wrong?"

The way she'd shrieked, I thought she'd sprained an ankle or suffered some other injury.

"Are you okay?"

"I broke the strap on my shoe."

I rolled my eyes. "I thought you were hurt."

"I can't walk in a broken shoe."

"You haven't been walking that much anyway." I groaned. "Maybe I can fix it." I dropped to one knee to examine the problem. "There's nothing wrong with your shoe, Gracie. What game are you playing?"

I looked up, expecting a mischievous smile, but she was batting her eyelids at a shiny red-and-black touring car easing to a stop at the curb. "Who are you grinning at?"

"I don't know—but it's the second time he's driven by."

"You are unbelievable." I seriously considered spanking her on the rump. If she insisted upon behaving like a child, I'd treat her like one. "Let's go—and stop staring at that automobile. You aren't doing nothing but encouraging him."

"Fiddlesticks. Ain't no harm in looking at the man." With a cheesy smile, she kept her sights on the car. "I mean, look at him."

I nudged her in the side. "All I can see is the Packard. Come on. Let's go. We're going to be late."

"You ladies n-need a-a ride?" the driver asked, poking his head out the passenger's open window. I started to give him what-for; hassling good girls was impolite, but there was something about his voice. Had I heard it before?

Gracie answered him. "Are you talking to us, sir?"

"Yes, ma'am." He'd scrambled out of the automobile and stood, towering above the roof of the Packard.

My jaw dropped. "I thought I'd recognized that voice. Is that you, Lenny?" I knew it. "Lenny Rhinelander. What are you doing here?"

He tipped the brim of an imaginary fedora, his gaze shifting from my sister to me. "Ooooh my! What a hoot running into you on a Saturday night. How's it shaking, Alice?" He smiled brightly. "Oh, my. S-seriously. I would love to g-give you gals a lift."

Gracie squeezed my arm. "You know him? From where? Who is he?"

I stepped toward the car with Gracie on my hip. "What are you doing in New Rochelle, Lenny?"

"Just out and about for a drive." He bent down, disappearing for a second, and killed the engine. Then he was next to us, standing on the sidewalk, his Oxfords doing a nervous shuffle.

"We're going to the cinema to watch Fairbanks in *The Three Musketeers*," I said. "But it's only a few blocks away."

"*The Three Musketeers*? I've s-seen it. It's one of Fairbanks's best." Then he shook his wrist, loosening the cuff of his shirtsleeve, and checked his wristwatch. "Sorry, but I'm pretty sure you've missed most of the overture."

I glared at Gracie. "I told you to hurry." Then I remembered my manners. "Sorry, Lenny. I should introduce you to my sister Gracie."

"I'm Leonard Rhinelander, but everyone calls me Kip." He shook her hand, adding, "Everyone except your s-sister. She calls me Lenny."

Gracie held on to him, covering his hand with both of hers. "Alice is older than me," she said, using her flirty, high-pitched voice. "I'm eighteen. She's twenty-two. How old are you?"

"Eighteen. Same as you."

She wiggled her shoulders in delight. "I figured you were my age, though you look older, being so tall and wide-bodied."

A smile spread across Lenny's face as he grinned sheepishly at Gracie.

It was as if I'd vanished. My sister always did this. Pretty as a picture. Smart as a whip and so easy to fall for. She had a perky personality and wore the latest flapper fashions, which she pieced together from Mummy's old dresses and the occasional ream of cotton she'd buy at the five-and-dime. My outfit was plain: a brown bag of a dress, brown pumps, and thick black stockings.

A car horn's *ah-ooh-ga* turned all three of our heads toward the street.

"I don't think I can park here," Lenny announced.

Gracie stomped her foot. "You're not going to leave us, are you? You said we'd missed the musketeers and could go for a ride, didn't you? So, let's do that, Kip."

"I would love to take you for a spin," Lenny said in a rush, but then raised a brow in my direction, giving me the older sister's right to refuse.

"Thanks for the offer, but we need to get home," I answered his unasked question.

"How come?" Suddenly, Gracie was choking back tears. "Daddy doesn't know we aren't at the Picture House. We have a couple of hours of freedom. Let's use them." Her eyes stretched wide. "Please, Alice. We haven't been to any place but the cinema in months."

"I know a j-juice j-joint, Muriel's Café," Lenny interjected. "It's a few miles down the parkway in the city," he added without stuttering.

"Oh, yes. Yes. Let's do that. Please, Alice." She was jumping up and down like a rabbit.

"Copacetic," Lenny grinned, clearly tickled by Gracie's bunny hop. "Come on, Alice."

He might've been talking to me, but his eyes were on Gracie. "I swear I'll g-get you ladies home on time."

"What do you say, Alice?" Gracie pleaded.

I thought about it. One evening—we'd never go out with Lenny again. So what was the harm? And besides, Gracie could use a night of fun.

"Two against one, I have no choice, do I?" I said solemnly. "Yes, we can go for a ride and make a quick stop at Muriel's Café. But we can't be late returning home."

Gracie had such a happy expression on her face. It was like I was the patron saint of juice joints and dance halls.

Lenny ushered us into the vehicle. I was in the rumble seat, and Gracie was in the passenger seat next to him. Then he cranked the engine and off we went.

* * *

The scenery blurred as Lenny sped along the parkway toward Brooklyn. The salty-sweet smell of the Long Island Sound faded as we journeyed closer to the city and traffic. When we reached the block where the nightclub was, automobiles lined up on the curb. On one side of the street, a half dozen women, arms linked, trotted along the sidewalk in rhinestone-studded gowns; diamond, emerald, sapphire necklaces; dangling shiny earrings; and crowns that sparkled in the moonlight. Another group of partygoers, their footsteps clumsy from too much hooch and too much hearty laughter, stumbled not far behind.

Lenny stopped in front of the café's awning, uninterested in the search for a parking place. The valet, a Negro man in a tuxedo and tails, opened the car door and extended his gloved hand, assisting Gracie and me from the Packard as if we were Queen Mary.

With the motor running, Lenny jumped out of the vehicle and shoved some cash into the colored man's palm. A breathless moment later, we were inside the nightclub. I was immediately struck by the stench of spilled hooch, cigarette smoke, and Chanel N°5 perfume. A wicked combination that pleased as much as it disgusted.

"This is a ritzy juice joint, Alice," Gracie whispered, sounding slightly nervous. "Kip must be loaded."

He was much more than that, but I'd tell her about him and his family later. I was too busy being in awe of our surroundings.

Chandeliers; bright white tablecloths; waiters dressed in red bow ties, white shirts, and black aprons rushed about, balancing silver trays over their heads, laden with cups of hooch, coupes of champagne, and bowls of steaming oysters or chop suey.

Looking around, I was more familiar with the club's patrons than I would've liked. I knew the type. Not quite the Rockefellers, Vanderbilts, or Henry Fords. They were residents of the homes, manors, and mansions I'd worked in as a domestic. But in this nightclub, they wouldn't recognize me. This was their place of fun, not some servant girl's.

Out of the corner of my eye, I saw Lenny reach into his pocket and pull out another wad of cash. He then slipped it into the outstretched palm of the maître d'. Yes, indeed. Muriel's Café was a very fancy joint.

The maître d' escorted us to a table next to the dance floor, across from the orchestra pit. Before I could cross my legs and pretend I didn't feel like a pauper next to the handsomely dressed couples surrounding us, a waiter delivered a bucket of ice, a bottle of champagne, and crystal coupes, which he filled to the brim without spilling a drop.

"Aren't you the high roller," Gracie said to Lenny with a devilish smile. "I figured you had money, but here you go, bringing us to this fancy nightclub and ordering champagne to impress us. What do you plan to do next?"

"M-my older brother always t-told me to order champagne when you're with beautiful young ladies," Lenny said. "The bub-bubbly tickles a lady's nose, my brother said, and the pretty ladies love how that feels."

"Then, you have a smart brother." Gracie lifted her champagne coupe as if she was about to deliver a toast. "You should bring him with you the next time we go out."

Oh God. Could it be, Gracie was trying to set me up with Lenny's brother without an ounce of shame? I kicked her in the shin under the table.

"What did you do that for?" She grinned knowingly. Then she said to Lenny, "How old is your brother? And didn't I mention that Alice is twenty-two? Is he that old? I'm sure she'd love it if the four of us went out on a date together. We'd have a blast."

I looked at Lenny. Something was wrong.

Gracie kept beating her gums about this date, not noticing Lenny's body seemed ready to sink into the floorboards.

"Gracie, please. I don't think Lenny's brother would want to be bothered with us."

"It's okay," Lenny said. "I'd love for us to g-go out with my older brother, but he d-died during the war." He winced at the words coming from his lips. "My apologies. I-I sometimes forget he's dead and talk about him like he's alive."

I heard the gulp in his voice, the effort of swallowing as painful as I can imagine. "I'm sorry for your loss."

There was so much pain in his eyes. I wanted to hug him but knew that wasn't right.

"You two must've been close."

A smile touched his lips. "Yes, we were. Very close indeed."

Gracie drained her glass of champagne. "You must have other friends or another brother?"

"Yes, I have another brother, but he's too old for Alice."

We were interrupted by an announcement. Another Negro in a tuxedo and tails had approached the stand-up microphone, introducing the Original Dixieland Jazz Band. I had one of their recordings, too. I played it all the time on my Victrola.

There was no more quiet conversation once the band started playing. Hearing that intoxicating music, the hoofers quickly crowded the dance floor. The jazz bounced, and the dancers followed. The Charleston knee-knockers knocked and the *Shuffle Along* fans shuffled. I sat in a chair close to the dance floor, enjoying the music and the bodies in motion, and ignoring the danger closing in. A flailing arm or rotating hip could strike me at any moment. I leaned back to save myself. But it might not have been far enough.

"Careful there. You almost caught an uppercut to the chin," Lenny shouted above the music.

"Let's dance, Kip." Gracie leaped to her feet, grabbed Lenny's hand, and tugged him out of his chair.

"Okay, Gracie. Okay," he said hesitantly as if he didn't want to leave me alone. But then there was Gracie with her bright smile of excitement. I seriously thought she might burst.

I lifted my champagne glass and waved them off. "Go on. I'll be fine."

And I was just fine, because as they danced away, I was hailed.

"Would you like a dance, doll?"

A young man, not bad-looking, stood in front of me with an outstretched hand. Without a second thought, I was on my feet. My last dance partner was the doorknob in our bedroom—and I loved jazz. It was the only kind of music I played on my phonograph.

Moving my body to live jazz music was glorious. The scratchy sound of my Victrola couldn't match the rhythms of the Original Dixieland Jazz Band. In Muriel's Café, I could hear each musical instrument, from the beat of the drums to the trill of the piano keys and the trumpet (God, that man could blow). My feet flew, my hips swung, and I was dizzy, not from champagne but from trumpeter Nick LaRocca, the band's leader, and all that jazz.

After two numbers, I thanked the man for the dances, returned to the table, and dropped into my chair, exhausted. Lenny was there, but someone was missing. "Where's my sister?"

"Last time I saw her, she was on the dance floor with a blond fella in a blue tweed suit." Lenny pointed toward the bar. "She's still with him over there."

"I cannot believe her. I thought you two were dancing."

"We were, but then . . ." He shrugged. "Then we w-weren't."

He passed me a handkerchief.

"I'm sweating that badly?" I wiped my cheeks and throat.

"Nothing about you is bad, Alice," he said. "C-can I pour you some more champagne? I ordered another bottle."

"We should head home. Our father will be mad if we're late, and he has a temper."

"I'd like to meet your father."

"Why? Whatever for?" I said, having to recover after almost falling off my chair.

"I want to see y-you and your s-sister again. And it would be easier for us to go out if he knew me. Then he'd know I'm not the kind of fella he has to worry about being around his daughters."

"You think that's why he'll be mad? Because we usually hang out with riffraff?"

Lenny's eyes hardened. "I didn't mean it that way. I want to see you and Gracie again, and fathers like to know who their little girls are spending time with. That's all."

Why was I so irritated? Could it be the fact that he made sense? Or damn it, was I angry because I was so happy he wanted to see us again? "Sure. We'll invite you over to dinner one day soon. I'll tell my father we met at the cinema and you gave us a ride home."

He pulled a pack of cigs from his vest pocket. "I like this plan." He grinned. "I can't wait to meet him. He sounds like someone I would want to know."

I didn't mention I had no intention of introducing them. It was far too soon for that. For if Daddy didn't like Lenny, that would be the end of it before it began. Even if the "it" didn't include me.

On our third outing to Muriel's Café, Lenny brought a friend, Carl Clacker, an electrician he knew from the Orchard School.

It took a few moments of awkward conversation, some feet shuffling, hemming and hawing, before I figured out what was happening: Lenny had set me up on a date.

Talk about being caught off guard. I thought Lenny enjoyed being with Gracie and me and was biding his time before he figured out which sister had stolen his heart.

Disappointment surrounded me, and I was crushed. Still, I did my best not to let on. I even went so far as to try to like Carl. Only problem: I wasn't that good of an actress.

After an evening of dancing and hooch at a nightspot in the Bronx, we headed home. But the Packard started sputtering, making noises like parts were falling from its underbelly and landing on the road.

Lenny drove the automobile off the main highway, pulled onto a side street, and parked. "I'm g-going to take a peek under the hood to s-see what's happening. Come on, G-Gracie. G-Give me a hand."

Now, why did he do that, I wondered. Gracie didn't know squat about automobiles. Did these two young men have a plan for something more romantic than a ride home and a quick peck good night? If that was the case, Carl was about to feel as disappointed as me.

The door slammed, and he and I were alone in the back seat. "Hey, doll." He snuggled up close. "You sure are a looker."

Grinning, he pushed his thin leg against my hip. I knew what would follow: a meaty hand on my thigh. And if that didn't draw a slap, he'd go further. All fellas made the same moves, and although I hadn't dated a lot, I'd dated enough.

Despite Daddy's effort to keep Gracie and me under lock and key, I knew a few things about boys. I usually didn't mind some petting, but not with this guy. Lenny could turn his head and see what was happening—and I didn't want that. No matter what he and Gracie might be up to while checking the hood.

I crossed my leg, lifting it so high I nearly brushed Carl's chin with my heel. That was clue enough, and he backed off.

"When Lenny fixes the car, we'll need to hurry home," I said.

"I don't want to go home." Gracie must've kept an eye and ears on what was happening in the car and called out, "Let's go to the Club Deluxe, over on 142nd Street and Lenox."

"That's not a good idea, Gracie." Lenny lowered the Packard's hood.

"Why not?" she asked, walking back toward the car.

"It's too far," Carl chimed in. "We should go to a juice joint closer to New Rochelle."

He draped an arm around my shoulder, his fingers dangling too close to my left breast, giving me a creepy feeling. Then he whispered close to my ear. "That's right, doll, I don't wanna drive halfway across the city. I wanna be with you right here, right now." Carl's white teeth were too big for his mouth.

I shoved him in the chest. "I would just as soon go home."

"Come on, honey. It's too early for that." Carl came right back, leaning in on me.

"What do you think, Carl?" Lenny closed the car hood, angled by Gracie, and opened the passenger door, helping her into the seat. "We could go for a ride. There are some spots near the beach over by the sound."

Carl didn't respond. He was sulking

"I want to go home." I spoke loud enough for Lenny and Gracie to hear.

"Nope," said Gracie. "I want to go to the Club Deluxe."

"That's all the way in Manhattan." Lenny had eased in behind the wheel.

"Then that just leaves the beach," Gracie pouted. "I don't wanna do that, Lenny."

I squinted at my sister, using my name for Leonard. She always knew how to get her way.

"Why not?" Carl sounded angry.

"Because Gracie said she didn't want to," I added, folding my arms over my chest.

Carl sighed and pulled away from me. Finally, he'd realized nothing would happen between us. "Okay, then. If we aren't going to the beach, let's get something to eat. There's a diner over on the other end of Pelham Road—and I've got a flask in my hip pocket. We could go to Henry's."

I knew the neighborhood where Henry's was located. Emily and Robert ate over there. "Why would we want to go there? Isn't Henry's in the colored part of town?"

"Yeah, but they got some of the best fried catfish you'll ever taste. I'm a Southern boy," said Carl. "When a colored woman is in the kitchen, you gonna get a fine meal."

"I'm not all that hungry, Carl," Lenny said. Then he looked at Gracie. "Are you sure you don't want to go to the beach at Glen Island Park? It's a n-nice night. Not too chilly. W-we can park." He touched Gracie's cheek. "What d-do you think, sugar?"

She shot me a glance. Her eyes screamed that the beach was the last place on earth she wanted to go.

I cleared my throat and said firmly, "Like I've been saying, how about y'all take us home? I'm not feeling all that well."

Now, it was Lenny's turn to sigh. "All right. If that's what you want."

"That's exactly what we want," I replied without softening my tone.

As much as I wanted to be around Lenny, the look of fear in Gracie's eyes was more important than him—at least that night.

A disgruntled Lenny took us home. When Gracie and I saw him again a week later, there was no Carl Clacker in the back seat. It was just the three of us, and Gracie insisted I sit up front with Lenny, for she preferred to stretch out in the rumble seat where she could stare at the stars in peace.

Bless her heart. Now and then, Gracie surprised me.

The New York Times

March 27, 1940

RHINELANDER LEFT ESTATE TO FAMILY
Daughter and 2 Grandchildren Are Principal Heirs

Disposing of property valued at "more than $20,000" in realty and "more than $20,000" in personally, the will of Major Philip Rhinelander, who died at Long Beach on March 18, was filed here today for probate with Surrogate Leone D. Howell. . . .

CHAPTER 8

———◆———

ROBERTA

1940

After my temper caught fire at Aunt Alice's house, I spent the weekend in my bedroom, avoiding my mother and sulking.

How can I explain my failure to Mr. Richards? How can I give him a reasonable reply to what went wrong?

How can I show up to work Monday empty-handed?

My aunt refuses to be interviewed by the newspaper.

She did not answer a single question about the commodore.

If she did I don't recall, because I was too angry. So when Mr. Richards asks me why I failed, the answer is simple: she and I can't be in the same house together without fighting.

That doesn't sound like the making of a newspaper-woman. I should've known better than to make the trek to Pelham Road.

Ashamed and disappointed, I needed a friend and called Ethel Ray.

"I lost my temper," I say soon after Ethel Ray answers the phone. "She makes me so mad. Why did she do it? Why did Aunt Alice pass for white??"

"I don't know, Roberta. There could be so many reasons."

"How can someone make that choice? There has to be a

reason." I am struggling with tears and press the receiver to my chest to muffle the sound of my sniffles. When I regain control, I ask her: "Why did Alice do it? Was it the man or the money?"

"It's not always about money, Roberta," Ethel Ray says. "Passing is complicated. Reasons are all over the map. For some, it's a chance to live a life without restrictions. A Negro with a slender nose, thin lips, and alabaster skin with a chance to marry into the Rockefeller, Astor, Vanderbilt, or Rhinelander fortunes is there for the money, or they might want to pursue their dreams unhindered." She paused. "You know, dreams don't come in colors for the Blacks in this country. Whites can dream often and dream bigger than coloreds, Roberta. With a much better chance of their dreams coming true."

"I hear you. But I just know that Holden Richards will prevent my dream from coming true. He's manipulative and unfair."

"He can be, but I'm sure he is a reasonable man. He might surprise you."

I wasn't ready to hear about Mr. Richards's attributes. "You make him sound like a man I shouldn't fear, mistrust, or judge too quickly. But you don't get it, Ethel Ray. I had a chance to impress the city editor, the golden boy of Negro news, and blew it."

"Do you even know how he got that name?"

"I've heard bits and pieces," I admit.

"He's earned the admiration of his colleagues through hardship, diligence, and courage." Her patience now sounds like exasperation. "I know this because some of the people he helped in Georgia were my people."

"You're not from Georgia. You were born and raised in Harlem, just like me."

"I was born here. My parents, too. But my father's parents and a bunch of cousins live in Gordon, Georgia."

Ethel Ray then told me Holden Richards's story.

Ten years ago, he wrote a series of articles about the film *The Birth of a Nation*. Holden was one of the first to condemn its scathing portrayal of the Negro man and grotesque glorification of the Ku Klux Klan. Then he followed those articles with a front-page story on two lynchings in Gordon, Georgia, where my father's family lives. It's near Savannah, where Mr. Richards was from—and he named names. City officials, leaders in the white community, the mayor, the sheriff, and the bank owner, to name a few of the men beneath the sheets.

The Associated Negro Press picked up the story, and more than fifty Black newspapers reprinted it. Holden was a national hero.

"Of course," she continued, "he had to pack his bags and slip out of town with his young bride, who died a few years later, or risk a Klan-knotted noose around his neck."

"Well, I haven't met the man who bravely faced the Klan. Not yet. I only know the one who took advantage of my bloodline and sent me on a fool's errand."

Monday morning arrives, and before I can settle in, I'm summoned to Mr. Richards's office.

"What are we going to do with you, Ms. Brooks?" He sits behind his desk, surrounded by cigarette smoke.

I glance at his ashtray; it's filled with butts. Despite the hour, he's been in his office for some time.

"You made a mess of things with your aunt," he said sharply, but I don't look up. "Are you listening, Roberta?"

No, I am not. "Are you firing me?"

He blows out a cloud of smoke. "No, but what happened wasn't helpful."

Wait a minute. Wait one damn minute. "How do you know what happened?"

In my lap, I squeeze my hands together. Mr. Richards massages the gray hairs at his temple.

"Do you know what makes your aunt an interesting subject?" He extinguishes what's left of his cigarette. "Her story is about more than a young colored woman passing as white. She represents something that New Yorkers weren't prepared for."

"Which is what?"

"You think about it. See if you can come up with an answer. Meanwhile, I'm not firing you," he says. "Your aunt said she'd give an exclusive to the *Times* if I even thought about it—which I hadn't."

I am stunned for several reasons. "You spoke to her?"

He wipes the lens of his glasses with a handkerchief. "She called me over the weekend, and we talked."

"Over the weekend?"

"Yes. Didn't I tell you I met your aunt years ago?" He lights another cigarette. "You got off to a rough start. But she'd like you to stop by again. And this time, try not to fight."

Back at my desk, I reach for "The Lighter Side" folder, where I keep my notes for the next column. I am considering what Mr. Richards shared about meeting my aunt years ago. Is he one of the reporters who wrote about her? Is he one of the reporters who wrote about my parents? I didn't ask. I don't want to know. Not today.

I instead think about men who have upstanding reasons for doing what they do.

Ann Petry will write about the men behind the Negro Playwrights Company. Canada Lee founded it along with Langston Hughes, Paul Robeson, Theodore Browne, Richard Wright, and Alain Locke—and soon will launch its first project, a revival of Theodore Ward's *Big White Fog*. The long list of male writers and playwrights at the company's helm are luminaries of the New Negro movement, an inspiration to many Black New Yorkers, including my boss, Ann Petry, who is not only a columnist but also a novelist and playwright.

So I'm not surprised we're covering Canada Lee's company as an exclusive. Still, I'd rather write hard news. For example, a series like Marvel Cunningham's investigation into Jim Crow in the Federal Housing Administration. Groundbreaking for a female reporter to be at the forefront of a story of this magnitude.

Marvel Cunningham was one of the first Negro women to work at the *Amsterdam News*. She's also a stringer for the ANP (Associated Negro Press) and has written for *The Crisis*, too.

If I was doing that kind of writing, I wonder if Mr. Richards would have come to me to talk to my aunt.

Chewing on my lower lip, my swirling thoughts come together. What if my aunt Alice was my hard-news opportunity? What if I did the digging and found the truth behind her story? Does it matter if I like her or not? If I control my temper, I bet I could convince her to do an interview for the *Amsterdam News*. I have to believe in myself. Hell, I could even write the story. An impartial story, too. That's a news reporter's job—write the truth without adding my personal opinions.

On the other hand, she refused to speak with anyone else at the *Amsterdam News*? The only reason to see me has to be about mending the broken fence between us. Is that a sacrifice I can make for my career? Damn. I wish I knew.

A week later, I am back on Pelham Road, and Aunt Alice and I are in the living room.

She is seated in the lounge chair closest to the fireplace with a book in her lap, slowly turning the pages and ignoring me. I sit on the sofa, except for my legs, which keep jiggling nervously. The rest of my body is tense and stiff, as if I were stuck in cement. It's uncomfortable for her and me to be in the same room. But I can't leave. There can be no more black marks on my report card.

I'll get her talking. I'll skip any mention of the Rhinelanders. That's how the mess began the last time.

What conversation can we have that won't end in a screaming match? Not that Aunt Alice yells. Her tone is always restrained. The pitch of her voice doesn't rise too high or fall too low. The middle ground is where she sounds strongest. But I think she's holding on to her sanity with a thin rope. Cooped up in this house for ten years, the last two alone. From what I can tell, she may dress in the latest fashions, have the cutest hairstyles, and wear expensive jewelry, but I wonder when she doesn't have what she wants delivered to her front door.

How do I get her talking? If I don't, she'll spend the rest of our time together with her eyes glued to the pages of that damn book.

"What are you reading?" It's an innocent question.

She looks at the cover. *Their Eyes Were Watching God* by Zora Neale Hurston.

I am surprised. "That's such a controversial book."

"Why is it controversial?" she asks, looking at me as if no matter what I say, it will be the wrong answer—and we'll argue.

"She's a prominent member of the Negro movement, a writer and activist. But that book is full of stereotypes. Characters who reinforce white society's low opinion of the Negro, especially our men. These negative images, language, and relationships that whites have advanced about how we live."

She stiffens at the word *we*.

"I don't see it that way," she says. "It is the story of a woman's life that isn't as pristine or predictable as some men would like it to be."

"Wow." The limitations of her viewpoint on the subject

astonish me. I take a deep breath. "We should not have this conversation."

"Why not? We're talking. Isn't that why you are here?"

Okay, then. If she wants to talk . . . "The book has no purpose."

"You're reciting Richard Wright's opinion. I read his review. The novel has merit. Every story written about Negroes doesn't have to be about political issues."

"Why not? They should contribute to the fight against segregation, Jim Crow, and the laws that cripple the Negro. A prominent, educated woman like her should write substantive novels."

"The problems of women aren't substantive?"

"That's not what I'm saying." My voice cracks. It's a warning. I'm upset, and this discussion is out of the blue. "Sorry. Sorry. Let's stop and agree to disagree."

"I met her before."

"Who?"

"Zora Neale Hurston. Or I think it was her. In 1925, at a nightclub near the *Amsterdam News*." Aunt Alice puts the book on the coffee table and stands. "She'd been in town only a few months but knew everybody."

My mouth opens to ask her who was everybody. What group of Negros would sit at the same table with my aunt in 1925? With her face plastered on the cover of every newspaper in town, with ugly headlines—who would invite her? I go to ask this same question, but looking around, I realize I'd be talking to an empty room. Aunt Alice is heading down the hallway toward the kitchen.

"Would you like something to drink?" she says over her shoulder.

I hurry after her.

The kitchen is the same as I remember it. The appliances may have been replaced with shinier, more modern pieces, but the floral curtains, the vinyl flooring, and the green enamel drop-leaf kitchen table remain. The wooden legs likely carry the marks I scratched into them when I was young, eyes beaming as I watched my grandparents, aunts, mother and father, and friends. The house was so often full of people, neighbors, and more.

We'd sit at the long dining room table during the Thanksgiving and Christmas holidays, an extra leaf added to accommodate everyone. Clanging silverware and china cups, the smell of roasted chickens, baked hams, green beans, potatoes, and pools of gravy and melted butter. The memories I thought lost rush back with the smell of strong coffee percolating.

"May I have a glass of water?"

She points at one of the kitchen cabinets, where I assume I'll find glasses, and then at the refrigerator. "There's a pitcher of cold water inside."

I pour myself a glass, take a long sip, and flinch when my stomach gurgles. Hopefully, it isn't too loud. I'm hungry, too.

Aunt Alice grabs the percolator and another pot, filling them with water and placing them on the stove. She's making coffee and, perhaps, tea, too.

"What did Holden tell you to get you to come back?"

My hand jerks, and the water glass slips, but I hold on. "What did he tell you to get you to agree to have me back?"

"I met Holden years ago, a little while after he first arrived in the city."

"He hasn't been here all his life?" I say as if I don't know the answer. Ethel Ray has told me the story.

"He's from Savannah, Georgia. Came here after he started a commotion in his backyard that drove him north."

"Yeah, yeah. I may know something about that."

"You should know all about it if you work for the man. I suggest you ask around and get the whole story." Her tone drops an octave on the last word.

"So, what did he say to change your mind about me?" I ask.

"Sorry, dear, but it wasn't about you, exactly," she replies.

"Then what?"

Aunt Alice catches her breath. "I was at a nightclub with friends when we should've been someplace else. He was there, too, and could've written about what I was doing and with whom, but he didn't. I'd do almost anything he asked of me."

"Except be interviewed by the *Amsterdam News*."

"That is correct," she says. "Now you? What did he say to you to get you here?"

"That's easy. A promotion. My own byline. The usual stuff an editor promises someone like me. Someone hungry to be a newspaperwoman like Marvel Cunningham."

"Oh, yes, Ms. Cunningham."

"Did you know her?" I ask.

"I met many newspaper people when Lenny and I were front-page news."

I nod. "That's right. You called him Lenny."

When she speaks his name, there is a light in her eyes, but I'm having trouble deciphering the emotion she's feeling—sentimental, or pain and longing. Whatever it is, it is powerful and appears to consumer her. I am touched despite my feelings about her.

An hour later, I stand on the porch, hand on the railing, saying goodbye and agreeing to return next week.

CHAPTER 9

──◆──

ALICE

1921

Lenny stuttered. Sometimes a lot, other times only a little. I didn't mind, but Gracie did. It was part of the reason she wasn't sold on him.

"It's a shame he can't put a sentence together without his words stumbling all over the place," she said as we dressed for another Saturday night at the cinema. "He has so much going for him—of course—" She giggled. "Mostly his money, but the stuttering is embarrassing."

"It isn't that bad. I barely notice it."

"That's because you're sweet on him."

"He's a swell guy," I replied without denying anything. "And he and I have a lot in common. We laugh at the same jokes. Enjoy the same motion pictures, comic strips, and music." I check my lipstick on our vanity. "And he treats both of us nice. He is a real gentleman."

"Yeah. Yeah. Yeah." She fluffed her bobbed hair. "Where are we going tonight? I hope it's the Club Deluxe. I met a swell egg there last week who said he'd look me up this weekend."

"Gracie, you'd better watch yourself. I saw that guy. He looked seedy, if you ask me. And if we run into him again, don't think I won't break up any of your boy-crazy business. You hear me?"

"You mind your affairs, and I'll mind mine."

She marched out of the bedroom, and I followed with a few quick words to our parents about "going to the cinema."

We left the house and met Lenny in front of the cinema. But we skipped the picture show and ended up at Nom Wah Tea Parlor, a new restaurant in Manhattan's Chinatown.

Lenny explained how much he had enjoyed himself when he'd been there before, and when we stepped inside, we were greeted by the owner, who gave us a special table near the kitchen. Lenny insisted on ordering for us. Everything was unfamiliar—chow mein, egg-drop soup, egg foo young, fried rice and pork, and fried shrimp dishes.

"I know"—he smiled—"enough food to feed an army, but I want you to taste my favorites. See if you like them, too."

"It is delicious," I said after the food arrived.

Pride beamed from Lenny's face. "I'm glad you like it."

Gracie pouted. "I can't eat this. I don't know what's in it."

"Just try it," Lenny said.

She ate a few forkfuls of the pork and rice dish but separated out the snow peas. I kicked her underneath the table, scolding her to be polite, since we weren't paying for anything. "Eat up, Gracie."

After dinner, it was late enough for a trip to the Club Deluxe, but the man Gracie had met a few nights before didn't show.

She searched for him, distracted by any man who resembled the short, black-eyed, curly black-haired Italian. It didn't take long for her to pout and complain. "When can we leave? I'm bored."

And we left. Lenny liked to be surrounded by happiness. I believed he enjoyed our company, but only when we were both smiling.

That night, as we often did before heading home, Lenny

took us for a ride. The night was beautiful, although a bit cool, as expected for an October evening. But we were bundled in layers, and Lenny kept thick blankets in the rumble seat.

We parked in a lovely spot near a clearing overlooking the valley. With the moon shining bright, we could see the outline of the faraway hillside and the moonlight shimmering over the water.

Still grumpy and pouting, Gracie begged Lenny to let her sit in the passenger seat. I moved to the back, unbothered. I, like Lenny, was enjoying the view and didn't want Gracie to ruin the evening.

Once I was settled, Lenny turned sideways with a big grin. "I've got a surprise for you." He reached into his breast pocket and withdrew a small black box. He didn't stop to build anticipation or anything; he flipped off the box lid, and there it was.

I jerked forward to get a better look. But the moon's rays were perfect, shining down like a spotlight on the silver band with a sapphire stone, immaculately cut and sparkling.

"For goodness' sake." My voice trembled. Was he asking one of us to marry him? To my heart's dismay, I assumed he was speaking to Gracie. "She's too young to get married."

"It's not a proposal," Lenny said with a laugh.

"Why would it be? I didn't think it was." Gracie grabbed the ring from Lenny's fingers. "Stop panicking, Alice. I knew it wasn't a proposal. These aren't diamonds, silly."

"It's lovely," I added, leaning over the seat. "Absolutely gorgeous."

"Yes, I thought you'd like it." Lenny's eyes glowed with pleasure beneath his nose glasses. "It's just a g-gift. I thought it was pretty and w-would-would look nice on your finger." His glance slid from Gracie to me.

"It's for both of us?"

He nodded, his eyes on Gracie.

She slipped the band on her ring finger. "Gosh, it's too big."

I almost suggested trying another finger but clapped my lips together. The ring would fit me perfectly. I just knew it. All I had to do was wait.

Gracie stretched her arm in front of her, eyeing the ring that would fall to the ground if her fingers weren't pointed toward the sky. "How much is it? I mean, how much did you pay for it?"

"Gracie, my goodness. How rude," I said sharply. "It's impolite to ask how much something costs. Sorry, Lenny."

"No problem. I didn't buy it. I inherited the ring. It's a family heirloom. My sister passed it down to me. She said I could have it, and now it's mine to do with as I please."

I tapped Gracie on the shoulder and reached out my hand. "Give it to me." She handed it to me. "Just so we're clear, it's not an engagement ring, but we've still got to ask Daddy if we can keep it."

Gracie tried to take the ring from my clutches, but I held on.

"Stop," I said. "I like it, too. Why don't we share it." It fit me better but saying that might bring back her bratty behavior.

She turned to Lenny. "If I had this ring in my jewelry box, I'd never give it up without a fight. Did your sister give it to you for your girlfriend, or did you take it without her permission?"

"He doesn't steal," I said.

"She's right, Gracie. I've never stolen a thing in my life. Especially not from my sister, Adelaide. She'd punch me in the jaw. She's very p-possessive. Keeps a death grip on everything she owns."

I still had the ring. "What are we going to say when Daddy sees it?"

"Come on, Alice. Don't be such a baby," Gracie announced.

"We don't have to tell him. I'll hide it in my pocket when we get to the house. We can keep it in our underwear drawer. He'll never find it there." She winked at Lenny.

"Daddy is afraid of our bedroom," she teased. "He stands in the doorway and fusses at us from there."

A few days after Lenny gave my sister and me the sapphire ring, I insisted it was time for Lenny to meet Daddy. Gracie wasn't too keen on the idea because she didn't want to risk Daddy getting into a stink with Lenny and preventing us from our weekends at the nightclubs and dance halls. But I loved the ring and taking it off every time I put it on didn't feel right. And I didn't like hiding it in the dresser, either. And if Daddy saw it before we told him about Lenny, his reaction could cause a problem.

"Daddy, I'd like to introduce you to Leonard 'Kip' Rhinelander. I call him Lenny."

We stood in the dining room, my parents, Gracie, Lenny, and me, mumbling through introductions and half smiles.

"We met him at the movie house a couple of weeks ago," I said, my gaze fixed on my father's face, studying every twitch of his jaw.

"He's been meeting us at the cinema on Saturday nights ever since," Gracie added, talking fast; lies didn't stick if spoken lazily.

"It's a pleasure to meet you, Mr. Jones, and your lovely wife, sir."

Daddy grunted, shaking Lenny's hands before folding his arms over his stomach.

Mummy wore her apron; her hands were stuffed in her dress pockets. She managed to smile at Lenny but didn't speak. She never had much to say to anyone other than Daddy.

Lenny had done as I'd instructed and left his rich-boy outfits in Manhattan—no fancy suit, oxford wing-tip shoes, or felt fedora. A checkered cardigan, a nice pair of conservative slacks, and a pin-striped shirt with a white collar and cuffs looked swell on him, and it's what I whispered when he came in. His newsboy cap was fashionable, if out of season, but he looked like a college boy, or, better, a college man.

The less showy his appearance, the less likely Daddy would find fault.

"Your daughters speak of you both often," said Lenny, but Daddy ignored the compliment.

"Have a seat, young man." Daddy sat at the head of the table and pointed Lenny to his right. "Alice told me you were eighteen years old. You don't look it. You look twenty-five. Have you been lying to my little girls?"

"I have b-been a big guy since I was b-born, so folks think of me as older than I am. But I'm not lying. I'll be nineteen soon."

Lenny hadn't taken his seat yet. He pulled out my chair, which was to Daddy's left.

"Don't worry about her." My father waved his hand. "You girls go in the kitchen and help your mother like you always do."

Mummy had already left the room, and we hurried after her.

In the kitchen, I tugged on her arm. "What do you think of him?"

"Young Mr. Rhinelander?" She tightened her apron strings. "You don't care what I think," she said cutely. "You want to know what your father thinks."

"That's for sure." Gracie was at the stove, opening the oven. "The chicken is done."

"Move aside." Mummy patted Gracie gently on the hip, grabbed a couple of dish towels, and lifted the roasting pan from the oven. "I think your father likes him."

I removed a pot of boiled carrots and potatoes from the stove. "He does?"

"I don't know why, but he shooed us out of the dining room so he could be alone with him." Mummy shrugged. "He is polite. Very polite. He doesn't seem to be bothered by us in the least."

"Why would he be bothered?" I asked, dumping the vegetables in a serving dish.

"Goodness, Alice. You are such a dumb Dora. There are any number of reasons Lenny could feel out of place here," Gracie said. "He's wealthy. We're not. We're immigrants. He's not." With two large spoons, she moved the chicken onto a platter. "Our house must look like a barn to him."

"You and I are not immigrants," I said hotly. "The only difference between his family and ours is money."

"That's a big difference." Gracie lowered her voice, eyes wide, like she had some secret she was finally about to tell. "But I wonder what his family would say if he brought you home for dinner."

Mummy angled between us, carrying a serving dish. "Unless you've already met them."

"No way." Gracie waved her hands. "We haven't met any of his family or friends."

"Yes, we have," I objected. "Carl Clacker."

"He was an electrician at the Orchard School. He wasn't one of his New York friends."

"So what? He and Carl were friends," I said.

"Not what I mean, and you know it. Besides, we haven't seen Clacker since Lenny tried to pawn him off on you that night. We've never met one of his *Social Register* pals. Or been introduced to any of his friends at the nightclubs he takes us to."

"Nightclubs!" Mummy gasped.

I glared at Gracie and squeezed my mother's hand. "Don't say anything to Daddy, but we only went a few times and didn't stay long."

Gracie made a face at my lie but then riffled through one of the drawers and held up a couple of large wooden spoons. "Don't we have any silverware? These are splintered."

"What's wrong with you?" I asked. "Are you ashamed of what we have? Who we are? Lenny has never acted like he's better than us, Gracie."

"Maybe. Then again. Maybe not. You have a crush on him that blinds you. He's like every wealthy man we've ever cleaned up after, them and their wives and children. Full of themselves, flaunting their riches, and saying whatever they want to get their way."

"I like Lenny—you're saying these things because you don't."

"I like him enough. But I see who he really is. And you could, too, if you opened your eyes."

Mummy banged a pot on the counter. "Girls. Stop this bickering. The boy is in the other room. Just be polite. We can talk about him after he's left."

"Yes, ma'am," I said, moving behind Mummy, where I promptly, childishly, stuck my tongue out at Gracie.

The weather in November was clear and crisp and without a single breeze almost every day. A few clouds fumbled across the sky, but the season's first snowfall was weeks away.

It was the time of year for dreaming. My favorite holidays approached, and the days went by at a lovely pace. Short, thoughtless early hours cleaning, mopping, and doing laundry at my latest job, a manor in New Rochelle, near the sand and the smell of the ocean. But the evenings filled my heart with smiles. Gracie had found a new friend, leaving Lenny and me alone for nights of adventure, laughter, and kisses.

Before I could stop myself, my heart was so full of him that I forgot about the life I wanted, the plans I'd made—my dreams.

My education. The salesgirl job in Manhattan. My own apartment.

My commitment to living a life different from my older sister, Emily, and Mummy—women whose existence revolved around their husbands and cleaning, baking, and knowing when to speak from when to keep their mouths shut—had been replaced by an unmatched desire to be with one man and a throbbing heart that grew larger and louder whenever I was near him.

So I'd missed my chance to apply at Lord & Taylor again, and this time, I couldn't blame Gracie, her asthma, or Mummy. She hadn't forced me to remain in the house, helping her can the fruit or the vegetables she'd bought by the bushel at the market. No, the reason I'd skipped my visit to Lord & Taylor was Lenny.

Specifically, a trip with him to Coney Island and a ride on the Giant Racer, a roller coaster at Luna Park, had my head in the clouds. And I didn't care how high I might be or if I ever came down.

On the days we didn't spend together, we'd talk on the telephone, but he'd also write me letters about what we'd do when we were with each other next. During the nights we did spend together, we'd drive through New Rochelle and eventually park near Hudson Beach or the Long Island Sound. In the back seat of his touring car, we'd neck. And at first, it was like my blood was on fire. I wanted him desperately, inside me, next to me, surrounding me—I breathed him in as if he were my first and last breath.

I was his Mary Pickford, and he was my Douglas Fairbanks.

A flirt, he loved to tease and tempt me, and the Packard became our sanctuary, where we kissed, made love, and made promises. I was falling in love without trying, and it was an exhilarating, delightful, frightening feeling. I didn't know what to do. I didn't know who to talk to, or if I did talk about it, what could I say that made sense?

But this much I did know—I didn't care about Leonard "Kip" Rhinelander's fortune; his family's opinion of us; his society clubs, private parties; his money, houses, fancy clothes, and new automobiles—none of it.

I just wanted to be with Lenny.

CHAPTER 10

On our own, just the two of us, Lenny took me everywhere: nightclubs, Coney Island, the cinema, a Broadway show (*Shuffle Along*). I was on his arm, and he didn't shy away from introducing me to the people he knew everywhere we went.

So Gracie was wrong. He wasn't ashamed of my family—or of me. And why should he? I was pretty, funny, and didn't mind a little necking in the Packard. He was a good kisser, too. His lips were soft, gentle, teasing. I longed for kisses that left my lips raw, and from the eagerness of his embrace, he felt the same.

One evening, we were parked near my house on Pelham Road. "I want to take you away for a weekend. Just the two of us."

"Overnight?" I feigned surprise, even a touch of shock, but I understood perfectly what he meant and wanted, which was what I wanted, too. "Where?"

"Newport, Rhode Island."

I knew enough about the rich to know Newport and its sandy beaches, lofty estates, yachts, and dinner parties weren't a place a real estate tycoon's son could go with a servant girl and not raise eyebrows. We'd been lucky and hadn't run into his friends during our outings.

"We've been a lot of places together, but Newport?"

"I k-know."

"It's the weekend vacation spot for half the New York elite. Every weekend is a who's who from the *Social Register*."

"It'll be fine," he said, his blue eyes sparkled. Then, an idea burst out of him. "I'll introduce you as Spanish royalty, a baron's daughter."

"Spanish? A baroness? I don't speak Spanish."

"Not the point, my love. I'll explain you've been in America, Los Angeles, let's say, since you were three." He pinched my cheek lightly. "With your dark hair, black eyes, and tanned complexion, you could very well be the descendant of a Spanish lord."

"I don't know, Lenny. Are you sure?"

"Jeez, Alice. Everyone in Newport is usually too drunk on hooch and jazz to remember what they did while they are in town, let alone who they did it with."

"Lenny, we're not going all that way just to get soused, are we?"

"Heaven's no." He pressed a palm over my breast and squeezed my nipple. A shiver went through my body.

"So you have something else in mind."

"We'll be fine, and I want you with me." He bent forward, kissing my lips tenderly, then roughly until we were lost in an embrace, drawing breath from each other's lungs, our kisses deep and lustful.

"What are you afraid of?" Gracie asked, perched in front of the vanity, brushing her bobbed hair.

It was late at night. The house was quiet; our parents were asleep in their room down the hall. I'd been on the telephone talking to Lenny about our trip and had just returned to our room to prepare for bed.

"I hear Newport is amazing if you're a part of that crowd,"

Gracie said. "And if Kip is taking you there, he is ready to introduce you to them as his. If it's Daddy you are worried about, tell him you are spending the weekend with Emily."

"She won't lie for me. As badly as Daddy treated her after she married Robert, she is still his precious girl, and Emily would never put that at risk."

Gracie's sigh was one of exasperation. "Then tell him the truth. You are of age, you know. There is nothing wrong with going away for a weekend with your boyfriend." She combed her bangs into place. "And if you're still worried, tell him you have separate rooms." She chuckled. "I'm sure he'll believe that."

"He'd never believe that."

"I know, but I'd love to see his face," she said. "You make too big a deal about Daddy's temper. He's not going to shoot Lenny. You are both of age. You in particular."

"He'll be nineteen soon."

"And you'll be twenty-three. Another reason you shouldn't be worried about what Daddy thinks. He has to know you've done some necking before."

"Daddy shooting someone doesn't sound that outlandish," I replied without commenting on what happened in the back seat of the Packard. "He does own a pistol and a rifle."

Judging from our wide-eyed moment of silence and a vision of our father, guns blazing like Billy the Kid, I wagered we both had the same image in our minds.

"Mummy had to hide his guns twice," I reminded Gracie. Then I remembered she wasn't there. It had been Emily. "Some man yelled at Mummy, called her names for being with someone like Daddy. And Daddy was standing right next to her."

"I recall you and Emily telling me that. The man thought Daddy was colored."

That day bothered me mightily for a long while. The man also called Mummy a disgrace and said that she should be ashamed. And he'd said this with Daddy standing right there as if my father had no right to tell him to go to hell.

Daddy was not a tall man, but he looked like a giant at that moment. He roared at the man, using words I'd never heard before and don't believe I've heard him say since.

He shoved the rude man in the chest several times and told him to run, or he'd get his gun and shoot him in the mouth. The man seemed so surprised that he had run away, shouting he'd return with his friends to beat Daddy's nigga ass. Nobody ever came, and when Emily asked Daddy why the man called him names, he'd said, because I'm mulatto. And in America, sometimes white folks make the mistake of thinking I'm colored."

"Are we colored?" Emily had asked.

Mummy answered. "My girls are white girls like their mother. You children aren't colored and don't have any Negro in you. You're white. That's what I put on the US Census, and that's what you are."

The second time Daddy threatened to shoot a man was on Emily's wedding day. We didn't go to the wedding. Daddy refused to let us. But Emily stopped by the house, and they argued. I was sixteen and eavesdropping. I thought they were loud enough for half the block to hear them. But I recalled hearing Daddy say he wanted to shoot Robert.

"What are you going to do, Alice? Will you tell Daddy about Newport or not?"

"No, I'm not. And it ain't because I'm afraid he'll shoot Lenny. He likes Lenny." I slipped on my sleeping bonnet and climbed into bed. "I'll come up with something, but I don't want to hurt his feelings. He believes we're good girls."

Gracie rolled her eyes. "You're such a prude. We aren't bad. We're just experienced."

"Well, you go ahead and tell Daddy how experienced you are. And I'll handle my life my way."

* * *

Newport was the bee's knees. Although Lenny and I spent most of the weekend in our hotel room, we had to eat. One night, instead of room service, we went to dinner, and while outside waiting for our limousine, who did we run into but Carl Clacker in a chauffeur's uniform.

Before he reached us, Lenny excused himself. "I n-need to chat with him for a moment. I'll be r-right back, honey."

I watched them and could tell the conversation was tense. I could see Lenny's jaw tighten as he listened to whatever Carl had to say. But I did hear Lenny's last words to him.

"You need to mind your own business, Clacker. Nobody asked you to mind mine."

He returned to me then, his face red with anger.

"What was that about?"

"Crazy Carl Clacker thinks he can scare me. Just because you didn't care for him, he wants to screw things up for us. I told him to bug off."

"I thought he was your friend?"

"Yeah, but he used to chauffeur around my family, including my sister, Adelaide. He threatened to tell her and my father that I was here with you this weekend."

I squeezed his hand. "So what if they knew we were here? Would that be such a problem?"

He shook his head. "My father hates immigrants and people who aren't like him. He doesn't even like me that much. And my sister is just like him. So, yeah. If Clacker somehow got word to him, it might mean trouble for me. But honey—" He kissed me. "I will always protect you and what we have together."

I didn't ask any more questions. Whatever else Clacker had said, I was sure Lenny would tell me if I needed to know.

In hindsight, I wish he'd told me more, or I had been more determined to understand what he meant by needing to protect me from his sister and father.

Why did I need to be protected?

* * *

The day after Christmas, Lenny had another surprise for me.

"We're going to Keens steak house for dinner, and I've booked us for a week at the Hotel Marie Antoinette."

Lenny had taken me to plenty of lavish spots like Newport and shopping at Saks and Lord & Taylor, but I still wasn't comfortable with the extravagant lifestyle he took for granted.

"Do you think I've ever been to a place like Keens? Damn it, Lenny. Until I met you, I'd never had a steak in a restaurant." I didn't mention how often I ate steak in the kitchen of one of those wealthy tycoon families where I took care of their little ones or mopped their floors. But that wasn't the same.

Still, I was wonderstruck, thrilled, and tingling all over. A week. Alone with Lenny. What an amazing time we would have, but I had to think.

How could I disappear from Pelham Road for an entire week without a damn good explanation? My father would never allow it. But my sister Gracie, forever the girl who knew how to get around Daddy's rules, gave her unsolicited two bits.

"He's taking you where? Wow. He's pulling out all the stops." Then she came up with a crackerjack idea.

Her plan went like this: one of my former employers, the Dunns, whose estate overlooked the Long Island Sound, had an out-of-town emergency and asked me to take care of their pets and perform some chores while they were away.

Gracie added, "The Dunns are out of town and left the house empty. Daddy won't call or check up on you if he believes you're working."

A car engine roared, and I peeked out the window. It wasn't the Packard but a touring car much larger than the one Lenny owned. Most surprising, Lenny wasn't in the driver's seat. A chauffeur was opening the rear door, and Lenny stepped out, holding a bouquet of red poppies like the ones in West Park Garden.

I didn't wait for him to make it to the front door. I grabbed my bag and coat and rushed out of the house, meeting him midway up the sidewalk.

"My, those are lovely," I gushed.

"Not as b-beautiful as you." His lips lingered on my cheek. "Are you ready?"

"Absolutely."

Once in the limo, Lenny introduced me to Ross Chidester, the Rhinelander family chauffeur. The man, in his proper uniform and a brimmed hat, had little to say, but I saw him staring at me in the cop-spotter mirror to his left. Although I didn't dwell on him for too long, Lenny was still talking about surprises.

"Wait a moment." He stepped outside, closing the front door slightly. I couldn't see what he was up to. But the next moment, there was a huge box with a big bow.

"For me?"

"Th-there's no one else it would be f-for."

"What is it?"

"Alice." He grinned. "O-open it."

The next moment, my cloth coat was on the floor of the limo and I was snuggly wrapped in a mink fur coat.

"Oh, Lenny, you didn't have to do this. I don't need gifts from you."

"I know." Facing me, he adjusted the collar around my throat. "That's exactly why I got it. But promise me"—he lowered his voice—"never tell anyone I bought you this coat, other than your family, of course. It will be our secret—no matter what."

"I promise."

I sat close to him in the limo's back seat, our legs and arms intertwined. We touched each other constantly, even if only holding hands or rubbing a hand through the other's hair.

"Okay, then. What's next? Tell me."

"All right. We're going to a Broadway show."

"What are we going to see? Another musical like *Shuffle Along*?"

"I'm not sure, but we have tickets at New Amsterdam Theatre. It's beautiful. The ceiling, the seating, the stage, just the best. The Cat's Meow."

It wasn't that long of a ride, but the limo driver wasn't taking a direct route into the city. "What time is the show?" I asked between kisses and sighs.

Lenny planted another deep kiss on my lips and stole most of my breath. "I have another surprise," he said.

"Oh, Lenny." I grinned. "I swear you don't have to keep giving me gifts."

He leaned forward and took the tip of my earlobe between his teeth. A slight squeeze and I sunk into him.

CHAPTER 11

I pressed my nose to the limo's rear window. "Where are we?"

"The Marie Antoinette. On Sixty-Sixth Street and Broadway. And by the w-way, we're Mr. and Mrs. Smith."

"Mr. and Mrs. Smith, huh?"

"Y-Y-Y-yes." His stutter struck so hard we giggled.

"I don't have enough clothes," I said, horrified that my bag of clothes didn't include anything elegant and would spoil everything.

"I-I planned this well, and everything you'll need is already in the suite."

Relief poured over me.

"Oh, Lenny. You treat me like a princess."

The limo had stopped in the circular driveway, and I reached for the door handle, anxious to get inside the hotel, but Lenny grabbed my wrist.

"We aren't going in yet. I just wanted to show you where we'll be staying, but remember we've theater tickets, a steak dinner at Keens, and then we'll be back here for as long as you like."

I gave him a wry smile. "And what will we do with ourselves while we're here?"

He murmured something about bed and then, "'To sleep,

perchance to dream, ay, there's the rub, for in this sleep . . .
what dreams may come.'"

"Shakespeare? When did you start reciting Shakespeare?"

"How do you know who Shakespeare is?"

"My parents are British, remember? My mother has been
reading it to my sisters and me since I was a kid."

We laughed and kissed again. Indeed, we kissed all the
way to the New Amsterdam Theatre and whatever play we
watched. Then there was more kissing at dinner until finally,
we were back at the hotel.

The lobby of the Hotel Marie Antoinette was exquisite. I
was dumbstruck by its splendor. The sparkle of crystal, shim-
mery gold, and flickering candlelight reflected off polished
hardwood floors. Walls were covered with lavish paintings
and portraits of people who looked like kings and queens,
and intricately woven fabrics seemed to be everywhere else.

I took in everything there was to see. It overwhelmed me,
and my head spun, and my legs trembled. I held on to Lenny's
arm with both hands.

When he stopped, I plowed into him.

"I'm so sorry." I was embarrassed, knowing that everyone
in the lobby—the women in their fur coats and sparkling jewelry, the men in their top hats and tails, and the finely dressed
man behind the front desk—must all think I was a fool.

The heat of my graceless tears blurred my vision.

"N-not to worry, my d-dear." He squeezed my hand, and
I felt suddenly at ease. I wasn't out of place as long as I was
with him. His thumb caressed my knuckles, and his encouragement kept me from disappearing beneath the floorboards.

He used a skeleton key to unlock the hotel room door.
When he opened it, I had to hold in my gasp.

The room was as gorgeous as the lobby.

There was a bed, a desk, a love seat, and a fireplace, but
before my gaze could take in more, Lenny swept me into his
arms, bumped his hip against the door, and pushed it wide

open. Then, with another swing of his hip, he shut the door behind us.

I waited for him to put me back on my feet, but he didn't. Instead, he pulled me to him for more kisses. I would never tire of him devouring my mouth. We fell onto the bed, with his hand in my hair and the other on my bottom.

"Is this why we are here?" I said teasingly.

"I love you, and I want to be with you, and I am tired of making out in the rumble seat of my Packard. The two nights we spent in Newport were wonderful, but I've booked this room through New Year. And if it were possible, we would never leave."

We hadn't wanted the busboy to bring up our luggage. Lenny carried a small suitcase, but as promised, the room was stocked with nightgowns, undergarments, fancy dresses, and more. But I only glimpsed a bit of the finery.

"Are you going to let me look around before we undress?" I asked gayly. "There's so much to see. The room is gorgeous."

He laughed and released me so I could rise from the bed.

On my feet, I practically skipped from spot to spot, closet to closet.

What I wanted was to be at Lenny's side, in bed, making love.

Lenny only left me once that week. He had to have dinner with his family on New Year's Day, but it must've been the quickest meal in holiday history. I didn't expect to see him until the wee hours of the morning, but he returned before ten.

Otherwise, we were in our hotel room, in bed, in each other's arms, kissing and making love, talking and laughing, feeling as free and unbothered by the world as a couple could be until two days after New Year's Day.

* * *

We'd spent more than a week together when a knock on the door tore us apart.

Frankly, it was more than a knock. The room shook as heavy fists pounded. So loud that I thought I was dreaming. It wasn't someone at our hotel room door but an explosion, a crash of thunderbolts.

I snapped upright in bed, trembling with fear. My first thought was *fire*. The Hotel Marie Antoinette was ablaze, and a maid rushed from room to room, warning the guests to flee for their lives.

But it wasn't a maid, a butler, or a fire chief.

A man's voice yelled, "Kip! Kip! I know you're in there. Open the goddamned door, or we'll break it down."

I pushed Lenny to the side. "Who is that? What does he want?"

Lenny groggily pulled his feet from beneath the blanket and swung his legs over the edge of the mattress. "I don't know who it is."

I held on to his waist, not wanting to let go of him. A crippling fear squeezed my chest. A storm was approaching, and the beast was about to land on top of us with the weight of a mallet.

"Is it your father?"

Lenny stared at the door as if the banging would stop of its own accord. "No. It's not the commodore. He'd send one of his lawyers. But how could he have found us? Why would he even look?"

Finally, Lenny rose, grabbed his silk robe from the chair next to the nightstand, put it on, and headed for the door.

"Kip!"

The voice on the other side of the door called him. Lenny faced me. "I recognize the voice. It's not my father. He sent one of his henchmen—his l-lawyer, Leon Jacobs."

Lenny opened the door. There were two men on the

other side. The one I didn't recognize was older, impeccably dressed, gray-haired, and too thin for his height. The other, I knew. Our chauffeur, Ross Chidester. The loose-lipped driver of Lenny's had betrayed us.

But, of course, I imagined the chauffeur didn't think of it that way. He was doing his duty to God and his country. How dare the young Rhinelander have a fling with a girl like me? A one-night stand was okay, tolerable. A weekend in Newport he could stomach, but ten days with me, a harlot, making love to the man-child "Kip," the stuttering imbecile who was unable to wipe his nose, let alone handle such a vixen as myself without assistance.

Leon Jacobs stepped forward, leaving Ross cowering in the archway, and entered the hotel room, looking around like he owned it.

"Pack your bags, Leonard."

Lenny shook his head and tried to speak, but words failed him.

"I said, pack your goddamned bags, boy. Your father has instructed me to take you by force if necessary."

The chauffeur looked as sheepish as Lenny, but each man in the room would do as instructed. None of them, especially my Lenny, had the guts to defy the commodore, Lenny's illustrious father.

I saw a weakness in Lenny I'd not noticed before. He cringed away from this man in his tailored suit, stern features, and breathy voice.

"He is your father's lawyer?" It was the only sentence I could muster. I was still in the bed, the sheet covering me. At least Lenny had put on his robe before letting them in.

"And my friend, the chauffeur," Lenny said quietly without the slightest stutter, as if his nervousness had been replaced, not by courage, but shock.

"Chidester will take her home."

I looked at Lenny. "What does he mean?"

"Don't worry." Lenny reached for me, but Mr. Jacobs cleared his throat.

"Your father wants to see you within the hour."

A few minutes later, Lenny was dressed and his things gathered. I still lay in the bed, watching the men creep around our love nest, disturbing the items I had thought of as keepsakes. The vases where fresh flowers had been delivered daily. I wanted to slip at least one of them into my suitcase. There was also the last rolling cart of desserts, fresh strawberries, and champagne Lenny had ordered. I wanted to keep the flutes as a souvenir.

"Do you have everything?" I asked Lenny as he stood in the doorway, the agony of what had transpired showing in his sad, droopy eyes.

"Yes, and don't worry, I will call you. We'll make plans for next weekend." He then turned to walk away, dropping his bags and moving toward me. Mr. Jacobs attempted to block his path, but Lenny pushed the lawyer's thin arm out of his way.

"I'm so sorry about this, Alice. I didn't know Ross was such a louse. I swear." He kissed me on the cheek, and he and Mr. Jacobs left the room. The last words I heard Lenny say were to the limo driver. "Get her home safe."

Then they were gone except for Ross Chidester, who stood in the hallway. The hotel room door was still wide open. He was waiting for me.

"Do you mind closing the door so I can get dressed?"

The door closed, and I was alone. Lying in bed, in my silk slip, my feet so cold I searched for something to cover them, but I had to get a move on.

I bundled up the toiletries, the nightgowns I barely wore, the dresses I'd never worn. Fifteen minutes later, I sat alone in the back of the limo.

For two days, I waited for a telephone call from Lenny. I was distraught with worry. What if his father had beaten him? I recalled stories at the Orchard School about how poorly his father treated him. Wealthy people were undoubtedly violent—undoubtedly, many of the ones I had worked for. Anger and frustration looked the same in the mansions as on Pelham Road.

Finally, the telephone rang, and it was Lenny. I was beside myself with relief and joy. We talked every day for a week, but the conversations felt strange, like someone was listening to Lenny, and he had to pick his words carefully. Then he said the scariest thing. He was off to warmer climates for the rest of the winter—a ranch school in Arizona.

Where in the hell was Arizona?

"I'll write you. I'll write you every day. But don't you leave me. Don't go off with some other fella. I'll be back. I promise." He stopped talking, and all I could hear was his breathing. Heavy breaths that sounded hard to control. Something was wrong. Very wrong. Then he whispered, "I love you, Alice. Please don't forget that I love you."

Then the phone line went dead. He was gone, and there was no word, no sign of where in Arizona he'd been sent. For weeks, I could barely get out of bed in the morning. I'd been destroyed from the inside out, abandoned, left on the side of the road like a bag of spoiled eggs, used up and no longer desired.

Still, I believed he'd keep his promise. I waited for his letters, longed for them, but nothing came. Not for two months.

What was I to do? Die? No. No. I wouldn't do that. I'd just have to find a way to survive without him. I had a life before Lenny. I just had to remember what it was, where I'd lost it, and how long it would take me to get it back.

PART 3

A BEAUTIFUL LOVE AFFAIR

The New York Times

April 11, 1941

SUES RHINELANDER ESTATE
Special to *The New York Times*

Papers have been filed in the Nassau County Surrogate's Court here in a suit by Mrs. Alice Jones Rhinelander for an accounting of the estate of her father-in-law, Philip Rhinelander, millionaire real estate operator, who died last year in Long Beach, L.I.

CHAPTER 12

ROBERTA

1941

I worry about my aunt. The incident at the Hotel Marie Antoinette was horrible, and the next two years of her life—a nightmare. I may not respect the things she's done, but hearing that story, I feel sorry for her.

Still, she isn't the Jones sister I worry the most about. I told my mother that I'd visited Aunt Alice, and her reaction surprised me. She said my relationship with my aunt Alice was my business—not hers.

The following morning, she told me she wasn't feeling well but wasn't sick enough to miss work. That afternoon at Baylor Castle, she slumped over. They rushed her to a hospital; the diagnosis was exhaustion and something about her blood pressure and sugar levels. I called my father to let him know she was ill. He asked if he should come and see her. They hadn't talked since my grandmother Elizabeth's funeral. But I told him I just wanted him to know. There was no reason for him to drop by. She was getting better every day, although that was a lie.

She'd taken ill a month ago and has been resting at home ever since. The doctors say her pressure and sugar are much better. She could go back to work. But she doesn't want to. She just wants to take a bit longer to rest and get stronger.

So I invited her to join me for lunch. I admitted I was meeting Aunt Alice, and for a moment, I thought she might say yes. I've already coerced my aunt to leave her house and eat at a restaurant near her home in New Rochelle.

But Momma's eyes darken suddenly. "I'm not in the mood to sit in a public place with her, especially if she's going to be all nostalgic about something she never should've wanted in the first place."

I have not heard my mother speak with such bitterness about anyone, not even Aunt Alice, before.

"Okay, then," I say with a smile. "Maybe next time."

With that, I am out the door, hightailing it to New Rochelle and Pelham Road.

Alice answers the door and says she'd rather stay in. I tell her she needs to get out of the house. Too many bad things have happened inside these walls.

It is as though the memories are lodged in the walls, seeped into the floorboards, and attached to the cobwebs in the ceiling. They are always there, closing in, cutting off hope of her having something other than what she once had on Pelham Road.

My speech is successful. An hour later, Alice is dressed in her latest fashion, her hair styled and her makeup on, and we are ready. I think.

Then she puts on a hat with a veil that covers her face.

"I don't want to be recognized."

I want to say she won't be, for no one cares about her fifteen-year-old story, but I don't. I've spent several months in a row seeing her now and then—and arguing only half the time. Why risk my track record now?

We arrive at the Greek restaurant and settle into a rear booth close to an exit.

I order a cup of coffee, moussaka, and a Coca-Cola. "What do you feel like eating, Aunt Alice?"

"I don't eat at diners like this one. You don't know where these people get their food."

She is thin as a rail, and I want her to eat, but her prejudice against immigrants would be funny if she weren't serious. I would challenge her if I hadn't promised myself I wouldn't argue with her. She is too frail for me to yell at. "Order the soup. They make a great chicken soup, or a hamburger. They have a lot of American food on the menu. I don't think you've been eating regularly, Aunt Alice. You look rather pale and thin, tea at least."

She orders the soup and tea. When our drinks are served, I ask her about Lenny and what she did after he left her in January 1922.

"I did what I had to do. I was young but not a child. So I returned to work, cleaning houses and caring for rich people's children. I didn't say much at home. Everybody knew what had happened by then. My sisters felt sorry for me. Your mother and her husband didn't have much to say. Except your father insisted the reason Lenny's father hated me wasn't because I was colored but because I was poor. He said this in front of my mother, and she nearly kicked him out of the house. I remember her saying, 'Just because Emily took on your skin color on her marriage license doesn't mean me or my girls aren't white. So you stop talking like that in this house.' Aunt Alice laughed, a deep chest-clearing laugh. "I'd never heard Mummy speak so forcibly to anyone about anything."

"What did my mother say when Grandma talked to Papa like that?" I can't help but to ask.

"Emily treated my hurt. She'd stop by to wash my hair, paint my fingernails and toenails, and bring me music to play on my Victrola."

"That sounds like Momma."

Aunt Alice plays with the tea bag in her hot water, dipping it in and pulling it out. "After a while, I wasn't as melancholy.

And I'd agree to go when Gracie wanted to drag me out of the house instead of refusing. She knew many people, most of them men, and her boyfriend back then, Footsie Miller, was quite a character.

"He introduced me to several of his friends who were like him. Italians from Hell's Kitchen, fast talkers who always had a fistful of money. I figured they were bootleggers or racketeers. They liked having girls who looked like Gracie and me in their arms. Back then, I had some meat on my bones, but after a few weeks, going out with Gracie made me sad. I missed Lenny."

Our food arrives. She doesn't say much more about that year she spent without Lenny after that, at least, not today. Perhaps the next time I see her, we'll talk about the Rhinelanders, and maybe she'll bring up Lenny again.

My aunt Alice telephoned the apartment, and my mother answered the phone. I don't know what they said to each other. I didn't even know it was Aunt Alice on the line, but within seconds of my mother picking up the telephone receiver and shouting for me to grab the phone, the pitch of her voice told me the person on the other end wasn't someone she cared to talk to.

And yes, she said "someone."

That was two days ago. Now, I am seated at the kitchen table on Pelham Road on a Saturday afternoon, sipping tea and watching my aunt try her best to keep from punching a wall.

"Do you know I have not received a dime, not one red cent of the money owed me since that old man died?" She is pacing, cigarette smoke trailing behind her like helium balloons. She turns left, then right, and marches from one end of the kitchen to the other and back. She doesn't seem to care where the ashes land. "If Adelaide Rhinelander Thomas thinks I'll hide in the bushes, she's lost her ever-loving mind. I will not go quietly."

I've learned the best way to chat with my aunt and avoid a shouting match is to remain calm and let her carry the burden of hysteria. When I first met her, I thought she was the one who held everything inside, which meant I couldn't tell what was really on her mind. Then I learned she has two temperatures: heating up and on fire. "Then what do you intend to do?"

"I've already done it." She stops near the stove, holding the cigarette to her lips—puff, puff, puff. "I have a lawyer. We're going to get my money back. You watch, you just watch."

"Why would she do such a thing? I mean, it's money that the courts agreed you were owed. What makes her so angry?"

"What makes you so angry at me?" She lights another cigarette. "You've come by here every other month for the last year with nothing to do but listen to my story, a story you can't write, and don't you dare forget that."

It was another deal I felt I had no choice but to accept. Perhaps down the road, I'll get what I wanted from her. Meanwhile, the stories are compelling. If she is lying, she has a talent for it.

She stands with her ankles crossed, wearing a lovely pair of alligator-skin pumps, an A-line skirt just below the knee, and a broad-shouldered white blouse. Her outfits are always the best.

"Why do you keep coming back?" she asks. "I know how you feel about me."

"I didn't come here to discuss how I feel about you. I came because you called, and I figured you needed my assistance. I'm not interested in listening to you gripe. Now, why did you call me? What is it that you want me to do?"

"The *Amsterdam News* must print an article about how the last of the Rhinelander family, Ms. Adelaide Rhinelander

Thomas, wants to renege on a promise made by her father to me. What kind of woman would do something like that after all these years? I want your newspaper to discover the root of her vindictive behavior. It has to be more than not wanting to give me my three hundred dollars a month. What did I ever do to her that she would go to all this trouble to keep me from what is mine? That's why you are here. To get me some answers and have those answers be interesting enough for Holden Richards to fill the front page of his newspaper with my name, her name, and why I don't have my money."

"Well, I guess I've got a job to do."

"Then you'd better get to it."

CHAPTER 13

ALICE

1922–1924

Lenny was gone. Our last night at the Hotel Marie Antoinette was the last time I would ever see him. I believed that in my heart, and the pain was indescribable.

Loneliness and love go together like a cloudy sky on a rainy day.

The day that would never leave me be. A cold, wet day that would turn into years of sorrow.

There was joy on the day before. There was peace in my heart, lying in his arms. We ate food that tasted heavenly, filling our bellies and our souls. The music we played on the Victrola was Joplin, the Original Dixieland Jazz Band, and Marion Harris.

I used to love rainy days. I recalled coming home from school when I was around eight years old, and I knew I'd make Mummy angry if I were late. But as long as it wasn't too cold, I wanted to feel the raindrops on my skin, the moisture clinging to my eyelashes. I knew I'd get a good whupping for ruining my plaid pinafore (which covered my long-sleeved white dress) and muddying my patent leather shoes. But I didn't want to be a good girl.

That's how I felt with Lenny away in Arizona. He broke my

heart, but I remembered that little girl, and every day, she could feel the rain, even though there was nothing but sunshine.

Now, at twenty-three, I was drowning from loneliness and the love I thought I'd lost forever. But then I received a letter, and then another. Soon, I wasn't as lonely. I was still very sad, but I was also hopeful.

My sweet Alice,

I do not know why I am here. I walk around the school campus feeling like a dead man, knowing you are not around the corner waiting for me. That you are not lying in my bed. I am so sorry and so sad that we parted the way we did. You must understand that none of it was something I imagined ever happening. My father needs to control every inch of my life. I can't get away from him or any of my family. Not until I turn twenty-one.

I love you—more than anything on this earth. Promise me you will wait until I return and that you will not stop loving me, my dearest. I need to know you will wait for me.

Yours forever,
Lenny

My dearest Lenny,

I received one of your sweet letters this Saturday morning. It's so good to get your letters, one each day for the past week, dear.

You have my correct phone number. But please do not call me in the evening, as I will not be here. Call me in the morning or afternoon, up to five thirty. You will be able to reach me until then, but after that time, I will be gone.

No, Leonard, dear, I am never disappointed with you as long as I hear from you once a day. I hope my

*letters cheer you up as yours do me. They make me
very happy.*

*If I say so myself, Lenny, dearest, I shall always love
you.*

*Yours as ever,
Alice*

Dear Lenny,

*I have finished supper, and I am ready to sit down
and write my dear beloved a sweet letter.*

*Daddy has gone out, with it being election night, and
Mummy and I stayed home. I am writing you this letter
with the Victrola playing beside me, and on the other
side is your loving photograph. It's just that your beautiful face looks so lonesome, and I miss my angel child.*

*But never mind, my honey, I love you. I also hope
you are taking great interest in your studies as it will
be good for your self-esteem. Just know that your girl,
although miles and miles away, thinks about you every
day, hoping and waiting patiently to see you return to
me one day soon.*

*I moved away from home for a bit. Up in Green-
wich with Mrs. Anderson. She isn't a nice lady. She
made things very hard on me. She always wanted me
to clean up every mess she made, which was plenty,
mend her clothing, and cook for her all day. But I'm
home again.*

*Oh, I am going to New York again on Wednesday
with Gracie. We have it all planned. I'm even going to
pass by your house. That's what we did last week. That
big old house looks funny because I know you're not
inside. God. I miss you terribly. With you gone, I feel
as though I don't have a friend in the world.*

*Yours always as ever,
Alice*

Dearest Alice,

If you want to marry me, as you've said so many times, let's get it over with, or else break the whole thing off right now before I grow fonder of you. As things are, I believe I can get along very nicely without you. I would miss you, of course, for you have been the sweetest thing in my life for nearly two years, during which, every day, I've learned to love you more and more. I need something definite done now so that there won't be any possible suffering for me later on because that would happen if I didn't have you.

Yours,
Lenny

Sunshine days and moonlit nights. Laughter, tears, and passion. It had been three years since Lenny and I first met. However, two of those years, we'd spent apart, and all I had to show for them was a thousand love letters.

The months stretched into years. Gracie married her Italian lover, Arthur "Footsie" Miller. My sister Emily announced her second pregnancy but lost the baby a few months later, and I wrote a thousand love letters to a man in Arizona or on a voyage to Alaska, I later learned, whom I prayed I'd see again one day.

In April 1924, a few weeks before his twenty-first birthday, Lenny returned to New York. Even if I hadn't seen him in almost two years, I hadn't stopped caring about him, loving him.

I didn't see him right away. Instead, we talked on the telephone several times a day for two weeks, his words reassuring, pleading for my patience.

"Just a little while longer, my love. We will be together soon," he said. "We've made it this far. We will have everything we've ever dreamed of. You'll see. I promise."

On Lenny's birthday, his family's lawyer hand-delivered a

check from a trust fund his mother had created. Then Lenny drove to New Rochelle, where I was waiting.

"Honey, we are solvent," he said, sweeping me into his arms.

I had no clue what he meant by the word *solvent*, and my ignorance had to show on my bewildered face.

"I have money! My own money." He lifted me off my feet and swung me around, his laughter filling my heart. "I can do as I please. My father won't be hounding me to do his bidding."

"And what is it you wish to do?"

"Be with you." The kiss was ecstasy, our hands groping the other's back and waists. Our bodies trembling with desire and joy.

After our reunion in the foyer, we sat in the kitchen, where Mummy had prepared a feast.

He stuttered less and had put on some weight. He'd always been tall; his muscles suited his lean frame. But now, he was larger, stronger, his physique harder and more pronounced. Lenny had acquired a calmness, too, a confidence I hadn't seen in him before.

Was it the money or me that made him more of a man? Did it matter as long as we were committed to each other?

From May through September, we were together. I thought we couldn't be happier. Then, happiness surprised me by giving me even more.

One night in October, we drove to Hudson Beach, the first time since he'd returned from his travels. He picked me up at home in his new automobile, a Rolls-Royce Silver Ghost.

At our spot, we necked for an hour. Every caress, every kiss, and endearment was as passionate as the first time he pressed his lips against mine.

A full moon filled the black-and-blue sky with light and shadows. When we paused to breathe, he faced me with moist eyes.

"I love you, Alice. I thought everything was perfect between us."

"What do you mean? Is something wrong?" My voice trembled with worry.

"No, honey bunch. Everything is right," he said. "But it can be more perfect." He swallowed. "I have decided to ask you something, and I want you to answer me h-honestly."

"Of course I will. Always."

He took hold of my hands, and I could feel his heart beating through his fingertips. I was afraid. What now? What new bend in the road would we need to avoid?

"I want to be with you, only you, forever," he said. "I love you, and if you love me—"

"Of course I love you."

He let go of my hands and reached into his vest pocket. The box differed from the one that had held the sapphire ring. He flipped open the box's lid, and inside was a ring. A beautiful diamond cut in the Asscher style with a platinum band, just like the one I'd seen in *Vogue*.

"Will you marry me?"

With my hand over my mouth and tears in my eyes, I said yes. But he took my hand from my face and asked me again.

"I want to see you when you answer me," he said, kissing my fingertips. "I want you to be my bride. Will you marry me, Alice Jones? Will you become my Mrs. Rhinelander?"

I had dreamed of marriage to Lenny but had left it at that, a dream. The horror of how his father's lawyer had made our love ugly still haunted me. But Lenny had asked me to marry him despite his father, family, or friends.

"Yes. Yes. Yes," I said, looking deeply into his eyes.

We kissed and embraced and kissed again.

"When?" I asked. "When should we do it? Get married?"

"Tomorrow. Next week."

"Oh my." I laughed, but his expression wiped away my

smile. "Are you serious? Lenny, are you insane? My dress. My sisters. My mother. We won't have time to prepare."

"We must be quick. Please, Alice. Let's go to the courthouse. We can get the license and wed today."

There was a desperation to his voice, an edge that could be determination or panic.

The thought flashed before my eyes that we should wait, marry in the spring. We should have a church wedding, bridesmaids, groomsmen, the works. But I couldn't deny Lenny.

"Okay. But we can't do it tomorrow. The courthouse isn't open on Sundays and Mondays—I can't get ready in one day."

"Then, Tuesday. I'll arrange everything with the judge and the courthouse in New Rochelle."

When Lenny brought me home that night, I woke up my parents and told them my news. They were as excited as I was.

By then, Lenny was the family favorite, especially with Daddy. They spent hours discussing the stock market, gambling, horse races, and baseball. I'd sit knitting while listening to them go on and on about the New York Yankees and how they dominated baseball. My mother showed her love for Lenny the same way she did with everyone she cared for, not so much with words but by treating him to her best recipes. His favorite desserts—he loved pie and strong coffee spiked with bootleg whiskey: the best Daddy could afford.

"What kind of pie is this, Mrs. Jones?" Lenny sat at the dinner table, sniffing in the aroma. "I believe this is my favorite meal."

"It's a pork pie. Very popular in England, and you love my pot roast, so I thought . . ."

"I've never heard of such a thing, but I do love it, Mrs. Jones."

"I've baked some pastries for you, too, made with plenty of butter, fruit, and alcohol," Mummy added gaily. "I'll make you a cake for dinner tomorrow. What's your favorite?"

"Thank you, ma'am. I love chocolate cake."

Lenny was part of the family, my family. I didn't care about his family or their reaction to Lenny marrying a girl from a working-class family—immigrants to boot, with no place in polite society, not as long as my parents and sisters loved him as I did.

"Where would you like to live?" Lenny asked.

We sat on the back porch steps, his arms wrapped around my shoulders, my head tucked against his neck, watching a million stars twinkle in the night sky.

"I've only lived in New Rochelle," I said. "I don't know where else we could live or where else I'd want to live."

"I've been all over the world but never had any say in where I went. But there is one place I love more than any other." Lenny pulled me closer, which I would've thought impossible. "A group of Hawaiian islands in the Pacific. The trees and beaches are beautiful. But the sand is what I love. There are a variety of colors from island to island and beach to beach—black sand, white sand, and red sand, even a beach with green sand. I want to live there. You'd love it there. The people are beautiful. The weather is fantastic. Their skin is tan, like yours, year-round. A shade of gold in the moonlight, soft and splendid in the sunshine."

"It sounds beautiful but so far away."

"We spent the summer, my mother and I, on the beaches, moving from island to island, just the two of us. It was a perfect summer."

I heard the love and the pain in his voice, but I didn't ask him to share more about that summer. I didn't like seeing him hurt. "But what about your father? I think he'd chase us no matter where we went."

"I am free of him. My trust fund has kicked in, and we, you and me, will have plenty of money and can do whatever we want to do and live wherever we want to live."

"But you want to live in the Pacific. How many miles away is that?"

"Come on now, Alice. Do you want to stay in New Rochelle for the rest of your life? What about adventure? Seeing places you've never seen before. Why stay here when we can go anywhere?"

"I'd miss my family."

"You do love me, yes?"

"I love you with all my heart and everything that is in me."

"So, I'm your family, too. Right?" He removed his nose glasses so I could see nothing but crystal-blue eyes looking into mine. "If you love me, you will do as I say, and I say we need to leave New York."

His tone had changed. The tender request was a demand.

"That's not fair, Lenny. I love you, but I don't know if I can leave home or my family right away."

"The way you talk, I fear you won't ever want to leave New Rochelle." He took his arm from around me and clasped his hands together.

"Lenny, please." How could I tell him I was afraid? I'd never been away from my family. I wanted my own apartment and a job in Manhattan, but I never thought that meant not being able to see my parents every day. "It's just that I'm so used to being around them and helping them."

"So you won't move? You want to stay in New Rochelle forever?"

"Lenny, don't be mad at me. Please."

"What about Emily? She and her family work and live in a castle in the Hudson Valley in Westchester County. She doesn't have a problem not residing in your father's house."

"Emily's different. She made a mistake and married a man Daddy didn't want her to marry."

Lenny frowned. "She married a Negro. So what? How can your father have a problem with Robert when he is not a white man himself?"

"You're wrong, Lenny. I've told you before that Daddy is from Jamaica. And if he does have some colored blood, it's barely a drop. It's island blood. Not Negro. Robert is brown." I tilted my head, looking at him from the corner of my eye. "Besides, it's old news. Daddy forgave Emily for marrying him once Roberta was born."

"If that's how your family explains it."

"What do you mean *explain*?"

"Let's not get into that," he said sharply. "I want to move out of New York. You don't. Not yet, but I will convince you one day. And you'll do as I say."

I still didn't like his tone, and I didn't understand why he had practically called my father a Negro. "Is this our first argument? Are you angry at me?"

He stood abruptly and paced for several moments before stopping to comb his fingers roughly through his hair. "Yes, it's our first argument, and I'm angry. But I'll rent us an apartment near here, and we'll live there, but only for one year. Then, we must find a city where it's just us. Not your family, and nowhere near mine."

CHAPTER 14

My wedding day was a feverish dream.

It was a fantasy with a simple white dress, bridesmaids, and a knight in shining armor—who occasionally stuttered and wore nose glasses.

We all knew that before the wedding, you picked your dress, a gorgeous gown of white silk and lace, and you were the princess of your dreams. Your bridal party—your sisters and girlfriends from school, the prettiest ones, for they looked the best in the lace lilac and lavender dresses. The groom and the groomsmen would be adequately tucked and stuffed into tuxedos and tails with tall black hats on their heads and starched white shirts with rounded collars and silk ties. But there were no lilacs nor the smell of lavender and roses.

And here I was, questioning the terrain.

Why were courthouses built on small hillsides with a hundred steps to climb? Did it make the building any more special? Did what happen inside need to be closer to heaven? Or was the long climb to give the bride and groom time to change their minds?

At a courthouse on a Tuesday morning in October, after walking up the tower of concrete steps, I stood in a judge's chambers—next to the man who would be my husband.

My heart was my guide. And marriage could happen without the white lace dress, the bridesmaids, or the groomsmen. All that was needed besides the groom was a man in a robe behind a desk who asked if we took each other for man and wife.

"I do," Lenny said.

"I do," I replied when asked.

Shaking with excitement and anticipation, Lenny and I married on October 14, 1924, in a civil service at the New Rochelle courthouse.

After the ceremony, we didn't go out on the town. We didn't gather a group of friends at Muriel's Café to celebrate our nuptials. Instead, we had dinner with my parents at our house on Pelham Road.

After dinner, we gathered in the living room, sipping port, eating slices of yellow cake with buttercream frosting, and smiling into each other's eyes.

I sat on the stool next to the wingback chair where Lenny was seated. We talked about nothing, but I recall how we kept touching each other. Our fingers intertwined, a sweet caress on the back of my neck, a gentle pat on his knee. Eventually, I sat on his lap, my fingers in his hair.

I caught my mother and sisters smiling at us. With whimsy in her gaze, Gracie married for a little more than a year, seemed happy for us, too.

We stayed for a few hours before taking the short walk to our new apartment, a block from my family's home on Pelham Road. On the outside, the building looked like any other on the block, but inside was magnificent. From the day he proposed until we moved in, I believed Lenny had his maids and butlers and chauffeurs fix up our new apartment, and I swear it could've been on Fifth Avenue.

I was very nervous about our wedding night. We may have slept together many times before, but this would be our first time making love as husband and wife. And I sensed that Lenny was as nervous as me.

With shaky hands, he reached into his pocket for the keys to unlock the apartment door. Once that was done, he lifted me into his arms, bumped the door with his hip, and carried me over the threshold.

He placed me down gently and danced through the apartment, mimicking the judge at the courthouse. "'I now pronounce you man and wife.'"

His long limbs swung by his sides as his big feet hopped from one to the other rhythmically. He had a wonderful sense of rhythm, making his chaotic movement fit with the music, even if only in his mind and mine.

After a few moments, Lenny ended the excited dance and the stripping off our clothes, and the frantic lovemaking began.

Later, lying in bed, hugging each other tightly, I couldn't help myself. I had to tell him something he may or may not believe, but I needed to say it. "I don't need your family's money to be happy."

"I know that."

He sat up in the bed but didn't let go of me. He pulled me closer, and my head rested on his chest. "However, the problem with money is me. I don't believe I can live like a poor man. I'm not poor," he said solemnly. "I'm sorry, but that's why I had to go away for so long, to make sure my father couldn't keep my inheritance from me."

"Can we live on your inheritance?"

"Yes. We can. We will, for a long while," he said, stroking my head. "Long enough. We won't be beggars. You won't have to work. And I am keeping my job at the Rhinelander real estate offices, so I will have some income."

"Your father will come around. I know he will. He has to see how happy you are. You don't stutter anymore."

His body tensed when I said that, so I amended it. "Well, not often, and then it's only a word here or there. Now, you can focus on what you have to do every day. Your father has to know you are no longer a boy. And he must respect you man-to-man."

"That's another reason I love you. You are a dreamer."

"You're right," I said, massaging his bare chest and rubbing my thumb over his lips.

Lenny had a faraway look.

"We are married to each other, and we are happy. So, let's stop talking about your father. There's no room for him in our bed. There's just the two of us, and maybe someday we'll add a bundle of joy."

Lenny cupped my chin and stopped me from talking with a fervent kiss. Then he pulled me to him as I draped a leg over his hip.

"You are right. The only people in this bed are you and me."

That was the end of our talk about his father and money. I don't believe I slept that night, and, of course, neither did Lenny. My wedding night was perfect. A bride could not ask for more.

Lenny and I were in a bubble. A magical, mystical, floating-above-the-sky, feet-never-touching-the-ground bubble. Exactly how a newly married couple should feel about their lives.

The outside world might be tarnished, dirty, crowded, and unforgiving. But in our bubble, we controlled the colors of the rainbow, the birdcalls, the breeze through an open window, and the rhythms of the most beautiful music. We inhaled the sweetest fragrances. Honeysuckle and lavender filled our nostrils, and we cherished each other.

I adored him, and he adored me.

The bubble showed its first crack a month after our wedding.

Lenny woke up early and picked up the morning editions of the *Standard-Star* of New Rochelle, the *Daily News*, and the *New York Times*. Somehow, all three papers had found their way to our front door.

Before unfolding the *Standard-Star* (it always came rolled), Lenny slipped off his robe, climbed back beneath the sheets, and lay next to me.

He pulled out the sports section and handed me the rest of the newspaper. I went directly to the women's fashion pages and checked out the sales at the department stores: Blooming-dale's, Henri Bendel, Lord & Taylor, and Saks. Stores where I once sought a job. Stores where I couldn't afford anything before Lenny.

Thumbing through the pages, I caught a headline that curled my stomach with knots. A reporter had made our marriage a front-page news story.

The date burned into my brain: Friday, November 14, 1924. The headline made me dizzy: RHINELANDER'S SON MARRIES CABBY'S DAUGHTER.

I can't remember what kind of noise I made—a groan, a curse. Whatever came out of my mouth caused Lenny to drop the sports section as he shot upright in the bed.

"What's wrong? What does it say?"

I couldn't look at him. "They mention my father is of West Indian descent. Why are they doing that? Are they questioning my race? Trying to imply that I'm not white."

Lenny threw the sheet off and swung his long legs over the edge of the bed. His feet struck the floor with a loud thud, but he said nothing.

"They are saying I'm colored, Lenny. It says my father is a swarthy, West Indian colored man." I scanned the newspaper in disbelief. "They know about Emily—that she married a Negro." I felt my breath rush from my lungs, and I couldn't breathe. "But I'm not colored. I'm not Negro. I'm white, Lenny. My father may have a drop of mulatto blood, which is why his skin is darker. That doesn't make him colored or

Negro. And it certainly doesn't make me anything other than white."

Lenny sat on the edge of the bed with his head in his hands. His back hunched, his eyes hidden from me.

"What are you thinking? Dear God, what are you thinking?" I scooted to the edge of the bed, barely controlling the desire to grab his face and force him to look at me. "Say something, Lenny. Please. Don't you believe me? Is it your father? Will he be upset?"

The longer it took for Lenny to speak, the more I felt like everything was ending. Our perfect world had broken, split in half.

Was my husband broken, too?

"Lenny!"

Finally, he raised his head, and I wished he hadn't. A look of despair filled his eyes.

"Don't stare at me that way, Alice. Don't you understand? This is more than a problem. It is trouble."

Problem. Trouble. The words he used frightened me more than the headlines. "What do you mean?"

"My father was only adjusting to the news that I'd married you, a cabdriver's daughter. Now there will be a family meeting. Everyone will come to the mansion to throw in their two cents on dealing with the disgrace." Lenny snapped to his feet. "Damn it."

"Do you hate me because of the newspapers?"

The anger in his eyes vanished. "Honey, I've had an idea about your bloodline from the moment I saw you at the Orchard School. You looked and acted so white, but there was something different about you, something that seemed especially beautiful. I thought you were maybe Spanish. Then I saw your father, and I understood."

"You understood what? Is this what your father thought when he sent the lawyer to the Hotel Marie Antoinette? Is that why I've never met him? Or why you have never invited me to your father's house? Why didn't he attend our wedding? Was it that he hated you married a girl with a supposedly colored father?

"Or will it be the first time he learns about any of this— about us—when he reads the newspaper articles?"

"He didn't care about you being colored. Not at first. He cared that I had the nerve to defy him over a servant girl. If he could've found a way to add anyone in your family to the *Social Register*, he would've gladly passed you off as a Latin heiress. He got mad because I wouldn't treat you like a tramp. I had the nerve to take you to the best places and show you off at the finest resorts. So, your father's skin color is only one of the items stuck in my father's craw."

"Will he be mad about the story or not? And what should I do? My parents have never been in the newspaper. Now these reporters have printed their names and addresses. The world will know them and me. You're accustomed to the limelight. We aren't. I'm not."

Lenny's laugh chilled my blood. "Then you shouldn't have married a Rhinelander."

"That's an awful thing to say, Lenny. I'm sorry your father is mad—"

"Mad? I wish that were the worst of it. I can handle his anger, but the man doesn't get mad. He gets . . . shit . . . shit. He gets even."

He sat back on the bed and pressed his palms into the mattress, his fingertips gripping the sheet. His body sagged, and he squeezed his eyes shut. I thought for a moment he was about to cry.

I hated seeing him upset, but I was hurting, too. I had the same feeling in my gut I saw in his eyes: fear and dread.

I knew how vindictive his father could be. He'd had Lenny carted off to Arizona and a voyage to Alaska for two years to keep him from me. I shouldn't have been surprised by anything his father did.

"What should we do, Lenny?"

"I don't know what we'll do. Not yet. Give me a day or two to figure this out. I need a few days."

It was the *Social Register*; those people mattered to Lenny's father. As long as they felt slighted by young Rhinelander's fascination with low-class people, which would be me and my family, and then went as far as marrying one, also me, and flaunting her under their noses the way he'd done—it would mean trouble for Lenny.

I swear his father cared more about what those people said than he did his flesh and blood.

Lenny was on the telephone. His posture let me know he wasn't enjoying the conversation. I didn't interfere, although I wanted to. Married a month, and we'd had more drama come our way than anyone else in my family. Even Gracie, who married her bootlegger husband Footsie Miller over a year ago, didn't have her face plastered on every newspaper in Manhattan.

I went to the bathroom. Not wishing to overhear whatever bus Lenny was being thrown under, I sat on the settee in front of the vanity, grabbed a bottle of red polish, and started to paint my nails.

"A-Alice. Where are you?"

I heard him and hoped whatever he wanted was better news than how he sounded. "Lenny, I'm in the bathroom."

The door creaked open. He stood in the archway, wearing the silk pajamas I'd bought him as a wedding gift. But they looked wrinkled.

"Are you okay?" I was still facing the vanity when I turned and looked at him closely. "Oh God. Now what's wrong?"

I glanced at the newspaper he clutched in his fist. Whatever he had to tell me had to do with reporters and newspaper people. I prayed I could survive what he had to say, but I wasn't sure. "Please, Lenny, you look ghastly."

"Yesterday, the story was in three papers. Today, it's in ten, picked up by the Associated Press and Reuters. My father is pissed as hell and wants to see me."

"Is that what the telephone call was all about?"

"That he wants to pin my ass to a skewer and roast me over an open flame." He waved the newspaper at me with a mocking expression. "'Look at the goddamn headlines!' He yelled at me so loud, I had to put down the bottle of nail polish and cover my ears."

I stood and held his hand, easing the paper from his grip. But letting go of the paper seemed to release his feet. He paced back and forth, moving in circles and straight lines, going nowhere but looking exhausted as he kept moving.

Then the expression on his face, the one I recalled from that night at the Hotel Marie Antoinette, reappeared. Fear and panic. Panic and fear.

Where was the strong man who had carried me over the threshold and made love to me three times a day every day since?

"So what?" I growled. "There's nothing he can do now. It's probably better that everyone knows we're married, right?" I touched Lenny's face. "It will be okay." I cupped his chin, forcing him to look at me. "I just have to make sure my family is fine. But this won't last forever. Eventually, the newspapers will lose interest in us, and your father will, too. Don't you think?"

Suddenly, he knelt before me, his arms around my hips, pulling me close. "I don't know. I hope you're right. But we can't talk to the press. No matter what questions they ask— we don't say a word. Understood?" A slight smile curled his lips. "Sorry, I know you better than that."

"You do. Whatever happens with your father, my family, or the press, we'll deal with it together." I wiggled free of his embrace, gently massaging the top of his head. "Let's not worry about this now. You've had a long day, and guess what

I did?" By now, I had him by the hand, leading him from the bathroom through the bedroom into the kitchen. "I made dinner."

"All by yourself?"

I wasn't sure if I should be bothered by his response or laugh at his joke. "What are you implying?"

"Nothing sinister, other than your mother has brought us dinner daily for the past three weeks. I thought she did that because you can't cook."

"It's true, I can't cook as well as my mother, but I know my way around a kitchen," I said. "Come on, let's eat and worry about those newspapers later. Besides, this may be the end of it. Your father can't do anything now that we're married."

On the table was a pot of stew and a loaf of freshly baked bread. And I'd lit a candle and placed a rose in a vase.

"This is lovely." He didn't pick up his fork. Instead, he closed his eyes, his fingers rubbing his eyebrows, moving in circles over his forehead as if he was pushing something out of his mind, pushing something away from his thoughts. Then his hands dropped, and he sat rather tall.

"Let's eat," he said finally. "It looks delicious."

CHAPTER 15

In one day, our names appeared in the headlines of three newspapers. Two days later, hundreds of papers had the story. Chicago, Detroit, Pittsburgh, and every city and town, north and south, were talking about Mr. and Mrs. Rhinelander.

Everywhere, people were reading about Alice Beatrice Jones and Kip Rhinelander. The millionaire, son of a multi-millionaire real estate tycoon, a white boy, had married the daughter of a taxicab driver with West Indian colored blood.

Then the headlines upped the ante, and it wasn't just my father's blood that was news; it was mine, too.

Lenny and I couldn't leave our apartment without reporters flashing their bright lights at us or shouting questions, demanding answers that were none of their business. And it wasn't only our apartment under siege. My family—my parents; Gracie and her hubby, Footsie; and even (but not often) Emily and Robert and their little girl, Roberta. Reporters weren't as interested in what two Negroes had to say about Lenny and me, and since my sister and her husband were "both" Negro, according to their marriage license, their comments held less value.

My parents were followed when they left their house. My father's taxicab couldn't pick up fares. Reporters pestered anyone who came near him, and passengers didn't want to risk ending up on the front page of the *New York Times, Daily News, Standard-Star,* or *Amsterdam News.*

The biggest insult was how the articles acted as if New York society elites were the actual victims—those individuals, families, and heirs in the *Social Register,* having their good names sullied by a Rhinelander who married beneath him.

I could envision the conversations in the breakfast nooks and fine dining halls on Fifth Avenue and Astor Place. Poor Lenny's wealthy relatives had to deal with reporters who wandered into their fancy homes, fancy office buildings, fancy restaurants, and limousines, behaving as if they were entitled to the details of the darkest moment in their lives—an unbelievable crime: a boy who fell in love with a girl suspected of being colored. And even if I wasn't 100 percent white or 1 percent colored, it wasn't a crime for Lenny and me to marry, not in the state of New York.

Everyone I loved was being chased, harassed, and disrespected. I had to do something. They hadn't asked for their lives to be scrutinized or ruthlessly examined. What they were going through was my fault, and it was up to me to fix it. Or at least try.

One day, Lenny left our apartment before sunrise to escape reporters, and frustration consumed me. I might even have lost my mind for a stretch of time. How else could I explain what I did next?

I took the train to Manhattan and the offices of the *Daily News.* I entered the building, went up to the reception desk, and demanded to speak with Grace Robinson, the reporter writing most of the articles about Lenny and me.

"Is she here? Where is she?" I stood in a noisy newsroom. Defiant and bold, I had stormed into the *Daily News* to call the woman a liar, gossipmonger, or whatever nasty words came into my head. Typewriters pounded, voices raised and lowered like a choir singing an anthem.

After a few minutes, a woman no older than me, with

short blond hair cut in the latest bobbed hairstyle, waltzed up to me, pen and paper in hand.

"What can I do for you, Mrs. Rhinelander?" She asked the question with her pen poised over the notepad she held. But I didn't answer. I just stood there with my hands balled into fists (a habit I had when I was angry). With my arms at my side, I pounded my thighs.

"Are you going to write down everything I say?"

"That is my intention," she said casually. "I am a reporter, and that is my job. So, tell me, the word on the street is that you are colored. Is it true?"

"That's a lie! I am as white as you. Why do you spread rumors? Why are you even interested in what my husband and I do or say!"

"You and your husband are news, Mrs. Rhinelander. And we'll write about you as long as you remain news."

Staring at her calm, perky features and confident stance, I lost my nerve. I was on her playground. She ruled here.

I walked out of the *Daily News* office, feeling like the dumbest dumb Dora ever born. Grace Robinson, the reporter, had shown no emotion as she lowered her news hammer on my head. She didn't care about me, Lenny, or my family. She had no concern about how her news stories hurt me or my family. No concern in the least.

I didn't mention my trip to the *Daily News* to Lenny. What would be the point? I had embarrassed myself and didn't need him to console me. I deserved to feel the way I felt.

But when I woke up still embarrassed by my conversation with Ms. Robinson, I made myself a promise: I would never do such a harebrained thing again.

Since the article about our marriage broke on November 14, reporters and photographers had camped on the stoop outside our apartment building. The morning following my meeting with Ms. Robinson, when Lenny left our apartment to meet with his father, I slipped out the rear exit of our building while reporters chased him to his limousine. I cut through a row of bushes and edged into the backyard, slipping by the press before ducking through the basement entrance to my parents' house.

"Aren't you a sly one," Gracie said as I stumbled into the kitchen.

"What are you doing here? Why aren't you home with your husband?"

"Footsie's out of town. Had a delivery to make, but he'll return soon enough."

I elbowed by her, the scent of fresh coffee drawing me to the stove. "A delivery. Right. You and Footsie should be in the news, too. I see the headline: BOOTLEGGER AND HIS BRIDE ON THE LOOSE."

"A lie. He's not a bootlegger, but that would be a better story than what I read in this morning's paper. Have you seen it? Or have you and your wealthy hubby become immune to front-page gossip disguised as news people should care about?"

"Immune?" I said, my temper flaring.

"To headlines. In newspapers. That's what!"

I poured a cup of coffee. "Never mind. What paper? What are you talking about?"

She shimmied to the kitchen table and flung a newspaper at me, which I caught.

"Read the headline," she ordered.

I read it with my hand over my heart.

RHINELANDER'S COLORED BRIDE FLITS
WITH BLUE BLOOD MATE
("I AM NOT COLORED!" CRIES THE
BRIDE OF RHINELANDER)

"When did you talk to a reporter?" Gracie asked, hands on hips, judging me with knitted brows.

"I didn't. Or I did. But she caught me off guard. She shouted at me, called me a name, and I yelled back. How could she put that in the paper?"

"Just like that." Gracie pointed at the paper.

My knees were suddenly weak. I sat in a chair at the kitchen table. "Lenny is going to go bonkers."

"Forget about Lenny. These reporters are hounding you and us because of him and his family—and I think they're the ones feeding lies to the reporters, saying people who have known us for twenty years have a problem with Daddy's skin color. No one in New Rochelle has ever said a thing about it, and he walks into the same church every Sunday, the same clubs, the same restaurants and neighborhood stores. The Rhinelanders make us look like scammers, as if we deliberately tricked Lenny. A man who has sat in this kitchen too many times to count, eating our mother's cooking and playing cards with our father. Hell, Lenny and Robert, a real Negro, have sat at this table, chewing the fat like they're brothers. So, yeah. I am sick and tired of opening the paper and seeing our family dragged through the mud."

Gracie was always getting riled up and saying things to make trouble, but this time, some of it made sense.

"I'm sorry," I said. "I never imagined something like this would happen. I swear. I'll talk to Lenny. There has to be a way to fix it."

That evening, Lenny stormed into the apartment with a rolled newspaper in his fist and his blue eyes black with rage. Any hope I had that he wouldn't see the *Daily News* article before I could explain dissolved.

"You spoke to r-reporters—?"

"I'm sorry. I made a mistake. I just got so angry." I followed him as he paced through the apartment, from the living room into the hallway, into the bedroom, and back to the living room. All the while demanding that I explain.

"I went to the offices to face that reporter who keeps writing all those stories. I just thought if I talked to her—"

"Why w-would you do such a thing? I told you n-not to talk to reporters." He stopped parading through the apartment and stood opposite me at the end of the sofa. "I warned you. And now look at this mess." He waved the newspaper at me. "Don't you understand that you should never be quoted saying something like this?"

"Lenny, I shouldn't have gone. I know that now. But I didn't lie. I'm not colored."

"That's not the p-point, Alice. This paper was on my father's desk this m-morning. And on the breakfast tables and serving trays of every f-family in the *Social Register*.

"Look at this copy of the morning edition of the *Daily News*." He threw it at me, almost hitting me in the chest. When I gasped, he didn't apologize. He kept yelling. "Look at the headline. You talked to a reporter. It is like hand-delivering the stories to them. Reporters are bloodhounds. They keep sniffing until they find something to dig their teeth into."

"You're being so mean to me, Lenny. You've never talked to me like this. I told you I was sorry." I stomped my foot, my voice cracking and tears blinding me. "I didn't mean to get quoted in the paper. I—"

He wiped his face and inhaled deeply. "I've m-made plans. We have to pack. We'll leave in the middle of the night and won't tell anyone where we are going, including your family. We need this story to die down. We can't stay where reporters can ambush us each time we step out of the house."

He walked off, heading for the bedroom, and I hurried after him.

"I can't tell my father?"

"You can't t-tell anyone, Alice. And since I can't trust you to do as I say, I'm not telling you where we're going until we g-get there."

"That's not fair, Lenny."

Ignoring me, he rooted around in the bedroom closet, removing suitcases. Then he dug through the dresser drawers, pulled out undergarments and other items, and tossed them in the suitcases.

His movements were jerky, and too fast, and too big. It was as if his body was as out of control as his temper.

"This is not like you, Lenny. Getting this mad and fussing at me like I did something wrong on purpose. My name or my picture has never been printed in a newspaper. Suddenly, I'm in a fishbowl, and all eyes are on us, our marriage, and our families. We've been married four weeks, and I am devastated that I didn't listen to you, I'm so—"

"Stop." He held up a hand. "Don't tell me you're sorry again. I know you are. But I had a tough day at work." Lenny's shoulders relaxed as he walked toward me. The anger in his eyes had also dulled. "I'll tell you this much. We'll be staying with some friends I know from the Orchard School. People I can trust to keep their mouths shut and not talk to reporters."

His sarcasm hurt, but he'd stopped yelling. "I said I was sorry."

He returned to the dresser, removing clothing, and I joined him, tossing our belongings in suitcases.

"You can telephone your family tomorrow after we are settled."

"Thank you, Lenny. I just don't want them to worry," I said, looking around our beautiful apartment. "What about this place?"

"I'll write them a check. They w-won't have a problem as long as they are paid."

"Lenny, are you sure? Are you sure running away is the best choice?"

"I don't know if it's the best, but we've got to try it," he said. "Now, hurry. We've got a long drive ahead."

I wanted to argue, to tell him he couldn't order me around and not give me any choices, but he was being so strong, so manly, I let it go. We had enough to worry about and fighting each other wouldn't help.

The New York Times

November 8, 1941

ENDS RHINELANDER CASE
Court Orders Annuity Paid to Leonard Kip's Ex-Wife
Special to The New York Times

Surrogate Leon D. Howell, in a decision filed today, ordered the estate of the late Philip Rhinelander to pay life annuities of $3,600 to Ms. Alice Jones, former wife of Mr. Rhinelander's son . . .

CHAPTER 16

———◆◆◆———

ROBERTA

1941

I've seen my aunt off and on over the past year. Most often at her house on Pelham Road, promising her that I wouldn't as much as whisper to Holden Richards. But I keep coming, hoping one day soon, I'll crack through the wall and she'll let me write her story. And who knows, she might also confess to what she did to break up my parents.

Today is Sunday. It's early afternoon, and I've visited with my aunt for the second weekend this year.

I am stunned when I am barely through the front door and she's barking at me.

"Let's pick up where we left off." She directs me to sit on the sofa, but first, I slip off my coat, hat, gloves, and scarf and toss the bundle on the bench in the foyer before entering the living room.

Well, if this is what she wants, I'll dive in. "You and your husband were under a lot of pressure after the news broke about the marriage."

"I don't care to discuss that today. I want to know what you found out about Adelaide Thomas."

"Oh. That's right." I hadn't forgotten. Not exactly. Aunt Alice had given me marching orders to get to the bottom of why Adelaide Rhinelander Thomas was making such a stink about the money the Rhinelanders owed my aunt. But I've been busy with other things, like writing my first hard-news article for the *Amsterdam News*.

However, I don't mention that she only cares about what she cares about.

"What do you have to tell me?"

"Not a lot just yet. I can't exactly walk into one of her private clubs, order a gin and tonic, and say let's chat."

"You aren't funny, Roberta. I know perfectly well what you can or can't do on Fifth Avenue. A good newspaperwoman is part detective and part researcher. She loves old newspapers, books, and occasionally old people. Did you go to the library? I wager there's plenty of information there about Adelaide Thomas."

Oh my, she is in a fighting mood. I settle on the sofa, my hands in my lap, fingers intertwined. "Here's what I know. She's been married since 1921 to a Wall Street broker, a wealthy man, of course. And she stays busy being a socialite, supporting charitable organizations, attending museum openings, and she's a member of the women's guild, and does her duty as the wife of a board chair, coordinating charity auctions, food drives—you know, the routine."

"No, I don't, since I never fully lived the life of a Rhinelander." She pushes a curly strand of hair from her face.

"Okay, then," I say. "But so far, I don't know what else Adelaide Rhinelander Thomas does other than be a Rhinelander."

"You make her sound like any other wealthy white woman in Manhattan. I wanna know why she doesn't want to pay me my money." Seated across from me in one of the lounge chairs, she reaches for her gold cigarette case but stops midway. "Goddamn. I'm out of cigarettes."

Should I offer to buy her a pack? I don't want her to go all cockeyed or worse. "You know it could be one of her lawyers telling her what to do."

"I've never known a Rhinelander who didn't keep tabs on their money. So, no. I don't buy that." She opens, and then slams shut the empty cigarette case. "Three hundred dollars a month shouldn't upset any apple cart. There's a reason she's not paying me other than money."

She exhales a long sigh and looks tired. Not the same flamboyant Aunt Alice I met a year ago. She is less polished, wears less makeup, and her hair isn't as coiffed. I can see a bit of gray at the roots along her hairline.

The style is short and sassy, but she's razor thin, more Katharine Hepburn than Hedy Lamarr, especially wearing the wide-legged cuffed pants and starched, white, broad-shouldered blouse. That money is how she survives.

"You believe it's personal?"

"Yes. Look harder, and you'll find it." She reaches for the gold cigarette case again. "I have a pack of Camels in my purse. It's in my bedroom, on my dresser. Could you get it for me?"

I have never been in her bedroom in the years I've come to this house. And I can't pass up the chance to look around. There's a canopy bed that barely fits into the room, a mahogany dresser drawer, a carved chifforobe, and a nightstand— all modern pieces of furniture and expensive. Heavy drapes hang before the one window in the room.

One of her dressers is full of picture frames. Photos of the family members I know, like my mother, Aunt Gracie, my grandparents, and the man I recognize as Leonard "Kip" Rhinelander. I double-check my memory to make sure I haven't missed anyone. If someone is missing, I don't remember who. We either never met, or they weren't around long enough to get to know.

There aren't any photos of my father or of me.

I don't know what to make of that. Before Holden Richards sent me to talk to Aunt Alice, she and I hadn't spoken in ten years—excluding the funeral, where I don't believe I even said hello. I can't be sure. It wasn't an easy day.

I retrieve the pack of Camels from her purse and rush back into the living room, hoping my absence hasn't caused her to become suspicious.

"Here you go." I hand over the pack and hustle back to the sofa.

She reaches for the cigarette lighter that matches the case. Gold and etched with painted flowers. Poppies.

Aunt Alice rips into the pack of Camels, empties the contents into the cigarette case, retrieves a cig, and lights up. "I hope she chokes on every damn penny," she says, puffing away.

Her words are laced with arsenic, and I don't have to guess about whom she is referring. "You are talking about Adelaide Rhinelander."

"Adelaide Rhinelander Thomas. Lenny's big sister. They do like to serve and protect, don't they?"

A conversation focused on Adelaide would lead us too far off topic, but it isn't for me to decide. "Would you prefer we discussed Mrs. Thomas today or what happened with you and Lenny between 1922 and 1923?"

A deep sigh appears to deflate the head of steam she is fueling. "Let's talk about those two years." She fingers her pearls, and I notice the ring on her left hand.

"Is that the sapphire ring Lenny gave you?"

She extends her hand and admires it. "Yes. Yes, it is." She lowers her hand to her side and moves to the end of the sofa, looking at me. "What was I supposed to do? Sit on my hands? No. I went out. I met people. Lots of people, exciting men from all over town. New York, New Rochelle, White Plains."

"I met some interesting men in Harlem, too," Aunt Alice continues. "Your father's friends. He knew a lot of fine-looking men. In 'twenty-two, Gracie had started dating a fella from Hell's Kitchen, an Italian named Arthur 'Footsie' Miller. Your father introduced them. Footsie. That man was something else back then."

"Didn't Grandpa have a problem with him? My mother told me he didn't like men from Hell's Kitchen."

"He didn't, but Footsie was a white boy. I think it's fair to say that my father wasn't so fussy about who we dated as long as they were white. He felt marrying a white man gave us a better shot at life. But your mother dismissed that kind of thinking." She walks over to the tray with tea, coffee, and the water pitcher and refills her cup of tea. "I refused to sit around and wait for Lenny Rhinelander to return. He wasn't the only fish in the sea."

"So, you saw other men and didn't miss Lenny."

Aunt Alice slowly walks toward me, taking careful steps. I've said something she doesn't like, and she is winding down her displeasure.

"How about a boyfriend?" Aunt Alice asks, causing me to gag on my swallow of coffee.

"Excuse me?"

"A pretty girl like you must have plenty of men chasing after her." She sighs. "I should know these things about you."

What's the big deal about today that she even wants to drill me with questions? I don't like it. And perhaps that's the reason she's doing it. Should I answer her questions to stop her from badgering me? None of what I might say is her business, but I need her to stop.

"I have a fella I'm seeing."

"What's his name?" She stands beside the still unlit fireplace, holding her cup of tea. "Wasn't your birthday last week?"

"No, it's coming up. This week. Next week, technically. It's Sunday, March thirty-first."

"It's a big one. You'll be twenty-one."

"Yes, ma'am." I bite my tongue. She remembers my birthday, and I feel a pang of satisfaction as if she's done something for me. Who am I now? The child sitting on her aunt's knee, marveling at her beauty?

"Do you and your boyfriend do anything special? Go to Coney Island? Perhaps see a Broadway show?" She moves from the fireplace to the coffee table where the gold cigarette case resides. "What's playing?"

"I wouldn't know. We rarely go to Broadway shows," I say, but I have no desire to talk with her about my boyfriend. "I'm sorry, but I won't be able to spend as much time with you today. Busy schedule at the newspaper."

"Oh, that's fine. I understand."

And from the twinkle in her eyes, she understood completely.

I am back on Pelham Road, prepared to be interrogated, and my aunt doesn't disappoint.

"Did you do as I asked?"

"Visit a library?" I say with a smile. Having stripped out of my coat and accessories, I hold two brown paper bags filled with sandwiches and chips. "Yes, I did. Ethel Ray, my high school friend, is now a librarian, and she dug up a few things for us."

"Like what, Roberta? I'm all ears." She stands at the window in the living room, but noticing the bags in my hands, a puzzled expression comes over her. "What's that you're holding?"

"I came bearing sandwiches for lunch. Ham and cheese. Potato chips and two Coca-Colas from a diner a couple of blocks from here."

"I didn't ask you to bring me anything to eat." Her tone is sharp, but her eyes linger on the bags. "But since you bought it, we might as well eat it. Come on." She strolls off toward the kitchen.

I traipse behind.

She moves about the kitchen, removing plates, glasses, silverware, and napkins and placing them on the table. I remove our lunch from the bags, grab a can opener from the drawer, and sit down. Although, I don't have a chance to bite before the questions begin.

"So, why is she trying to take my money?"

"I learned that it's not lawyers pushing her from paying your annuity. Mrs. Thomas has been chatting, upset about items her mother left her, which are missing. And she believes you have a lot of that missing jewelry and have been selling it off to finance your appetite for fancy clothes, travel, and inappropriate young men."

Aunt Alice let out a roar of a laugh. "You are lying. She must be losing her mind. I'm running amok on three hundred dollars a month. What an ornery, vengeful beast she is." Aunt Alice sips her Coca-Cola. "Where did you get this information?"

"One of her chauffeurs overheard her talking with another woman after some fancy event, and that chauffeur knows my father. She'd had a few coupes of champagne."

"Oh, so Robert is helping me?"

"I don't think he considers it help. Just passing along some gossip."

"How is your father these days?"

I don't know why I hadn't thought she'd ask how I obtained these tidbits about Mrs. Thomas, but I am not prepared for a conversation about Daddy. "He's fine. But as I was saying, I think that Mrs. Thomas is . . ."

I pause for an instant, hoping she'll get my drift. "She is bitter, too. She's had a few hard knocks in her life, you know." I say this as gently as possible, hoping to avoid an outburst. "It's not that I am taking sides. She's the last of the commodore's children and your age. Her mother passed away when she was a girl. Her other brothers died one after another."

Aunt Alice pushes her plate away. "So what? Am I supposed to mourn for her losses while she's trying to take everything from me?" She is suddenly on her feet, opening and closing drawers, searching for God knows what. She finally stops her frenzied dance. "I will not feel sorry for her. That money is the last thing Lenny promised me. And I want him to keep at least one of his goddamned promises."

I don't get to finish my lunch. Aunt Alice leaves the kitchen, marches toward her bedroom, and slams the door. I take that as my cue to grab my things and go.

I do call her a few days later to congratulate her.

ALICE WINS—COURT ORDERS RHINELANDER TO PAY

Aunt Alice beat Adelaide Thomas. I figure that will make her happy or less unhappy. But she doesn't answer the phone.

I don't visit her for a few weeks after that. But when I return, she feels like talking. So, I settle back on the sofa and listen to what she has to say.

CHAPTER 17

ALICE

1924

The estate in Connecticut belonged to one of Lenny's class-mates from the Orchard School, whom I recognized when he and his wife opened the door.

"Come in, come in," the man said, smiling at me. "My name is Bernard Hilliard, and this is my wife, Christy."

"Welcome," Christy said. "We are glad to have you as our guests."

I didn't know what to say. They were young, like us, and, like us, they were attractive people, too. And Christy was also very pregnant. But from our first ten minutes in their home, they proved themselves an excellent host and hostess.

Hiding from reporters might not be as awful as I thought. Staying at the Hilliard home felt like the honeymoon Lenny and I never had. Every moment was freedom. And we tried to cherish it. We sincerely gave it our best shot, and I believed our plan was working.

The only new articles about us were trying to solve the mystery of our disappearance. Where were we, and how come no one could find us? Everything was going exactly as we'd hoped. Soon, the newspapers would grow bored with Kip Rhinelander and his bride, the daughter of a taxicab driver. They'd latch on to another couple's woes. We only had to be patient.

By the beginning of the fourth day, Lenny and I felt normal, like we were married. I even offered to cook his favorite breakfast, but I didn't know what it was. He told me toast and eggs with sausage would be fine. But the Hilliards' kitchen maid was beside herself when I tried to go near the stove.

Christy warned me to stay out of the kitchen. It was the house staff's dominion. If we needed anything, to use the chimes and a servant would be at our side in a jiffy.

So a maid named Trudy served us tea and eggs for breakfast—the perfect meal. Frankly, every meal was delicious.

I felt slightly embarrassed being treated so kindly by the Hilliards' servants.

"Most of the wives I know have servants," Lenny said with a wink.

"I keep forgetting about your money."

"That's because you weren't raised with it. I can never forget it."

His tone changed on that last part, and I didn't like what I heard. Misgivings? Longings? Not for me, but most likely for the prestige his family name gave him when he was on Fifth Avenue.

I woke up early, but Lenny was gone. I wasn't worried. He still had to slip into Manhattan to do business for his father's real estate company. Few reporters would chase him when he was in the Rhinelander Building. That location was sacred for some reason.

I had breakfast with Christy and Bernard and then walked through the garden. There was a light snowfall, but it wasn't too cold. The fresh-fallen, sunlit snow was beautiful and reminded me of Thanksgiving and Christmas in New Rochelle.

Lenny returned in the afternoon, stuttering almost as badly as when I first met him. And immediately, I knew he'd seen his father.

"What did you talk about?"

"Th-they put a picture of him in the newspaper with a headline about you and me, making him f-feel f-foolish. He was angry, and my father is a bully."

"What does that mean? What does he propose to do?"

"Let's take a w-walk," Lenny said. "I need some a-air."

The sun shone on the horizon, a golden glimmer in the late afternoon, helping us see where we were going.

Lenny held my hand as we moved along a paved path. "No one knows where we are, and that's been good. But he threatened me."

A cool breeze turned into an iceberg in my lungs. "How so?"

"To begin with, he said he'd disinherit me. Cut me off. Leave me a pauper." Lenny shrugged. "The particulars don't matter. But he, his friends, and other family members act like I've committed blasphemy. Destroyed the family's good name, turned my back on my heritage, shamed people long dead that I never knew or cared to."

"But you have your mother's money, Lenny. The trust fund. We don't need your father's money."

He chuckled bitterly. "It's not as m-much money as I th-thought."

The lines on his face had deepened. "What can I do to help?" I squeezed his hand.

"There's nothing you can do but keep loving me. If you promise to do that, I'll get through this. We'll both get through." He sighed. "Father is holding another family meeting, and I promised him I'd be there. So maybe if I find a way to cooperate, he'll back off."

"Cooperate?" I said softly. "When is this next gathering? I fear something might happen to you while you're away from me. Who would call me? Your family members have never met me."

He stopped walking, held my shoulders, and turned me to face him. "N-nothing is going to happen to me. My father won't physically h-harm me. It's just that he messes me up inside my head. That's all. Remember, you k-keep loving and t-trusting me, and I'll worry about him."

The press was not happy about their newest piece of scandal candy vanishing without a trace, but we were hiding, for the most part.

Lenny had a job in Manhattan at his father's real estate firm, and he went to work each day collecting a paycheck every two weeks. I never understood why he worked. He had enough money, but his father would likely find a new way to make his life miserable if he didn't show.

So he left our Connecticut getaway for Manhattan in the morning and returned every evening after dark. If I asked what happened during those hours he spent in the office with his family, doing whatever real estate tycoons do, I would get a sharp-tongued response.

"Don't worry about it. I will handle them. Be patient, and everything will work out."

I didn't like it when he talked to me like that. So I stopped asking.

I had other things I could do to keep myself busy. Our host and hostess doted on me, making sure their servants were at my beck and call.

Behind Christy's back, though, I coerced Trudy into showing me how to use the new sewing machine model, the drawer Singer. I'd never tried it before, although I'd seen it in a few wealthy homes where I had worked.

But quickly, my days felt long and lonely, and I missed my parents. I begged Lenny to take me to New Rochelle. He said no the first few times I asked.

Too risky, he claimed. "The news stories are dying down. Let's stay out of sight a bit longer."

I almost asked why he didn't need to hide, but I didn't

want to be snapped at for asking a question he didn't want to answer. But I missed my family.

"Drop me off at my parents' house, please. We never get caught if we travel in the middle of the night."

Finally, I struck the right chord because he agreed.

"I'll pick you up tonight or around four in the morning." He kissed me and drove away before I reached the back door. I slipped into my parents' home through the basement entrance just before dawn, and no reporters were in sight.

Mummy was already in the kitchen.

"At least you called us; otherwise, I would have been worried sick about you, Alice."

I rushed over to her, wrapped my arms around her waist, and hugged her back. "I've missed you, Mummy."

"We've missed you, too."

"Where's Daddy?" I moved toward the living room.

"Don't bother. He's already on the road, trying to make up for money lost when those reporters were hunting down you and Lenny every day and night."

"So it's better now?"

"They are still around. You can never tell if one is hiding behind an automobile or following you to the grocery store. Two of them nearly scared me to death, pulling stunts like that."

She patted my cheek. "You look tired, Alice. Aren't you getting enough rest?"

"I miss being in our own place, going out and having fun like we used to. We're in hiding because of his family's attitude toward poor people—and colored people."

"You are not colored, not like what they mean. But you aren't high society, either," she said. "Have a seat and let me fix you some breakfast."

*   *   *

That night Lenny was late to arrive at the Hilliards' home in Connecticut, and I was worried. Still, I didn't want my first phone conversation with his father to be: *Do you know where my husband is?* So I hadn't called the mansion, and my calls to his office went unanswered.

When the telephone rang around ten o'clock, and the call was for me, I was beside myself with worry followed by a decent dose of anger.

"Sorry, but I've been with my father all day," Lenny explained. "I will be home soon. Stay up and wait for me, babe. We've got to talk."

Then the line disconnected, and I had a different kind of concern.

What did it mean? *We had to talk.* We talked all the time. And if we couldn't talk, we wrote letters because we couldn't bear it when we didn't have the other's words in our heads.

I was waiting in the hall when he walked in.

"Why would you say something so silly, Lenny? We will talk when you get here. We don't need to make an appointment."

Christy and Bernard had already gone to bed when Lenny staggered toward the parlor. I dismissed the servants when I smelled the liquor on his breath. Once we were alone, I guided him to our room.

But when he finally entered our suite, he did the strangest thing.

He didn't sit in a chair or recline on the mattress. He pressed his back against the wall and slid to the floor, his body crumbling like a crushed flower. He had lost the strength in his legs. His trembling fingers covered his face as he pulled his knees into his chest, his body shaking.

Lenny was sobbing. "I won't have anything. I don't know how to live if I am broke."

I hadn't seen a grown man cry before. Daddy never shed a tear. So I didn't know what to do for Lenny. Did he want to be left alone or consoled? Smothered in kisses, his head held in my lap?

"How can I help you? What do you want me to do? I don't understand. Is this what your father talked about all day, taking your money? I don't need your father's money. You know that. I don't care if you have money or not. I've told you that before. So don't give your father's threat any never mind."

Lenny's chuckle was dark and ugly, void of humor, almost lacking sanity. "You don't listen, Alice, do you? I'm the one. I'm the one who cares about the money." He removed his hands from his face and glared at me. "I don't want to be poor. And I don't want him to win. He is a bastard, always forcing me to do things I don't want to do. Th-things that make me hate him m-more a-and m-more every goddamned day."

I sat on the floor next to him but didn't touch him. "I thought it was enough, the money you received from your trust fund in May when you turned twenty-one. Can't we live off of that?"

He huffed out a low, harsh laugh. "That's pennies compared to what he's trying to keep from me."

"How can I help, Lenny?"

"W-we have to find a way for me to keep my inheritance." He looked at me with tears in his eyes. "I thought of something, but I n-need to w-work it out b-before I give you the details."

"You can tell me anything, Lenny."

"Not this, not yet. Be patient. Soon. This will be fixed. Soon."

After that night, Lenny didn't return to the Hilliards' manor until after ten o'clock almost every night. I didn't like it, but thankfully, he wasn't always soused. Still, it wasn't an accident in the least. It happened so often that I started referring to it as a habit, one I could set a clock to.

The night he stumbled in after one o'clock in the morning, looking ruffled and reeking of bootleg whiskey, I didn't want to sound like a jealous wife, unhappy with her husband arriving late, coming home drunk. But it was impossible to keep that tone out of my voice.

"Where did you go? What nightclub? Did you hear anybody good?"

"Stop fishing," Lenny said. "I wasn't at a nightclub. I drank whiskey with my father."

"Is that a good thing?"

"It was a necessary thing." He removed a pack of Camel cigarettes from his vest pocket. I hadn't seen him smoke in years.

"I was putting a plan into action."

"Another plan? What does this one call for?"

"You won't like it, but we can pull it off if you trust me. I've been talking to my sister and brother, and they agree this might get my father off his high horse for a bit." He held my face between his hands, his thumb caressing my chin. Then he explained.

"We pretend to hate each other."

"No. I don't want anyone to think you hate me. I would feel bad if people had doubts about why you married me."

He sighed. "That you might've been more interested in my money than in me."

"That's ridiculous. You've given me plenty of beautiful gifts, but I haven't asked you for anything. Except maybe the sable mink coat, but it was so beautiful in the store when you took me shopping at Saks, I couldn't help it."

"I love buying you pretty things." He sidled up next to me and kissed my cheek, making a loud smacking sound. "And don't forget the diamond ring on your finger wasn't cheap, my love."

"Oh, yes." I held my hand so the ring caught the light. "I

also have the sapphire ring, which I love, too. But you didn't buy it."

He dropped his cigarette butt in the sink. "That sapphire ring is causing me some serious grief with my sister, Adelaide." He shook his head. "But I shouldn't have even mentioned it. Nothing for you to worry about, my sweetheart."

He wrapped an arm around my waist and cupped my chin. His eyes moist and his voice shaky, he said slowly, "We won't have to keep secrets forever, just long enough so my father doesn't cut me off. The damn newspapers got my father's ego charged up. But he won't always be over me. I'll have everything once he thinks I've recovered from my rebellion."

"Am I your rebellion?"

He nodded. "It's bullshit. But he can't take you away from me. I won't let him. I just have to find a way to keep my inheritance." He licked his lips, his eyes hooded. "If we got an annulment, that would satisfy my family. The stigma would be gone. I would be redeemed for having the nerve to marry you, which is what got them riled up."

I placed my hand on my chest. Annulment? Had he said "annulment"?

"So, to keep your money, you'd leave me without a husband?"

"No. I want you to win. To fight the annulment and win."

"Then why do it? You'd still lose your inheritance."

"My father is embarrassed and angry now. Once a higher court declares us wed, it will take the fight out of him."

"And if I lose?"

He kissed my cheek. "We'd remarry in Europe if it comes to that."

"I don't like this, Lenny."

"Don't worry, love. It will work. It has to work." His voice sounded suddenly far away.

"But an annulment, Lenny? Why?" I steeled my spine, bit

my lip, wiped away his tears with my hand, and made him look at me. "If you believe this is the only way, I'll do it. I won't be upset. I won't panic. I trust you."

He dropped to the floor, stretching his long legs out in front of him. Then he spread his palms on the floor. "We have to beat my father at his own game. That means I must take this risk to get my money and appease him, at least for a while. I need him to trust me again. It will take time, just a little, I promise. But you'll have to be strong. We will both need our strength and wits to fight him."

"Go on, I am listening," I said, surprised and proud at how mature I sounded. There was no crack in my voice, trembling lips, or teary eyes.

"Are you sure?"

"If you love me, which I believe with all my heart that you do, your plan will keep us together. So, go on. Tell me what you have in mind."

"Here it is. I will go to court and claim that I'm seeking an annulment, let's say, because you tricked me into marrying you or something like that. It'll work. I'll get the lawyers to figure out the language. But I swear to God, I know it'll work, Alice. You just have to trust me."

"Okay, but I don't want to be in Connecticut for the holidays. Please, Lenny. I love Thanksgiving. It won't be the same if we're here. I adore Bernard and Christy, but we should spend our first Thanksgiving as husband and wife with my family. They won't turn us away."

CHAPTER 18

We made a pledge the night before Thanksgiving. No newspapers. No matter what, if you were coming to 763 Pelham Road for dinner, that was the price to pay.

Not even the sports section, Mummy told Daddy. He looked stricken. But for his middle daughter, he would miss one day with his nose buried in the latest news about baseball, boxing, horse racing, or whatever sport was popular in November.

Everyone would be under one roof. I squealed with delight. Even Emily and Robert were coming to dinner. Nothing would spoil this day for Lenny and me.

My mother, my sisters, and I cooked for two days. Mummy started preparing some items a month earlier. And by the end of the evening, we were as stuffed as the turkey we'd devoured.

It was a feast with chestnut dressing and cranberry sauce, noisette of lamb, tenderloin of beef, baked winter squash, hot asparagus tips, and boiled potatoes. The desserts were sublime, too. Mummy went all out. We had cranberry sherbet, English plum pudding with brandy sauce, vanilla ice cream, pumpkin pie, and chocolate cake for Lenny.

After dinner, the men excused themselves and gathered in the living room to listen to Little Orphan Annie on the radio—one of Daddy's favorite shows. Footsie, Gracie's husband, had brought a few bottles of hooch, and Lenny had confiscated a half dozen bottles of his father's best champagne from their wine cellar. Add that to the brandy sauce in the plum pudding, and they were having a raucous time.

My sisters and I finished helping Mummy clean up the dishes. However, Emily had to keep an eye on her daughter, Roberta, a four-year-old who liked to get into everything. But after we finished, I slinked into the living room and headed straight for Lenny, causing Emily to chuckle. She recognized the purpose behind my sly approach. I wasn't swishing my bottom for anyone other than my husband.

He sat on the sofa, and I squeezed in next to him, tucking my legs beneath me and resting my head on his shoulder. He put his arm around me and tugged me close.

I was content to spend the evening with my head on his shoulder, drifting in and out of sleep. After such a big meal, we were all droopy-eyed.

But a knock on the door made us all jump.

Mummy was the first on her feet, but Daddy cleared his throat and gave her a nod. She sat back down to let him answer the door.

"I'll get it, dear. You rest yourself."

Lenny and Robert leaned forward as Footsie, standing, rested a hand on his breast pocket, all watchful in case Daddy needed their assistance.

Mummy's gaze followed Daddy until he disappeared on the other side of the wall between the foyer and the living room. "Who is it, Daddy?" she called.

"Western Union telegram delivery," he said.

"Oh Lord," said Gracie, her tone expecting tragic news.

I wasn't worried. Everyone I loved was in sight.

"Mummy, come on out here," Daddy called.

A confused expression took over my mother's face. "On my way, Daddy," she replied.

I couldn't even remain cuddled up with Lenny. We un-tangled, and I eased toward the opening between the living room and the foyer.

"I have a personal message for Mr. Rhinelander," said the Western Union messenger, craning his neck to see what he could of the house.

Mummy moved quickly, blocking his view. "Daddy, ain't nobody here with that name."

"I didn't think so. You'll need to return that message where you got it, son."

I covered my mouth to squelch a giggle. We'd gotten skilled in safeguarding our privacy.

The door was closed in the boy's face, and I hurried back to my comfortable seat on the sofa, in Lenny's arms.

"I wasn't rude," Mummy said, returning to the living room. "I smiled at the boy the whole time."

"She did a fine job," Daddy said, settling back in his over-stuffed rocking chair.

"I'm sure it was one of my father's ploys or his lawyer's. See if I was dumb enough to show myself."

"He doesn't know you're here?" Footsie asked.

"He suspects, but he can't prove it, and that bothers him. I've carved out a life without his stamp of approval, and that makes him mad." Lenny huffed. "That's what he calls it—*approval*. His firm hand and knowledge of what is right from wrong. My being here eating at your table in the company of Robert and Emily burns his bottom." Lenny grinned, and it was wide, fierce, and mildly scary. "I'm showing him." He nodded hard at Robert. "I can do whatever I please now that I'm a man. I'm twenty-one, and he should leave me be to do what men do."

"That's right, Kip," said Robert, up on his feet, shaking his fist, giving Lenny encouragement.

Daddy raised his glass, gesturing toward Lenny. "How long can you keep this up? Hiding from the press and your family's wishes. Sooner or later, you'll have to face your pops and resolve this business between you." Daddy drained his glass and started fiddling with his pipe. "You intend to stay with my daughter, Lenny? Through sickness and health?" He brought the pipe to his lips and struck a match, filling the room with the smell of sulfur. "I drive a taxicab all day, and people talk. They don't recognize me most of the time, and what they talk about is you and Alice. And I'll tell you, son. I don't like what I'm hearing." Daddy's eyes were trained on Lenny as he held the match to the tobacco bowl and puffed.

Lenny sat up straight and looked my father in the eye. "I'm not sure what rumors you've heard, sir. But I love your daughter, and the newspaper stories are unfortunate."

Daddy coughed as a bloom of smoke rose from his pipe. "People are calling my Alice a liar. Saying she deceived you."

Lenny rose and walked over to the fireplace. "I've heard that, too, Mr. Jones. Read it in the newspaper, too. But that's my father creating fiction for the papers so he doesn't look bad when he goes to the country club. He's even threatened to disown me. Cut me out of the Rhinelander estate." He lifted his empty glass from the coffee table. "Hey, Footsie, fill me up."

"Sure thing, Lenny." Footsie plowed over to the buffet where he'd put the liquor bottles and dumped some hooch in Lenny's glass.

"Make those two more fingers, pal."

"You bet."

Footsie handed Lenny a drink with the whiskey sloshing near the rim of the glass.

"Can he do that, Lenny? Cut you out of the estate?" Gracie asked, holding her cup up for her husband to notice, which he did.

"Hell no," Footsie said, filling Gracie's glass. "Pardon my French, Mrs. Jones, but that doesn't make sense for a father to take his son's future and stomp on it like that."

"The c-commodore is a different kind of man," Lenny said. "I h-hate F-Father for suggesting such a thing. Just because I'm in love with A-Alice."

I could see how upset he was. "Lenny, please. Daddy knows these people are just spreading rumors. Repeating lies they've read in the newspapers. Your father wouldn't keep you from your inheritance."

"You just have to be smarter than him," Gracie said.

"What do you mean?" Lenny asked.

"Make up your mind not to be controlled by him." Gracie crossed her legs. "He's trying to see if he can scare you into doing things his way. That's all."

Lenny rubbed his hand over his face. "You're right, I g-guess. He—he can't control me un-unless I let him."

"That's right, Lenny," Daddy said. "Stand up to him. You can do it, boy."

After Thanksgiving's late-night glasses of hooch, brandy-soaked English pudding, and champagne, I couldn't make it as far as the foyer, let alone a long drive back to Connecticut. So, I convinced Lenny to curl up with me on a spare mattress in the basement. It was warm and clean, and I promised we'd be safe and sound.

Thankfully, he was too sloshed to disagree.

I woke up late and tired. Sleep had come and gone in fits and starts. I kept replaying my conversation with Lenny in my head, and no matter how many times he'd told me not to worry and keep the faith—dread was glued to my sanity, and I couldn't escape it.

It was the morning after Thanksgiving, and the feeling of thanklessness was suffocating, but within an hour on that fateful morning, I would find a new pain.

"Are you reading what is written here?" Gracie was as indignant as I'd ever seen her. She paced in one direction and then circled the kitchen table as if on a racetrack. "These papers are saying he claims you deliberately deceived him." She pointed a shaky finger at the newspaper I held in my hand.

She read over my shoulder. "Colored. That is what this says—he claims you told him you were white and didn't have a drop of colored blood. He went even further, too, saying you are Negro. And we aren't Negroes. Are we, Daddy?"

My father stood from the kitchen table. We all stared at him, waiting for him to say something. His profoundly tanned complexion suddenly seemed darker than ever before.

"George, George," Mummy said. "Is there something you need, darling?" She walked over to his side, touching the small of his back.

"The man is a liar," he said. "Your mother is completely white. In the state of New York, that means you are white. We may have as much white blood in us as the Rhinelanders have in them. I may have some Spanish blood or something else, but it's so far back in my family that it doesn't matter."

I remained seated, staring at the newspaper, reading it over and over. Was this our plan? The one Lenny and I had talked about and agreed upon? Was this the way we were to ensure that Lenny and I remained married, and he not be denied his inheritance, his share of the Rhinelander family fortune? It had sounded less ugly, less painful, and less absurd when Lenny and I talked. Reading it now, it was offensive and humiliating.

I could see the deeply etched lines of mortification and anger on my family's faces. I wanted to tell them the truth about how the plan would work. Lenny's goal was for me to win. Then, his father couldn't deny our marriage. It had held up in a court of law. And in the long run, it would put more money in our pockets. We'd end up together despite his father's hate.

But I couldn't do it. I couldn't explain what Lenny and I had planned to my mother, my father, Gracie, and definitely not Gracie's Italian Mafia husband.

"What are you going to do, Alice?" Gracie had stopped pacing. Her gaze shifted from me to Daddy. "What is this family going to do? It's our name in the newspapers, too. They might as well be accusing all of us of living a lie. And we haven't done that. We've never pretended to be something we are not."

"Emily's marriage certificate says she is a Negro." I knew it was something none of us wanted to be reminded of, but I had to say it. "That was no accident."

Gracie waved her hand in the air. "Don't get that wrong, Alice. Emily chose to call herself Negro because her husband is Negro, and she didn't want him to be ostracized because he'd married a white woman."

I looked at my mother. She hadn't even blinked.

"You've never felt in any way that your life would be less if you called your husband mulatto?"

Mummy didn't move away; she took her hand from my father's back. "That's unfair. Don't listen to Gracie. This problem has nothing to do with her or me or your father. This has to do with Leonard Rhinelander. He is a liar. And if he is going to make these accusations, you must fight back."

I'd never heard my mother speak so forcefully.

"No, Mummy," I said. "This is not his doing. This is his family. His father. They are the ones who are forcing him to do this. I don't care what they're writing in that newspaper. I don't care what these papers are implying. This is not my Lenny. And I will never give him up. He loves me, and I love him, and all of the Rhinelanders' millions of dollars cannot take him away from me."

"So what are you going to do?" Mummy asked, but Gracie responded first.

"We should fight back. And fight the way they are fighting us.

"In the press. We should stop avoiding publicity. We should have a lawyer. And when needed, seek out reporters and make sure they hear our side of the story."

"I think you mean my side of the story, Gracie."

"I said what I meant." Grace snapped. "This is about family. And we will fight this together."

"Rumors. Rumors. Rumors. It's insane that we sit here and talk about them as if they had a bearing on the truth," I said to my mother and Gracie, in between gulps of hot coffee.

"If Lenny was planning to get our marriage annulled, don't you think I'd know?" I said with a straight face as if I was not in on the plan.

So many photographers and cameramen had set siege on the Joneses' family home on Pelham Road, and a crowd had gathered outside.

Lenny entered the kitchen. "Alice, we should leave."

I looked at him, alarmed. I leaned forward, my palms pressed flat into the table, my arms straight and rigid. Between gulps of anxiety and shock, I uttered. "Lenny, what have you done? And how can we leave? We can't get past that many reporters without being attacked."

I looked at Daddy. He has a stranglehold on the newspapers he held in his hands, and his jaw twitched like it might come loose.

"You're not going anywhere, son. Not until you explain this." He dropped the papers on the table—covering the one Mummy, Gracie, and I were reading—and spread them so the headlines were visible.

FRAUD! RHINELANDER TO BRIDE

BLUE BLOOD CHARGES WIFE WITH DECEIT OVER RACE

RHINELANDER SEEKS ANNULMENT

"It wasn't my idea. My father . . . says this is the only way I can save face. The only way to bring honor back to our family. I do not support this, but . . ."

The sickness in my stomach rose into my throat, and I waved, excusing myself, and took off at a dash, barely reaching the bathroom on time. Gracie wasn't far behind, holding back my hair and wiping my face with a damp, cool cloth.

"That bastard. He didn't tell you about this great plan of his?"

Of course I knew about his plan, but I couldn't help the hollowness in my chest or the twisting in my gut when I saw the newspaper headlines. But Gracie didn't know I knew, and all I could do now was stare at her.

Wanting her to know she had comforted me, I touched her cheek. She'd been there when I needed someone—someone who was not Lenny.

"I'm going to put a knife in his heart," Gracie said.

I smiled nervously and then proceeded to lie. "No, I'm sure it's his father's doing. He wouldn't come up with something like this by himself. That's not my Lenny."

"I don't think you've ever known your precious Lenny anyway."

Gracie tended to me, drying my eyes and fixing my hair, frazzled into a thousand twisty strands. And after a while, I felt okay enough to face Lenny.

I was a regular Mary Pickford; I thought my acting had been excellent, although part of it wasn't acting. I was afraid. The newspaper articles were far worse than I'd imagined them to be. It hurt seeing his plan in tall letters smeared on the front pages of every newspaper in New York and Westchester County. And though he objected, denied, and looked the part of a man betrayed by his family, I saw something else. Lenny seemed okay with it all. Appropriately upset, but to me, too calm. Had he envisioned the headlines? Had he and his family designed them?

Everyone was quiet when Gracie and I walked back into the living room. Even Footsie seemed dazed. With his dark curly hair, large black eyes, and swagger, he wasn't the type to be easily silenced.

"He's gone," Daddy said. "Lenny left. And good riddance."

A scream burst from my throat. I didn't even know it was there.

CHAPTER 19

Footsie earned my respect that day. He set up camp on the front steps, guarding the door against the milieu of newspaper people. He wasn't a man who played around with his words. He was direct and sometimes, I thought, downright scary.

But we needed help. Reporters were everywhere. And right alongside them were most of our neighbors. Some of whom we knew well enough, like the Masterson family. They brought over apple pie and a promise of prayers at church on the coming Sunday. We all belonged to the Episcopal church in New Rochelle. It was an all-white church, and no one ever bothered us about being there. But would they now—with the headlines screaming that I was colored?

Others dropped by, offering condolences as if someone had died. But not a phone call or a message from Lenny. I never thought I wouldn't hear from him all day and night. He had warned me it would be tough going, but I never counted on it being so hard, so painful.

I was in my bedroom when my friend Kitty stopped by. I figured she was there to get in on the gossip and catch up on the happenings of the Jones household, especially as it related to Leonard "Kip" Rhinelander. But I didn't care why she was there. I'd had such a rough day. I needed to be around someone other than concerned family, nosy reporters, or not-so-friendly neighbors. Someone I called a friend.

Kitty and I had grown up together, and her family, like mine, were working-class people originally from Ireland. A curvy girl with bright white teeth and red-crayon hair, she was covered in freckles and sunshine and always seemed happy. When we were kids, she was teased about the dots on her face and her hair color, but she explained that everyone in her family started with red hair and freckles due to the Irish blood that ran through their veins. Her family left the United Kingdom before 1922, the signing of a treaty with Britain that created the Irish Free State. Her mother still considered herself British. I took that to mean they were just like my parents. So we'd been decent friends.

"Why is he doing this to you, Alice? I've known you since you two met, and I've never seen anybody more in love with each other than you and Kip. I don't understand why this is happening. Is he that afraid of his father?"

"Look at these letters." I removed the shoebox of mail from beneath my bed. "We wrote to each other every day when he was away. Sometimes, we'd write to each other when he was in the next room. But you know that already." Kitty had held my hand during those months that turned into years after the disaster at the Hotel Marie Antoinette.

"Well, you buck up," she said, patting my hand. "It still seems odd to me, though. Did you two fight? Is that what prompted this nonsense? Did he learn about some of those boys you went out with while he was gone?" Kitty's laugh was full of secrets and conspiracy. She knew I'd seen a few fellas. But it felt like ages ago, and all of that was before we married. Therefore, in my mind, long forgotten.

"He knows everything he needs to know. I don't keep the truth from Lenny."

She raised an eyebrow and smirked. "Not according to

today's *Daily News*, *New York Times*, and *Standard-Star* headlines."

I pressed my palms together and shook praying hands at her. "Please. Did you come by to cheer me up or push me deeper into the hole?"

"Oh, I'm sorry. It's just . . . What's happening is fascinating. Watching how you and Lenny return from this will be fun. Because if you want it, and it appears you do, you will win."

I smiled. "That's an excellent comeback. You're the only one to talk to me as if Lenny and I will be back together one day."

"I'm an optimist, and I have known you for a long time," Kitty said earnestly. "You aren't a quitter."

"It's his father, you know. He's the one behind everything that's happening. That man is vindictive."

"With what we know about the rich, I hope you're not surprised."

"No, I guess not. I realized his father could be cruel when he kept Lenny away from me for two years. If that wasn't a sign of a vengeful man, what was?

"The only thing that helped me keep my head up, even a little, was that at least I wasn't suffering alone. I knew Lenny felt the same way. It wasn't easy on him. The letters proved that."

But that thought did not give me the solace I needed. I wanted our lives to begin as we'd planned—a young, happily married couple, starting fresh, in love, side by side, with dreams of holidays and a house—a home where we'd raise our children. But his father had taken that from us.

By Monday morning, I had lawyers. And not just any off-the-street lawyers. My parents and I were in the law offices of Lee Parsons Davis of White Plains, New York. And he said we had to fight back. My lawyers included Mr. Davis and a former judge, Mr. Swinburne.

I just wanted to lie in bed and sob.

But Daddy said no. "No one will treat my daughter this disrespectfully and get away with it."

He glared at the lawyer with fire in his eyes.

Mr. Davis was supposedly flamboyant in a courtroom, always ready to drill a new hole into whomever he had on the witness stand. But he was timid in his offices when squared up against my father, who was much shorter than him.

"I am going to fight the annulment. I am not colored. He has no grounds for an annulment."

"Why do you want to stay married to him if he doesn't want to be married to you?"

"I don't believe he wants an annulment. That's his family pressuring him into doing these things."

I reached into my purse and removed a gold cigarette case, a gift from Lenny, although I didn't smoke—or hadn't smoked until that week. As I lit up, my father cleared his throat, delivering a judgmental glare. I wasn't sure if it was my smoking or the fact that he had a sense of how ugly the next few months could be. I was afraid, and he knew it. But he wouldn't abandon his daughter. I could feel his thoughts; I wished I had his strength and conviction.

But I was married and had my husband.

"What's our next step, Mr. Davis?"

"Tomorrow will be a hectic news day. We will announce that you're fighting the annulment with a press release tonight. We'll talk to some of our favorite reporters to make certain the story is exactly how we want it, and then we're off to the races.

"We won't let him get away with this nonsense about your bloodline or anything else of that nature. He spent a lot of time with you and your family. If there were a question about your race, he would have brought it up."

Daddy left his corner of the room to stand beside me. "That is true," he said.

Lenny had said something about race before, but I decided not to mention that conversation. It wasn't a big deal to him then, and what he was claiming now was a part of the plan. Wasn't it?

Another hour passed with me sharing whatever I could remember about gifts given to me, places we'd gone together, and Lenny introducing me to his friends.

The last thing out of the lawyer's mouth was "And we'll make sure you're listed in the *Social Register*. You two are legally married, and the spouse of a blue blood is an automatic inclusion."

Blue blood, noble aristocrat, that's what Lenny had told me that meant. That's what his family thought of themselves. No wonder they hated me.

My knees wobbled. Thank goodness Daddy was within arm's reach. Otherwise, I wasn't sure I would've reached the door.

We left the lawyer's office, the three of us slipping through the back door that led to where our car was parked and got in. My parents hadn't said anything besides my father's grumbly sounds about Lenny, his family, and their lawyers. My mother had been deathly silent and ghostly white.

Daddy and Mummy sat in the automobile's front seat. I ducked down in the back in case reporters lurked in the bushes. I was sure someone would say something, and there was no point in my being the one to offer information before I heard what they had to say. My mother surprised me and said something first.

"Are you sure you're ready for this battle, dear? You could just accept the annulment and go on about your life. I know you love him, but, dear, this suit won't be easy to fight."

"I know, Mummy. But I'm ready. Trust me. I can do this."

* * *

The best-laid plans, as they say . . .

After Connecticut. After FRAUD! After lawyers and infuriating headlines. I had to talk to Lenny. I needed him to hold my hand. Tell me everything would be all right. Promise me that no matter what, he loved me. And one day, all of it, all the hell, the pain, the lies would be behind us. And we'd be together. Forever.

We met in New York's Central Park at the East Seventy-Second Street entrance.

It was tricky. Damn challenging to arrange. But sometimes, the risk doesn't matter if the reason is important enough. The danger only makes the effort sweeter. And that was precisely what happened. No one saw us, and I chalked it up as our Thanksgiving miracle.

Central Park was freezing, twenty-some degrees, with snowflakes and peace. I loved the smell of a park on a cold day. It's as if the scents were frozen in time, lingering in the air, covered in icicles, and waiting for a warmer sun and the spring thaw.

I was snuggly attired and unbothered by the chill. My mink had a thick collar that I turned up, so most of my face was hidden. I had on kid gloves but also a muffler; my hands were buried deep inside. I wanted to enjoy a long walk with Lenny in what might be the last time we would be together for a long while.

I arrived first and stood near the pavilion where we were to meet. I didn't like waiting. It gave me too much time to think.

Imagine how it must've felt to be in love with a man who wasn't the man you thought he was. The realization didn't happen in a flash. It happened slowly, like pulled taffy or molasses dripping from broken glass. I wasn't so blindsided to miss what had been in front of me all along. But I prayed I was wrong. I prayed that he hadn't done anything so terrible as to lie to me.

Someone had told me that rich people with money think

differently from the rest of us. That may be where I got confused. I needed to think differently but was too poor to understand how that worked. Having and keeping money mattered to people who thought less of you and how that made them look.

I opened my purse and removed my handkerchief to dab my eyes. I wasn't crying. It was the cold that had pulled the tears from my eyes.

"Hey, honeybunch. You look lovely."

"Old scout," I said, using one of the nicknames we had for each other. "You look quite dashing."

And he did, in a wide-shouldered, loose-back, half-belted cashmere coat and a couple of wool scarfs around his throat.

Lenny looped his arm through mine and pulled his fedora low, shielding his eyes and most of his face from the cold and prying passersby.

I laughed at how snugly we were wrapped. "It might be the dead of winter, but we aren't going to freeze to death. That's for sure." I leaned into his shoulder. "Something else may kill us."

"Like the morning edition of the *Standard-Star* or the *Daily News*."

"Or the *New York Times* or the *Amsterdam News*. They've started covering the story for the folks in Harlem. My sister Emily told me."

"I'm afraid I will lose everything. We won't have any way to live. No way to survive."

"I don't understand, Lenny. You received your inheritance in May. I thought that was what we were waiting for on your twenty-first birthday, and now there's something else? How many twists and turns will your father send us through? I wish we had just run away. Take whatever you have left, and let's go to Hawaii. Let's get out of here."

I could see his chest heaving. Deep, heavy, fast breaths, panting like he was trying to hang on to something elusive.

Why was he panicking? Where had my calm, calculating lover run off to?

"Lenny. Lenny? Please, Lenny. Take a deep breath." I patted his back and held his gloved hand. "There you go. Listen to the sound of my voice. Breathe in. Breathe out." I sighed heavily. Not because I needed to, I wanted him to watch me. See me calm so it could rub off on him.

I removed one of my gloves and patted his cheek with my bare hand before brushing a snowflake from the tip of his nose.

He stopped gasping for air and stood rigidly in the middle of the walking path.

"I'm sorry. I don't know what happened. Suddenly, my vision went haywire. Everything seemed to shrink, and I couldn't see farther than the end of my arm. I don't know, some hysteria." His laugh was a soulless sound.

I caressed his cheek.

"I need you to be strong. I believe in you," he said. "This plan will work."

I turned slightly, not wanting to look him in the eye. "There are things I don't understand. I won't burden you now with all my questions, but I have one I must ask. Lenny, in addition to everything in the newspapers. I am doing as you said, fighting for us to stay married."

"I know. My father didn't count on that."

"I don't understand why he publicly put you and my family through this ordeal. We're all in the limelight. Not that we'd ever accept a dime of his money—but he would've tried to buy us off before any of this became front-page news."

"Because he doesn't care about you; he's not ashamed of you. He's ashamed of me. I'm the one he wants to destroy. He doesn't care what happens to you."

Lenny was a Broadway sign of flashing lights and emotions. I had touched on a subject that pained him. "It's about his reputation and fixing his image. For that, he must have a public declaration, an annulment that r-renders our public love affair and marriage a lie and me a f-fool for falling in love with s-someone who sh-should've revolted me."

The words stung, but they weren't Lenny's words. They were his father's, a man I'd never met. "I could accept the lies being told about me. Agree to the annulment, and after a month or so, we could meet in Europe and find somewhere else to live on the other side of the world." I was choking on the words. Leaving my family not to be married to Lenny would crush me. But it would be easier on him. "He would never have to know we are still together."

"I told you when I was eighteen, I didn't want to have an affair. Not with you. I want the dream. I want us. I just can't believe so many people are angry at me. My father has never liked me, which I came to grips with ages ago, but now, even my sister, Adelaide, is mad with me."

We had reached the edge of the park, and in a few more feet, we'd be in the middle of a crowded sidewalk, surrounded by New Yorkers. Someone might recognize us, no matter how tightly we were bundled.

"I hate him for forcing us apart. For those two years we will never get back. For these days and possibly weeks until we can be together."

"Don't ever stop." He squeezed my hand. "Promise me. We can beat him. I can beat him. And I'll get my way. I'm a Rhinelander. Right?"

My smile trembled as I held back the inevitable sob. "I-I am a Rhinelander, too. And I won't give you up, either."

"Yes, you are." He looked around, making sure we were still alone, as alone as we could be in Central Park. He bent forward and kissed me softly. "I've got to go."

And then he stepped onto the busy sidewalk and disappeared.

CHAPTER 20

I had seen my friend Kitty two days earlier. But when she rapped on the back door, I saw salvation. With her perky eyes shining and a sly grin curling her lips, I thought of her as an angel coming to whisk me away. Not to heaven, mind you. I wasn't ready for that, but any place other than the house on Pelham Road was freedom. A chance to escape the weight of everything that had happened in the past fourteen days. A reprieve from the madness for a few minutes or hours, or whatever of my life that could be salvaged since that first article in the New Rochelle *Standard-Star*.

"How did you know?" I shouted over my shoulder while rushing down the hall toward my bedroom to grab my wool coat with its squirrel collar, my leather envelope handbag, and the new cloche hat my mother had embroidered. I didn't bother changing out of the brown shift I wore. I'd keep on my coat. Despite my dream of adventure, Kitty was probably taking me for a drive.

Did I mention Kitty had an automobile and knew how to drive it?

"Slow down," she said, trailing behind me. "I'm parked three blocks from here. We have time. Put on some makeup. We're going to a nightclub. We'll dance and let off some steam. You look like you could use it."

Kitty knew a different side of me and was a gal I could count on. During those first months when Lenny's father had shipped him off to foreign countries and eventually a ranch in Arizona, I thought I'd die without him—at first. Then I got pissed. And then I wanted to forget about him. Kitty helped me through it all. Not by sitting me down and lecturing me, either. If I said jump, she said how high.

I plopped down onto my vanity stool and quickly assessed my makeup needs. Then I worked with efficiency to apply the bare minimum.

Kitty sat on the edge of my bed. I could see her reflection in the mirror.

"I read the paper today. Are you going to do it? I mean, wow! That's awfully bold of you, suing Commodore Philip Rhinelander. That's something else."

"Everything you read in the newspaper is not everything that has come out of my mouth," I said, dusting on face powder and searching for my tin of rouge. "The lawyers are writing the rules for what happens next."

Although I considered Kitty a close friend I could count on, I couldn't trust her with the entire truth, which was the part about Lenny's plan. She might not believe it was a good idea, and my sisters already gave me enough grief.

"How can they just up and decide you're colored?" Kitty was saying. "You've lived your entire life in New Rochelle on Pelham Road—just like before I moved into the city. Everyone around here and at school, even at church, never questioned you or your sisters. You are white people. Nobody ever called you a Negro." She paused momentarily, measuring what she was about to say next.

I encouraged her. "Go on."

"Some folks think your father might have a bit of something else in his heritage, but not enough to make you or your sisters anything other than white. Not with your white mother standing right there."

Her point was not lost on me. Daddy's tanned skin didn't fade in the winter like with my sisters and me. So what could I say to Kitty? What I'd say to anyone. "You're right. My father does have some West Indian in him, but so what?" Then I added with a sly grin, "And it's not like Lenny hasn't seen me up close every season of the year. He knows there's no difference between you and me, for example, other than those freckles and that fire-colored hair. And even if there were, he would still love me! I may be guilty of making too much of the difference between white and colored. It's so confusing. It's just the way we all grew up, I guess. But I am the same person, no matter what people see in my lineage or want to call me."

Kitty sprang to her feet with a chuckle. "That's right, and you're too gorgeous to pass up on, right? Now, let's get out of here before something bad happens."

I wrinkled my brow. "Like what?"

"Like one of those newspaper people find out about our secret way outta here."

I quickly finished with my makeup, and we slinked out of the house through the backyards and bushes, sight unseen, until we reached a street three blocks from Pelham Road. It was the first time I'd used my getaway path, but it wouldn't be the last.

Everything was ready. My lawyers had lined up the counter-suit and were anxious to serve Lenny the papers.

But he'd disappeared. No one could find him.

Where was he?

He said we were a team, working together even when things got tough, and things were as jagged as concrete and as dangerous as an avalanche of ice. So why had he disappeared?

One of my lawyers, the former judge Samuel F. Swinburne, was confident that his process server would find Lenny.

I wasn't so sure. I knew if Lenny didn't wish to be found, he wouldn't be. But I needed to see him, hear his voice, and have him explain why he wasn't calling me. All he had to do was pick up a receiver and dial my number. Waiting by the telephone most of the day, I thought about our plan, which I had agreed to. But that didn't take away the hurt. A phone call and an I-love-you weren't asking too much, now, was it?

I was antsy. I pulled out some of the latest issues of *Photoplay*, *Good Housekeeping*, and *Vogue*, the latter a gift from Lenny. But my ability to concentrate was about as good as the neighborhood dumb Dora, which was me on that day.

I didn't know what to do with myself on a Sunday afternoon. Then Gracie and Footsie showed up.

They had gone shopping and came into the house around four o'clock, dropping off a few bags of groceries for Mummy, Daddy, and me. My parents weren't home, having gone to church for an afternoon service, and I didn't expect them until just before dinnertime.

Footsie came in briefly, greeted me, and extended his sympathy for my situation. Which he did every time I'd seen him since mid-November, when all hell broke loose. But he left right after, for which I was grateful. He was too much to handle most days, with his tough Hell's Kitchen talk and his telling me how he would handle the Rhinelanders if they butted into his affairs the way they were messing in mine.

At that, he lit his cigar, one of the smelliest things on earth, and left Gracie to keep me company while he handled some business back in the city.

"I always wondered why Daddy didn't have a problem with you marrying him," I said, glancing at the door he'd just exited. "He isn't the man I would've expected you to marry." I stuck my hand into one of the grocery bags and removed cans of peas, corn, beans, and tomatoes.

"After you started seeing Lenny so hot and heavy, Daddy was glad when I came home and introduced him to Footsie.

It was better than disappearing day and night and not telling anyone where I was. They didn't have to worry about me as much as they worried about you."

I emptied my bag and reached for another one. "I guess."

"And to think, now they've got a mountain of bushwa to worry about with you and Lenny going at each other and him talking rubbish about who we are. I hear newspapers as far as California are talking about your annulment."

"Your mouth, please."

"Don't mind me," she said, opening another bag. It had milk, eggs, and butter.

"Where'd you get that? I thought dairy was delivered on Mondays."

"Footsie knew where you could buy it from the warehouse, so we did." She placed the items in the icebox. "So, what happened this week at court? I'm trying to keep my nose out of the papers."

I side-eyed her. Those words didn't sound like my younger sister. No matter how often I asked her to stop talking to reporters, she seized any moment to be in the spotlight.

"I'm serious. I'm not going to say a word. Just curious about what went on."

My hands were in the last bag of groceries. "What did you and Footsie do? Go to a butcher on a Sunday?" There were several packages of meat wrapped in brown paper.

"Yeah," she replied. Having finished her bag, she sat at the table. "So what happened?"

"Mr. Davis or Mr. Swinburne update me as often as warranted each day. I'll be in court soon enough, and they want me to be there with my family—especially my sisters, but for now, they're just keeping me informed. Then I don't have to read it in the newspapers.

"The first witness my side called to the stand was the city clerk of New Rochelle. Not what I had expected, but William

R. Harmon was the man who signed our marriage license and performed the wedding ceremony.

"Lenny had arranged for the marriage license not to be listed publicly for thirty days, and the city clerk did exactly that. He held on to it. Thirty days."

"Will you ever get to go on the witness stand and set the record straight?"

"I don't know if they want to put me on the stand. Mr. Davis says he's letting the evidence tell the story. Based on Lenny's love letters, they told the judge that our relationship was no sudden infatuation or puppy love affair. Mr. Swinburne told the court that Lenny's love for me started years ago."

"How did they get the letters, Alice? Did you give them to your lawyer?"

I went to the cupboard for cookies and Lipton tea bags, avoiding eye contact. "I don't want an annulment, Gracie. I want to stay married and keep my husband."

I could feel Gracie's eye roll making a full circle. She had something to say, which I could tell I wouldn't like, but I gave her the reins.

"Go on. Speak your piece."

"If that's truly what you want. But I'm beginning to think you've got some brains in that big noggin of yours. You accept the annulment, and you'll walk away without a penny. On the other hand, if this keeps up, you might get a good deal of cabbage out of old Rhinelander. They might pay you off to make it stop—all the attention. It's like the only story in town. So, yeah, do what you must to keep the wheels turning."

"I don't care about money."

She laughed. "I bet you five dollars that sooner or later, that's all you'll be able to think about. This man and his family are loaded. And you've spent three damn years, nearly four, doing everything he's ever wanted you to do, and now, after marrying you, he's behaving like a spoiled child. He wants his cake, but he runs as soon as his society friends turn their backs on him."

"That's not true." It wasn't his friends or family; it was just his father. "Here." I filled her cup with hot water and dropped in a tea bag. "Drink this but add plenty of sugar. You need it."

"He took your youth, Alice. And he is putting you and your family through the wringer, which includes Footsie and me—lest you forget. We didn't ask for this attention."

"But you don't mind it."

She stirred her tea bag. "As I said, hang in until you hear some coins drop. Or hell, better yet, the sweet smell of a bucket of money."

"Don't talk like that," I said sharply. "You have been playing rather loose with your tongue lately."

After that, we didn't say much to each other. Footsie returned, and Gracie left with him. She'd helped me kill some time. But now, I could go back to wondering when I'd hear from Lenny.

CHAPTER 21

⸻ ✦ ⸻

I had to see Lenny—and I had to see him that night.

But first, I had to find him. He was still missing and hadn't been seen since the second of December. Mr. Swinburne had done as he proposed and retained services to deliver my counter-suit to Lenny, but his vanishing act so far had been successful.

But what concerned me more was that I hadn't heard from him.

No messages, no discreet telephone calls. He probably thought it would be too big of a risk. But unlike him, I was willing to chance it. So it was up to me.

If we were to see each other during this sticky time, I'd have to make it happen.

But who could I go to? Who would be willing to help me find Lenny?

When the name came to me, I wondered why I hadn't thought to seek her help before. I just had to make it to her place without a swarm of reporters on my trail.

Bundled up in disguise—a large floppy hat on my head, covering most of my face but still fashionable—I hoped to make it to the train unseen. I slipped out of the house and went through my favorite exit route, the backyards of four connected houses (like Kitty had shown me), except I ended up five blocks away from my parents' Pelham Road home instead of three.

Still, no one was around when I emerged from the bushes, and I hurried toward the train station and headed for the city. Once there, I'd take a subway to Harlem. My sister Emily and her family, Robert and baby Roberta, had rooms at the Baylor Castle, where they worked. But with the noise of my situation with Lenny becoming commonplace, they spent most of their time in Harlem, where my trouble with my wealthy in-laws didn't plague them.

But how would I get through to Robert? How would I convince him to contact Ross Chidester, the limo driver who had driven me home from the Hotel Marie Antoinette those years ago and, on occasion, still worked for Lenny? Limo drivers of the *Social Register* crowd were like a fraternity. Robert was one of them and could help me if he wanted to.

It took more than an hour to reach their address. It was nearly nine o'clock when I knocked on Emily's door. I knew her schedule well enough and knew she wasn't working at the estate that night.

She opened the door, and her cheeks instantly were wet with tears. "Oh, my dear girl, how are you doing in such a hard time?"

She showed me no animosity after all the news articles, after all the talk of race, skin, and such. She and her Negro husband had also suffered from the sting of the headlines. But I should've known better. My eldest sister was the calmest of us, the most kind, and the most loved, and once upon a time, the most vilified by our father.

We fell into each other's arms, and my emotions, the tension of the past days, overtook me. My body shook with sobs, and for a few moments, I felt cleansed. Free of the guilt of the lies I'd told my family, free of the fear that trusting Lenny could be a dangerous mistake.

But I regained control of myself. I hadn't come to her to weep in her arms for hours on end. I had to find Lenny.

I explained what I could to Emily about why I needed to

see him and how I thought Robert could assist, for I believed all the chauffeurs in Westchester County and Manhattan knew one another.

"Do you think Robert could help me find Ross Chidester?"

"Are you sure this man, Chidester, would even help you? Wasn't he the man Lenny's father used to find you at the Hotel Marie Antoinette that night?"

I had told Mummy and Gracie the story, and they'd, of course, told her. But all I did was shrug. "Could be he had no choice. Commodore Rhinelander is a powerful man. Lenny and I spent many hours in the back seat of the limo driven by Ross Chidester."

Emily gave me a look. She wasn't the type to abide back seat antics. She'd spoken up about her love for Robert and confessed to Gracie and me that she was a virgin on her wedding night. "Well, whether Robert can find Mr. Chidester or not, are you sure you're making the right decision, trying to see Lenny? This business in the papers is mighty ugly, and what he's been quoted as saying about you—and our family, doesn't sound like a man you'd want to see, even if he is your husband."

"You won't understand this, but we love each other—and what you read in the papers isn't always the truth."

Emily gently rubbed my shoulder. She always wore her heart on her sleeve and treated Gracie and me like lost souls she was born to help. "I'll call Robert and ask him if he knows anything about this Chidester fellow. If he does, he can swing by and take you to him if he's nearby. That is if he's willing to speak to you. But don't get us involved too much in this business. Robert will do whatever I ask. But at the same time, I won't ask him to do more than I should and still protect our family. My husband and daughter are the most important things to me, Alice. I love you very much, but I love Robert and Roberta, too."

"Thank you for whatever you and Robert can do."

Emily went to use the telephone and a few minutes later

came back, and I saw by the look in her eye it was not completely good news.

"This is quite a coincidence, but your Ross Chidester is part of a limousine pool Robert knows of, and he reached out to him, but you're not going to like what he said."

"D-does he know where Lenny is?" I swallowed. The question had stuck to the roof of my mouth. "Please. Did he know Lenny's whereabouts?"

"He is in Connecticut at a place called Hilliard cottage."

Air rushed into my lungs so fast the world started spinning. "I know where that is. We went there to hide after the first story appeared.

"This may be too much to ask, but since he keeps the limo overnight to clean it up and whatever, can Robert take me to Connecticut? I know where the Hilliards live. I won't stay long. But I must talk to Lenny."

"Robert won't be able to pick you up until late. The Baylors are at a concert of some sort. But he'll take you." Emily chewed on her lower lip for several long seconds. "But you should call Lenny first. It could be awkward if you just show up. There is the chance he doesn't want to see you, Alice."

"No. I won't need to call. I know Lenny. He'll want to see me as much as I want to see him. I do not doubt that."

While waiting for Robert, Emily and I played with Roberta. Their little girl was nearly five years old and quite the rascal, according to Emily. So we entertained ourselves and her with her toys, dolls, and other children's games.

"I want to have a child one day," I said, my fingers in Roberta's hair, pretending to make a ponytail from her curls. "A little girl. Boys are too much work, I believe. And a little girl with Lenny's eyes—she would be the most gorgeous young lady in the world."

"Mothers always think their child is the best and the most beautiful. As they should, because to us they are." Emily was sitting on the floor across from me, but then she stood and walked over to me and stroked my hair. "I am surprised Roberta has stayed awake this late. It's way past her bedtime."

We put her daughter to bed and returned to the kitchen, sipping tea and eating biscuits and jam until Robert arrived close to midnight.

He didn't even take off his coat when he entered. "Let's get going. It'll take a while to drive there and return before dawn. I have a big day tomorrow."

"You don't stay out there too long. Do you hear me?" Emily was talking to me, not her husband. She knew he'd come right back. I was the one who would dawdle.

It was a long drive, but mostly because I was anxious to see Lenny. It felt like the ride took a million years. When we arrived, I instructed Robert to park a little away from the main driveway leading to the Hilliard estate.

"Just in case a reporter is hiding in the shadows."

"Are you sure? It's mighty dark, Alice."

"I'll be fine. Don't worry. I know this property. I spent a couple of weeks in November here."

Robert nodded, and I was off, watching my step in the moonlight, my heart pounding.

I barely knocked before the door opened, but Lenny didn't greet me. Instead, it was the still-very-pregnant Christy. She touched my cheek and smiled. "He's dying to see you."

My heart warmed, but— "How did he know I was coming?"

"Chidester, his driver, called and mentioned you'd likely be heading this way."

I laughed. "I should've thought of that." I eyed her then, perplexed. "Why are you up? It's after midnight."

"The baby's due any day now, and I can't find a comfortable position when I lie down. So I take long walks inside the house. Bernard would have a conniption if I wandered outside alone. Speaking of which, you do know there are bears around here?"

I laughed. "You are such a tease."

"I'm serious, but enough of our chatter." She took my hand. "Come along. As I said, Lenny is waiting."

She led me to the suite we'd shared while staying there before. Lenny was dressed casually, standing at the fireplace, his hand on the mantel.

I raced into his arms, and we embraced, hugged, kissed, and murmured: "I love you." "I miss you."

"I'm sorry." Those words came from Lenny's lips. "I've been with my father and his lawyers day and night. I couldn't call. I couldn't do anything until I slipped away a few days ago but thank you for finding me."

"I thought you'd be here. But the chauffeur Ross is how I truly found you. But you already know that because he called and told you I was coming."

More kissing and clinging to each other as if we were drowning and each other's arms were all that could save us.

"I hope he doesn't squeal to your father," I whispered against his lips.

"He's not obliged to do that n-now." Lenny pulled away, but not far. "My father f-fired him a w-while ago, but he still drives for me on o-occasion."

We sat on the edge of the bed, hugging and kissing.

"I can't stay long. Robert, Emily's husband, is waiting," I said. "This is so hard for me, Lenny. The newspapers, the lawyers, the way the papers say that I lied to you about who I am . . ."

He massaged my neck and chest. "It's not me, Alice. It's my father and his lawyers."

I smiled. "My father says lawyers were born in hell."

Lenny laughed. "It could be they came to earth solely to do the devil's bidding."

"Are you calling your father a slave to Satan?" I gave him a wry smile.

"No, I think sometimes he's the damn devil himself."

That's when my smile disappeared. "I don't know how much longer I can take this, Lenny."

He pulled me close. "Trust me, honeybunch. It'll be okay."

"I do trust you, but you can't control everyone in your family, particularly your father," I said, and kissed his chin. "Promise me if things go haywire and get out of control, we can run away. I'll do it, Lenny. I'll leave everything to be with you."

He gently kissed my throat, my chin, my eyes. "We'll end up leaving one day. But it would be better if I'm not disinherited."

We wanted to make love; I could tell by the passion in his kisses and the trembling in my legs. But there was no time.

I love you. I love you more.

Moments later, I was in the limousine with Robert, quietly crying as he drove along the parkway to my parents' house in New Rochelle.

PART 4

———◆———

LEONARD "KIP" RHINELANDER

UPI (United Press International)

December 7, 1941

White House Announcement of Hawaii Attack

Text of a White House announcement detailing the attack on the Hawaiian Islands is: "The Japanese attacked Pearl Harbor from the air and all naval and military activities on the island of Oahu, principal American base in the Hawaiian Islands."

The Washington Post

December 8, 1941

HAWAII ATTACKED WITHOUT WARNING WITH HEAVY LOSS; PHILIPPINES ARE BOMBED: JAPAN DECLARES WAR ON U.S.

The United States of America and the Empire of Japan are at war. The conflict that Adolf Hitler started on September 1, 1939, has now truly become a death struggle of worldwide proportions.

CHAPTER 22

————◆————

ROBERTA

1941

The world is upside down. The United States has gone from a watcher to a doer in a day. The attack on Pearl Harbor cut to the heart of what makes America—America. The response to the treacherous act by Japan has everyone up in arms. Skin color doesn't matter. America does.

In the blink of an eye, our country is at war, which will make for one of the saddest but also most patriotic holiday seasons in history. Still, I am in New Rochelle on Pelham Road the Saturday before Christmas, not knowing how my aunt Alice will react.

When I arrive at her house, I wonder if she'll be as reflective as everyone else, or at least the people I know. But she can't keep track of how many packs of cigarettes she has left, so her staying abreast of the latest news on sunken US carriers, Japan, or Pearl Harbor would be a surprise. Her thoughts are trained on Rhinelander. If it doesn't have that name stamped on its forehead, it's of no interest to her.

When I enter the house, I don't mention what is happening in the world. I let her lead the discussion because it's about the only thing she controls these days.

Adelaide Rhinelander Thomas is at it again. Alice won

the first round, and now the woman has taken her case to a higher court. What is the matter with her? What has Alice done to her other than marry her brother? Why would Adelaide bother with lawyers, court documents, and the like to cut off Alice? The commodore had been paying the annuity for more than a decade. Why put on the brakes now? It's not as if Adelaide Rhinelander Thomas is broke. She just wants to see Alice penniless and heartsick.

The situation has hurt Alice. It's evident in her sunken eyes, protruding collarbone, and the loose skin threatening her neck. She was thin a few weeks ago, the last time I saw her, but now she is skeletal.

I hope she has a little nest egg to tide her over. But after caring for two sickly parents until they died and refusing help from her sisters, she misses that monthly check in more ways than I can count.

Today, she answers the door in a silk bathrobe, her hair covered with a sleeping net and wearing no makeup. Not even a dab of lipstick.

Thankfully, I've anticipated her lack of appetite and disinterest in shopping or cooking meals. So I show up with a bag of groceries.

"Did you speak with the lawyers?" I edge by her, heading for the kitchen, and am pleased when I hear her padding behind me.

"Of course," she mutters. "Don't you listen? I told you she wouldn't give up easily."

I place the grocery bags on the counter. "I hope you like canned peas and the Imperial canned meals. You don't like to cook, so everything I have here is canned or frozen but easy to prepare. And if you feel like having breakfast, I also bought eggs, sausage links, and a loaf of Wonder Bread—you know, building strong bodies eight ways."

I smile, but she doesn't. I should've figured she isn't one for knowing advertising slogans.

"Did you bring me some coffee and cigarettes?"

"Of course. Would you like me to make you a cup?" I say, placing the last can of peas on the shelf in the cabinet.

"Yes. Sure, but can you pass me my smokes?"

I remove the coffee from the grocery bag and the cigs from my purse. "I got you two packs."

She nods and sits at the kitchen table. "I think it's the ring that she wants."

"Who?"

"Adelaide. The sapphire ring that Lenny gave me in 1921, weeks after I met him," she says. "He got it from her."

"And now you think she wants it back? Jeez. And with zeal, too. The way she's fighting the annuity suit, I swear she acts like you stole it." I found a skillet for the sausage and eggs. "Do you have a toaster?"

"I have a Sunbeam toaster." She points.

"Got it." I open the loaf of bread and drop in two slices. "Why did you trust him so much?"

"You mean Lenny?" She yanks open one of the drawers and removes a book of matches. "Why wouldn't I? We were in love with each other and had been for three years. Whether together, or with him in Arizona and Alaska, were we still in love—even when our lives began to unravel the first time."

"The Hotel Marie Antoinette."

"Yes. It was humiliating. Disgusting and cowardly, too—sending his lawyer. His father didn't even tell him to his face that he had a problem with him dating a woman like me." She sighs. "It was a hard lesson to learn. Especially for someone who cared the way I cared and loved the way I did."

I sit in a folding chair at the card table in the living room, where my mother has the pieces of her latest jigsaw puzzle before us. When finished, this one will show a group of golden retrievers on their hindquarters with tongues wagging and eyes shining with a forest in the background—the picture on the lid of the box, but now it's a thousand un-matched pieces.

"How was your day, Roberta?" my mother asks after I've plopped into the chair with a heavy sigh. "You've been so quiet lately. Is it the war? I know it's scary."

I pick up a puzzle piece but have no idea what to do with it. I just wish I did. "I feel anxious all the time, Momma. It's like I'm waiting for the sky to fall."

She studies the jigsaw puzzle, picking up a piece and putting it down in favor of another. "During the Great War, everything that happened occurred on the other side of the Atlantic. We thought it would be the last war. A second world war was never imagined. And it hurts even more."

"The war is frightening. But it feels far away, which makes it difficult to know when or what to feel, other than anxious." I exhale a heavy sigh. "There are so many stories just in Harlem these days about Negro nurses and soldiers, ready to fight, but because of segregation, unable to join the fight in Europe. . . ."

"Can we talk about something else?" I say shakily.

"Of course, dear. Whatever you want."

"Ann Petry stopped by the paper today. She won't be returning. She's working on a novel and getting more involved with the Negro Theater Ensemble."

"Who's going to write the gossip column?" my mother asks, her tone shifting as if I'm about to announce I've been promoted to a new position at the paper.

"Not me. Not anyone. The city desk focuses on the war and what changes it might bring to Harlem."

"Oh, I'm sorry to hear that about the society column. During times like these, people need normal things to distract them from the scary things." She examines a puzzle piece closely. I then place it in a pile with other pieces that look the same to me.

"The newspaper won't stop covering sports and the goings-on in Negro high society. But we always have written stories about issues and problems in Harlem's Negro neighborhoods."

"And that sounds like a righteous calling, but you also have advertisements about skin lighteners, false teeth, and nightclubs."

Too often lately, my mother has shown how much she is not a woman of the modern world.

"Do you want to help me with the puzzle?" She eyes the puzzle piece I am squeezing between my thumb and forefinger.

I chuckle. "Yes, I'll help. Although I don't like the look of these dogs."

"They're lovely, Roberta. Just a group of friends together, looking happily at the photographer." She pushes some of the puzzle pieces aside, making room for her elbows, which she places on the table, resting her chin on the knuckles of her hand. "How is your aunt doing?"

I am only slightly surprised by her question. I have spent six months not mentioning my visits with Aunt Alice to my mother. Of course, I should've known something would happen I hadn't anticipated, like my mother reading about her sister suing Adelaide Thomas to reinstate her annuity.

"Is she okay?" Momma doesn't look at me; she examines the puzzle pieces.

"Honestly, I can't tell some days. She will seem fine, and then it's painful to be around her. I wish the Rhinelanders would leave her alone."

"My. Your attitude toward your aunt has changed."

"What do you mean? How did you know what my attitude might've been?"

"I'm not blind, Roberta. You two were close when you were a child. She was your favorite aunt. She'd take you to amusement parks and shopping at the fancy department stores. She spent time with you until things got so bad she couldn't do anything but . . ."

"That didn't have to do with the Rhinelanders."

"It's a shame those people are still messing in her life," she says.

"Lately, she seems tired."

"I wish she'd let me come by and see her."

The surprise on my face doesn't compare to the feeling in my chest. It is the first time my mother has said such a thing about Aunt Alice. "What do you mean she won't let you see her?"

"The only person she agrees can visit her is you."

"When did you ask her if you could stop by?"

"I call her on occasion, and on occasion, she will answer the phone, and that's when I ask—before she hangs up when she hears my voice. But if she stays on the line, she says no. Clear as a bell. Voice loud and strong. So there's no mistake."

"Why in the world would she hang up on you? She's the one who should be embarrassed. She hurt you. Not the other way around." I push away from the card table and rise. "I thought you were enemies."

"How could I be enemies with my sister?"

"Because of what she did to you and Papa?" I say incredulously.

She frowns. "What would your father have to do with my relationship with Alice?"

"She was the reason you two split."

"Who told you that?" she asks. "I bet it was your aunt Gracie. I know those words never came out of your father's mouth."

She is right about that. My father has never said an ill word about my mother. Even when I try to encourage him to do so. When I was younger, it was a game in my childish mind to see if he'd join me in criticizing her for some parenting choice she inflicted upon me, like not dating until I was sixteen, not drinking Coca-Cola until I was sixteen, not wearing silk stockings until I could buy them for myself. An entire horrible list of things I couldn't do. But he never cooperated. They might be apart, but he was always respectful.

"Aunt Gracie told me a few things when I talked to her on the telephone."

"Whatever she said is wrong. Trust me." She fits a couple of puzzle pieces together, leans against her chair's bridge, and exhales. "Why is it most of the conversations in this family take place during a holiday?"

I stare at her. "That's odd, because Aunt Alice doesn't like holidays."

"I'm not surprised. But that's a shame. She used to love them. Thanksgiving and Christmas were her favorite times of the year."

CHAPTER 23

—◆—

ALICE

1924

The meeting took place at my lawyer's offices in an elegant conference room with dark brown leather chairs, crystal vases, a chandelier, and polished mahogany furniture glowing from every corner.

Seated around a long table with legs shaped like a jungle cat was Mr. Davis's secretary, Mrs. Sage, an older woman with gray hair and a pillbox hat she never took off, and a young lawyer who helped Mr. Davis with my case, Pritchard Anders. He was a tall, string bean of a man with a crop of yellow hair whose five-o'clock shadow arrived during breakfast. My other attorney, Mr. Swinburne, was digging up facts on Kip and wouldn't be joining us, whispered Mr. Anders as he helped me into my chair.

My mother and father were at my side, and none too surprising, the first words out of Lee Parsons Davis's mouth were about the *Daily News*.

"An article will help clear up some of this business about you seducing Kip to get your hands on his money. It'll show how stingy he was. How he never bought you gifts or took you to fancy restaurants."

I stared and nodded, knowing full well that the article would be filled with lies, but that didn't bother me.

"Who is the reporter?" I asked as I sat at the long table, although I knew what he'd say.

"Grace Robinson."

"Of course." A name I'd hoped I'd never hear again. "Why would you talk to her? I told you what happened."

"You shouldn't take reporters seriously," Mr. Davis said. "They're doing their jobs, and sometimes those jobs can help us in the court of public opinion."

The words sounded like something Mr. Davis had said many times to clients. I wondered how often he fed information about a client to the press.

"If we get hammered in court," said Mr. Anders. "We'll hammer back in the press. It's important to give the public an opportunity to have an alternative perspective."

"What if someone finds out I lied? Won't that look worse?"

The men in the room, including my father, looked at me with bewilderment in their eyes.

"Lenny did give me gifts." And it was easy to prove. There were photographs of me in the mink coat he bought me, carrying a handbag you could only purchase at Saks. And the roadster he bought me for no reason whatsoever—considering I couldn't drive. And there was the diamond engagement ring and the platinum wedding band, which I intended to wear proudly until the day I died. These were only a few testaments to Lenny's generosity. So, who were we planning to fool? And speaking of rings . . .

"What about the sapphire ring," I asked my lawyer.

"That you don't have to worry about, either. We'll bring it up in court if we need to."

The ring was an heirloom for the Rhinelander brood. Lenny had given me a popular family heirloom, which, now that our marriage was known, had caused an uproar. My source, the chauffeur, Ross Chidester, through Emily's Robert, had a bushel of juicy stories from eavesdropping on the most elite conversations of the people listed in the *Social Register.*

According to Robert, the ring had belonged to Lenny's late mother, and his sister, Adelaide, was highly discombobulated—Chidester's word—about it not being in her jewelry box.

Of course, Adelaide and her society friends were spreading tall tales. Lenny told me and Gracie the ring was an heirloom passed down to him by his sister.

Still, to squelch this gossip, all Lenny had to do was remind high society of the facts. Instead, he allowed rumors to become legends among the servants and chauffeurs. Fabricating an elaborate story about how I'd spent the night at the Rhinelander mansion one weekend when the commodore was out of the country and had slipped out with a bagful of goodies from his mother's jewelry box.

What type of treacherous creature was I to do such a thing?

"We need to change the picture Jacobs has painted of you in court," Mr. Anders said, drawing my attention. "You're not a gold digger."

"I know that."

"We know that, too," Mr. Davis said. "You are a victim of a wealthy man's desire and power. A heartbroken woman, we need the public to know. Not the salacious seductress Lenny's Mr. Jacobs portrays."

"But I love him. And he loves me. What happens in the newspapers and the courthouse is not him. It's his family, his father—they are the enemy, not Lenny."

"You have a point, Alice." Mr. Davis puckered his lips, head bobbing. "Your enemy is the four hundred. The wealthy snobs in the Hudson Valley and on Fifth Avenue. Those gents and their ladies need a good whack in the jaw now and then. And you, Mrs. Rhinelander, are just the little girl to deliver the punch."

I wasn't sure I understood what he meant, but I had to put up a good fight.

I was tired of letting go of everything I'd held precious just to embarrass Lenny in the courtroom.

I told the lawyers I'd lost it, but of course, the sapphire ring was in my jewelry box in my bedroom. On the other hand, I never mentioned the mink coat. I was keeping a promise. Some things, I told the lawyers, were off the table. They seemed to like it when I used smart talk like that.

Lenny's legal team had a counterattack to our articles. A few days after the story about how little cash Lenny had departed with on my behalf, the headlines went something like this:

RHINELANDER FIGHTS COLOR

MILLIONAIRE CALLS HIS BRIDE A COLORED WOMAN

My lawyers were ecstatic. It's what they hoped he'd do. Their glee stymied me.

Nonetheless, I was so damn tired of hiding in the house, reading newspapers, and peeking out the window to see nothing but reporters hoping to get a glimpse of the girl who married Leonard "Kip" Rhinelander.

They didn't understand that my insides were dying. I thought I was losing my mind. I didn't even think about love anymore. There were only lawyers and what was happening next in the trial, except they kept telling me it wasn't a trial. I wasn't on trial. It was a hearing to end my marriage—that much I'd understood from the beginning.

After a hellish week, I was exhausted, fretful, and lonely, and needed to get away from Pelham Road, or I'd lose my mind. So I telephoned Kitty—and she was game.

I used the same escape route she and I had used before and

was relieved when the trek through the backyards was not as challenging.

However, when I reached the spot where Kitty was to be parked, it wasn't her car; it was a pickup truck, and she wasn't behind the wheel. Her brother, Henry, was driving. I hadn't seen him in years, not since he returned from fighting in the Great War. Now he was twenty-three but looked ten years older. He was still as freckle-faced as his sister, but his hair was more blond than red.

"Howdy, Alice," he said.

My brows arched. "Howdy, Henry." I looked at Kitty and said teasingly, "Is he old enough to run around with us?"

"You stop that, Alice," Henry butted in. "I'm more than old enough to hang out with you two."

I piled into the front seat and sat on the door with Kitty in the middle. Henry cranked the throttle, and we were off.

"So where are we going?" I asked. "Not that I care. As long as we're heading somewhere away from New Rochelle."

"Let's go into Harlem," Kitty said. "There are plenty of speakeasies and nightclubs there. We'll blend in, too."

"We can go to one of 'em black and tans."

"What's that?"

Both of them gave me a look.

"I swear I don't know."

"I thought you got out more," Henry said. "It's a jazz joint that lets coloreds and whites come into the nightclub as customers. But, hell, we might sit next to a Negro couple."

Kitty was pensive. "Are you sure, Henry? What if someone recognizes her? With a bunch of coloreds nearby, will that mess up your trial?"

"It's not a trial," I countered, still stinging from my last conversation with the lawyers. "Besides, I have on my disguise." I tugged the wide brim of the fashionable floppy hat I'd worn when I went to Emily's. It had worked then. "And I've spent only a couple of days in court."

Henry glanced away from the road, confusion in his blue eyes. "For it not to be a trial, you are being judged mighty tough. You've been in court only a few days, and even without a jury, the news stories are condemning you and calling you all kinds of things. My mother would beat Kitty to death if she heard those things. So whatever you can do to defend yourself—you best do it."

"That's why I have lawyers." I sighed. "But I didn't call Kitty and sneak out of my house to spend the evening talking about trials, judges, or Lenny Rhinelander."

"She told you. Didn't she, Henry," Kitty said. "Hey, she's right. No more court talk. Okay?" She poked her brother in the side.

"All right. No need to punch me."

"Now, where are we going? Dancing. Right, Alice?"

"You bet."

"Hooch," added Henry.

"God, yes." Kitty and I said together.

"Jazz."

"I love dancing and listening to jazz—I always play it on my Victrola. Although, my Daddy hates it." I lowered my voice and scrunched up my eyes, imitating my father. "Damn, jazz music and Prohibition are allowing young people to misbehave. Everywhere you go, y'all drinking hooch, dancing in saloons, necking in the rumble seat of automobiles. The 1920s are dangerous times."

Henry and Kitty laughed.

"He's a hard man," Kitty said.

"I know. But my answer to jazz music is a loud, screaming yes," I replied. "Now, where are we going?"

"You'll see. I think I know a place where you won't be noticed, but I'm still glad you put on some kind of disguise."

I fluffed the scarf tied snuggly around my throat. "What do you think, Kitty?" I asked.

"You look like the cat's meow."

My smile wasn't the best, but I don't think either of them understood my desperation. I couldn't believe what was happening to me. Who was I before I met Lenny? I wasn't whoever I was now. The girl I was now wasn't fun. She was sad all the damn time and never did anything or went anywhere other than a courthouse. I was twenty-five years old and happily married a little more than a month ago. Married, but my happiness was vanishing.

"Are we going or not, Kitty? Otherwise, take me back home or let me out of the car."

CHAPTER 24

————◆————

Smalls Paradise was a misleading name. Seventh Avenue's newest "it" spot, opened less than a month ago, was about as sizable a nightclub as I'd ever seen, and it was packed.

The club was a black and tan, too, so it wasn't unusual for whites to sit beside coloreds.

I followed Henry and Kitty into the nightclub's main room as we weaved through the club's patrons. Henry was right. The place was filled with people of all colors. A Negro woman in a hurry brushed by me, jostling me to the side but abruptly stopping to say, "Sorry. Pardon me," with a smile before she continued on her way.

She must think I am colored, I thought. That was the only explanation for the smile and apology, I decided, inching closer to Henry and Kitty, shy of stepping into one of their coat pockets.

Henry spotted an empty table near a group of women seated toward the rear of the nightclub, and we settled right in. The large party of women were primarily dark-skinned Negroes, but a couple were almost as white as me. But they weren't strictly white.

Something about them and how comfortable they looked among coloreds told me otherwise.

The women were having a good time, laughing and backslapping one another. Their tables were cluttered with empty glasses, plates of chop suey, and an order of fried oysters. The smell wafted back to us, and I was hungry as a stray cat. "Let's order everything those girls got."

"Sounds great," Henry said. "I am starved, too."

"This is such a swell place," Kitty added.

Everybody was beautiful and decked out in their glad rags. The flappers were elegant, with layers of long beads and the cutest short bobs. I wore my long hair in a bun at the nape of my neck with loose curls around my face. It was old-fashioned, but Lenny once mentioned that he liked long hair. I never thought about cutting it after that.

Not until that moment.

The lively group of women had someone new join them. She was brown-skinned and didn't sit at their two tables immediately. She stood there and started talking about her job at the *Amsterdam News*, the largest, most successful Negro newspaper in Harlem, and a story the city editor had challenged her to write about—the Rhinelander trial.

I overheard someone call the name Marvel, and she answered. It was a surprising name, which I immediately liked. Too bad it belonged to a gal who worked at a newspaper, even a Negro newspaper.

Kitty and Henry had called over a waiter to order us food and drinks. And the band wasn't playing yet, so I eavesdropped.

This girl, Marvel, had a barrelful of opinions about several topics and had no problem sharing her thoughts on the Rhinelander case. However, I found myself more interested in her demeanor than her words.

She sounded smart. Educated. More so than Lenny or me, that was for sure. And she had friends—young women and men her age who went out together, laughed, talked, danced, listened to jazz music, clapped their hands, and stomped their feet. She was free to live her life.

She had all this, and she was a brown-skinned Negro, too. A knot in my stomach felt like it had grown barbs, and I recognized the feeling. I was jealous.

Marvel took a seat with her friends.

Pretty girls surrounded her with flashing smiles, dark eyes, and not nearly as much makeup as Kitty and I wore.

She talked about her day in court and loudly shared her opinion about the Rhinelander case, with apparently no concern about who might overhear or disagree with her. This, I found incredibly bold.

"She was a dark speck in a predominantly white crowd," Marvel said, talking about me, I presumed.

"What do you mean dark?" asked one of Marvel's friends. "She looks white to me."

"I was being sarcastic," she countered. "But she was prideful, no matter. With more than a hundred pairs of eyes upon her, she didn't tremble or shy away from their gazes. She kept looking straight ahead like an owl, sizing up their prey, waiting for the perfect moment to gobble it up."

She turned to her friends. "A wealthy white man is trying to get rid of his colored wife, except she claims she's not colored. It's salacious how the men in court look at her."

"It's a ridiculous case," said one of Marvel's friends. "A white man marries a woman who is passing, and now, because he and his family have money, high society is up in arms."

"They are embarrassed a Negro girl fooled him, got into his head so he couldn't let her go."

Marvel raised her hand, taking over the conversation again. "Look. She's either the smartest gold digger I'll ever write about—and I hope the last—or there is more to it than an embarrassed wealthy white man and a colored girl with the looks and the savvy to bag him."

She laughed. "Thanks to my big mouth, one of the beat reporters says I won't be able to write a story, let alone sell it, but I'm going to show him. So I'm traveling to White Plains from Harlem daily to figure out the truth. You know, the story behind the story—who is this Alice Jones?"

"You think she and her family are lying?" asked one of her friends.

Marvel paused, taking her time, thinking her response through before she replied. "When I first saw her, I had it in my mind that it would be easy to despise her.

"She is a Negro woman, like me, but nothing like me. She is pretending to be white but gets caught. But that story is too easy. Too plentiful. How many Negroes in New York are passing? Living on Fifth Avenue but sneaking back to Lenox Avenue and One Hundred and Twenty-Fifth Street to be who they really are behind closed doors?

"I want the hidden story about Alice Jones. Is she a colored temptress or a young girl whose life has been tossed and turned by a clever, wealthy white man whose life's ambition is to squash the life out of women, or a working-class colored woman?"

Marvel had a quick wit and a clever tongue. For a moment, she had me believing that Lenny and I were liars.

"Nothing was what it appeared to be. No one in the Rhinelander courtroom could be trusted to tell the truth.

"Besides, there were other things to be bothered by when it came to Alice Rhinelander sitting primly next to her team of lawyers—all those white men in the Westchester County courthouse. I swear they all wanted her."

At this point, a young colored man, pristinely dressed in a fancy tweed suit and with a meticulously trimmed mustache, joined the table of women. For a short time, he grabbed everyone's attention, including Marvel's. I didn't pay much attention to him other than to notice he was handsome for a Negro.

Soon, however, Marvel was speaking again, but now her words were directed at the young man.

"I'm a Harlem gal. Born and raised in one of the wealthier Harlem neighborhoods. You've heard of it, Sugar Hill. My father is in the banking business. He has nothing to do with racketeers or any of that ilk. My family's home is next door to W. E. B. Du Bois. So that should tell you a thing or two about my family."

The man must have said something I didn't hear that insulted her because she was mighty boastful.

The band started swinging right then, and Marvel and her friends leaped to their feet and shot to the dance floor.

I was glad I'd worn a disguise, but I was nervous now and pulled my collar up in case someone had better eyes than me in the dark. Thank goodness, Smalls Paradise was all candlelight and cigarette smoke.

Kitty and Henry were laughing about something, while I was trembling with nerves. When Henry asked me to dance, I was anxious to burn some energy.

I grabbed Kitty's arm and pulled her alongside us to the opposite side of the dance floor from Marvel and her friends.

The three of us danced until Henry dragged us back to our table. We ate our food and drank our drinks.

By then, I noticed another group had taken over the tables where Marvel and her friends had sat. I sighed a long breath of relief. I only had to be in the courthouse a few times, but the next time I was there, I'd have to look her up.

Wouldn't she be surprised when I called her by name? If I dared do such a thing.

After another hour, I asked Henry and Kitty to take me home. I'd had enough excitement for one evening.

I left Smalls Paradise more heartsick about the loss of the girl I might've been than grieving over Lenny.

The crowd, the energy of the people in that room, white, Negro, colored, mulatto—whatever they called themselves, in that nightclub, young people were enjoying their youth.

Listening to music, dancing, drinking, and sharing passions and dreams, flirtations and love affairs.

I may not have liked my name being bandied about the way it had been by the girl Marvel and the other people in her group. But I wasn't the only subject, just the newest, and they had something to say. They were living their lives, lives not put on hold by love.

What had I missed by falling in love with Lenny? What kind of young woman could I have been without him? Those dreams that I put aside. Education. My own apartment. A job at Saks as a salesclerk who knew everything about fashion, makeup, and the latest hairstyles. That girl could've met a nice boy. Someone who didn't have a father whose name was in the *Social Register*, a father who believed Alice would never be good enough for his son. It didn't matter what color or shade of white, brown, or black she might've been. Her name and address weren't listed in the *Social Register*. She didn't have a lineage that made her a French Huguenot. She had parents she loved and sisters, who sometimes were bratty and other times showed her so much love she wanted to weep. But now, all she thought about was him. What did that get her?

Nothing but headlines and people she'd never met who felt they had a right to judge her and tell her who she was and what she deserved from life. How could she get her life back from a sea of faceless, voiceless people who saw her only as words printed in black and white in the morning edition?

Maybe that was all she was now? Words on a page, written by people she didn't know, read by people who didn't care about her feelings, hopes, or dreams.

Maybe what she should do was give up.

For the briefest moment, I wasn't me. I was "her," and that's what I thought. Nothing would work out for me. I was used up, ruined at twenty-five years old.

I sat in front of my vanity, staring at myself in the mirror, turning from side to side, wondering what I'd look like at thirty, at forty, at sixty-five. *Why worry about the future?* I thought. *Today is all I have.*

And I couldn't give up yet. Could I? God help me. I wasn't even ready to give up Lenny. But I had to try to survive. I had to find a way to not give up on myself.

Then my mother knocked on my bedroom door.

"A messenger arrived and left this for you," she said. "I didn't tell your father. He wouldn't like it. But you read what it says and decide what you wish to tell Daddy."

When she handed it to me, I knew it was from him.

My Lenny had a keen sense of timing. As soon as I came close to getting a foothold on my life, he stepped in and mucked things up before I could gain a solid grip.

He had done it before. A week after my response to his annulment suit, Lenny sent me a telegram.

I closed my eyes and inhaled to calm my racing heart. It took a moment. Then I opened the envelope.

The note read that he had been a fool to trust Leon Jacobs, his father's lawyer. *As if that revelation is a surprise,* I thought bitterly.

The message said I should "fight like the devil" but don't try communicating with him.

Suddenly, my father was in the doorway of my bedroom.

"Are you okay?" He glanced at the telegram in my hand. "Is it from him?"

I nodded.

"May I come in?"

I looked at him and smiled. "Yes, Daddy."

He stepped in but seemed unsure about what to do next. "You can sit next to me on the mattress," I said.

I faced him and gave him the letter. Daddy took the note but didn't read it. He sat across from me as I wiped tears from my eyes.

"I'm not sure why I'm crying. It's just that I'm so confused.

We were together, and now we aren't. I've been married—" I counted on my fingers. "Two months? But the last month I've spent with my husband hiding from his father and the press or having him hide from me."

"I'm sorry this has happened to you, but he's a weak-minded boy, trying to keep you in his clutches. Writing you notes like this, after all the grief he's put you through." He sighed heavily. "I know it will be hard to do, but don't fall for his foolishness."

There was nothing for me to do but outwardly agree.

"Yes, Daddy. I know." I dried my eyes. "I'm going to go to bed. I'm too tired to think."

He stood and walked to the door but stopped. He was still holding the telegram. He went to place it on the dresser.

"No, Daddy. Throw it away. I don't need it cluttering up my room."

CHAPTER 25

The New Year was supposed to be about fresh starts. Whatever went wrong the year before could be made right. But 1925 wasn't interested in clean slates. Once the year started, the dirt piled up so high that I thought I lived in a dust bowl.

The mayhem began with the lawyers. Both sets. Lenny's and mine. They haggled from January first. And from the outside looking in, Lenny's team was winning.

At the beginning, I reasoned it was because he had more lawyers than me.

"Don't worry," said Mr. Davis before our session began. "They're just trying to intimidate you, but we have a solid case."

I wanted to believe him. But he didn't sound very confident and never made eye contact, a telltale sign of approaching lousy luck.

Isaac N. Mills, a gray-haired, seventy-four-year-old retired New York Supreme Court justice, led Lenny's team. A man with that title could wield enough fear in a courtroom. But he also brought his son, Roy Mills, and the man I encountered at the Hotel Marie Antoinette—Leon R. Jacobs.

Jacobs's opening remarks at the courthouse exceeded his vileness at the Hotel Marie Antoinette, mainly because he had an audience. It was as if he'd lit a match over an open jar of kerosene. Fire and smoke. That's all I heard.

My lawyer called him desperate and ingenious at once until he requested a trial by jury. Jacobs reasoned that for the "poor victimized Lenny" to be judged fairly, his annulment case must be heard before a jury of his peers. Once given the facts of the case, twelve white men would determine if his marriage to Mrs. Alice Rhinelander was worthy of annulment.

Justice Joseph Morschauser of the New York Supreme Court presided over the proceedings and, without much deliberation, agreed that a jury trial would be best.

"What does it mean?" I asked as we left the courtroom, heading for a rear exit to avoid the press.

"The burden of proof is on us, Mrs. Rhinelander," Mr. Swinburne said. "Your husband is accusing you of deceiving him."

"So what is this proof you have?"

"Proof that you aren't colored?" Mr. Davis said.

We reached the limo my lawyers had arranged for me. Mr. Davis, the shorter of the two men, gestured for the driver to remain in the car. He opened the rear door but blocked my entrance. "I'm sending one of my associates to Leicester, England," Mr. Swinburne said.

"Whatever for?"

"To obtain a copy of your father's birth certificate so we can end the race question."

"My father's birth certificate?" I wasn't sure how to feel. "But my father was born in Jamaica, not England."

"Jamaica's a colony."

"Your father spent most of his life in England," said Mr. Davis. "We'll start our search there."

It was at that moment I realized my lawyers didn't believe me. They didn't think I was white.

By mid-April, Swinburne's associate had returned from England. But he was empty-handed. I was relieved and confused by my relief. "What does it mean if you can't prove my father is white or colored?"

"Without proof of his heritage, it's Mr. Rhinelander's word against yours."

My father was in the room that day, seated quietly in a corner, holding my mother's hand. I expected him to speak up, but it was my mother who had something to say.

"My daughter is not colored," my mother said. "Mr. Rhinelander is wrong. That is all you need to prove in court."

Mr. Davis smiled sweetly at my mother, but when I walked out of the courtroom, no one warned me that the delay in proceedings would bring my life to a standstill.

I hated the spotlight and having every newspaper reporter, cameraman, and overly opinionated bystander in America hounding me.

But what would it be like without them? What would I do for six months?

Surprise. Even without the trial, it felt like the *New York Times, Daily News, Standard-Star,* and the Associated Press visited my doorstep every other day. I was still news.

And only a phone call away—if Lenny remembered how to dial my number.

The first few months, while waiting for the proceedings to resume, I waited for Lenny to send me a note or anything, letting me know we were still one, still together, fighting a battle we had to win.

During the long, lonely days and nights of what felt like an endless spring, surprisingly, I didn't lose my mind. I missed Lenny terribly, but there had been a letter that reached me. A telephone call that lasted seconds. A bouquet of poppies addressed to Gracie, but we knew they were for me. Still . . .

It wasn't enough. Not close to enough. Only enough to keep my heart from breaking apart completely.

* * *

In late May, we were back in court for a brief session where the news was especially thrilling for my lawyers. The judge announced the proceedings would begin in November.

The lawyers from both sides had collected what they needed to try the case in front of a jury. My lawyer sounded extremely pleased when he whispered, "We are no longer playing defense. We have the ball, and can be bold and aggressive on the playing field."

Seated at the defendant's table with my lawyer, while my sisters and parents sat on the other side of the rail in the benches behind me, I didn't mind comparing my life in court to a football game. But the judge had another surprise, which in hindsight, I should've expected it: my first victory.

Alimony.

A thousand dollars a month for me to live on and pay my legal fees.

I wanted to throw up. Instead, I slinked out of the courtroom, smiling sweetly, holding my head high whenever camera bulbs flashed.

Then I slipped out the rear exit of the courthouse and fled to the limousine waiting to take me home, but standing next to the car was Marvel Cunningham.

Astonishing how a day where you've won something you never thought you'd have to fight for turns on its head and gives you something else entirely unexpected.

Of course, I'd seen her before at Smalls Paradise. Listened to her go on and on about her opinion of me while I was there, too. But now, I knew her last name. I'd come across her byline in the *Amsterdam News*.

But here she was a few feet in front of me, and I was walking toward her, and she was square-shouldered, head high, looking at me.

She was stylishly dressed in a wool coat with a thick collar and fur stole—fox, judging from the head. Beneath the coat,

I saw the hem of a mint-green gingham fabric. Somewhat lightweight for a cold, breezy December day.

Bundled up in fur myself, I cocked my head, stunned at her boldness. "What are you doing?"

"My name is Marvel Cunningham. I'm a stringer for the *Amsterdam News*, and I'd like to ask you a few questions."

"No reporters are allowed back here," I said, unsure if it was true. But I'd been lucky and hadn't come across any in the days I'd been coming to court, so I had assumed the alley behind the courthouse was safe from newspaper people.

Marvel moved closer, notebook and pencil in hand, preparing to bombard me with a string of questions I'd answered a million times.

I'd decided to pretend to listen. She wasn't going to leave without something.

"'Blue Blood Weds Colored Girl,' 'Social Leader Happy with Colored Wife,' 'Bride of Rhinelander Called Mulatto,'" she rattled off the headlines. "Those are only a few of the stories that appeared in one day last month. How has it affected you as a colored woman to be publicly exposed for passing as white to wed a wealthy white man?"

"How dare you. I am not colored. And I love Lenny."

I stomped my foot, angry at myself for letting her get anything out of my mouth. But it didn't matter, since she ignored my response and asked me more questions.

"How about your mother calling the annulment case bosh? In the *Daily News* story, 'Rhinelander Annulment Talks Bosh, Says Mother-in-Law.' And your sister also earned a headline when she told the press that you and Lenny had gone into hiding for a bit, hoping the story would die down." She shook her head, brow furrowed. "It seems to me these headlines are making you out to be the victim in the case. What do you say?"

"Do you want me to answer your questions, or do you prefer to keep asking them until I finally pick one?"

I used my most forceful voice, which said a lot. For my voice didn't have a commanding flair.

She visibly swallowed, and I saw something I hadn't seen at Smalls Paradise—she wasn't all that confident or as commanding on her own without her group of friends around to entertain.

"What's a stringer? You're not a reporter for the *Amsterdam News?*"

"The *Amsterdam News* doesn't have a full-time female reporter on staff. A stringer is a freelancer who only gets paid per story if the newspaper decides to run it. And if it's not a major rewrite."

"Then, you're not a reporter."

"I am. Just not full-time with a regular paycheck from a newspaper."

"Oh. So why would I talk to you?"

"I don't know. Maybe because I saw you at Smalls Paradise a few weeks ago and didn't tell anybody it was you."

I was floored. "You recognized me."

"I'd seen you in the courthouse, and I'm observant. It might've been dark inside that club, but I'd been studying you. Not only your face and the clothes you wear, but your walk, the way you tilt your head when you want the judge to think you're hearing something for the first time. The way your eyes appear teary—"

"Come on, you can't see my eyes. I'm looking at Justice Morschauser the entire time I'm in court. That's what my lawyer tells me to do."

"You turn your head on occasion to glance at your sisters. Usually, when something is said about Kip Rhinelander calling you a fraud."

My driver, Jerry Redding, a close friend of Robert's, who'd said he was trustworthy, opened the limo door, studying Marvel and mostly checking to ensure she wasn't pestering me. That might not have been the case, but she had surprised me.

"You want to ride with me?" I asked, heading for the automobile's rear car door, held open by Mr. Redding. I was curious about something.

She stood staring at the driver holding the door open for her without taking a step. For a moment, I thought she wouldn't get in. Then she eased into the back of the limo and sat next to me.

"Do reporters, or stringers, excuse me, have rules?"

"What do you mean by rules?"

"Standards they must go by to be considered decent, I don't know, respectable members of the press?" I trusted she heard the sarcasm in my tone.

She pondered the question, twisting her lips sideways. "I guess we do. There's the Journalist's Creed. Why?"

"Since you didn't write about my friends and me taking a break from everything and hanging out at a black and tan, you might be a reporter or stringer who can help me."

"Help you with what?"

"First, tell me something about this Journalist's Creed."

"Sure, but I don't want to bore you by reciting the entire thing."

Hmph. "Then give me the highlights."

"Where are we headed, ma'am?" Mr. Redding asked.

"Into the city. We're going to give Marvel— May I call you Marvel?"

"Can I call you Alice?"

I nodded. "A ride to the *Amsterdam News* building on Seventh Avenue—" I looked at Marvel for the rest of the address.

"One Hundred and Thirty-Fourth Street."

The limo lurched forward, and I turned to Marvel. "Okay, your creed."

"How about I give you the short version." She took a deep breath and closed her eyes. "A reporter should write only what he holds in his heart to be true.

"We believe that no one should write as a journalist what he would not say as a gentleman; that bribery by one's own pocketbook is as much to be avoided as bribery by the pocketbook of another; that individual responsibility may not be escaped by pleading another's instructions or another's dividends.

"We believe that the journalism which succeeds best—and best deserves success—fears God and honors man; is stoutly independent, unmoved by pride of opinion or greed of power, constructive, tolerant but never careless, self-controlled, patient, always respectful of its readers but always unafraid, is quickly indignant at injustice; is unswayed by the appeal of privilege or the clamor of the mob; seeks to give every man a chance and, as far as law and honest wage and recognition of human brotherhood can make it so, an equal."

"I wouldn't have thought there was such a thing as a journalist's creed. You'll have to send me the rest of it so I can take a look. I'm curious. Though why aren't women mentioned?" I pulled off my gloves, waiting.

She laughed. "The man in the creed means human, that's all."

"Then why doesn't your Negro newspaper have a woman reporter on staff?"

"They will soon enough when they hire me." She still held her notepad and pencil. "You're not as ditzy as I thought."

"Why didn't you write an article about me at Smalls Paradise? You felt sorry for me?"

"I honestly wasn't thinking about the Journalist's Creed. I want to write for Negro newspapers, magazines, or the Associated Negro Press, and that means I want to share relevant news about Negroes facing challenges, conquering them, or, if they're doing the wrong thing, getting exactly what they deserve. A story about you having a drink at a nightclub isn't news. That belongs in a gossip column."

"Isn't that what the Rhinelander case is mostly about—

gossip, lies, things that have nothing to do with two people who fell in love and got married?"

"Well, if that is the story, so be it," she said flatly. "But there has to be more to Alice Beatrice Jones than marriage to a Rhinelander who accuses her of fraud, passing for white, and tricking this wealthy white man into marriage. Nothing about that sounds like love to me."

I stared at Marvel, wondering what she really wanted from me. One thing I hadn't done in the past few weeks was suddenly trust a reporter. "Isn't news supposed to be titillating?"

"Some of it has to be, but if you eavesdropped on what I had to say that night at Smalls, I was telling the truth. I was impressed when I saw you that first time in the courthouse," Marvel said. "I had it in my mind that it would be easy to despise you. A Negro woman, like me, but nothing like me."

"I wish you'd stop saying that. I am not colored or Negro."

"And you sound sincere when you say it, but I saw you in court with your parents last week, and your father is the same shade as my dad. And he's Negro."

"You don't understand my family."

"Then tell me about them and explain how your husband, Leonard 'Kip' Rhinelander, is suing you for fraud. Claiming you deliberately deceived him.

"If he and his lawyers prove that, you've lost more than a court case. You've given up any hope of keeping your dignity. Unless that doesn't matter to you."

I wasn't sure if it did or not. I'd spent the past four years thinking about only one thing—how much I loved Lenny Rhinelander. "I'm not sure. But ask me again in a week or so."

CHAPTER 26

After the jury trial was set for November, I still had to live through several months trapped in loneliness, but I figured out a way to make it through. For most of the summer and early fall, I ducked reporters, slipping out of the house to join Kitty and her brother for an evening out to a Manhattan, Harlem, or Bronx nightspot. I dressed in disguises, drank hooch, listened to jazz, and danced until my feet swelled. It was a winning plan and kept my mind off the courthouse and lawyers. However, Lenny had a stranglehold on my thoughts.

There was also my home life. I spent many hours in the kitchen with Mummy, cooking Daddy dinner, or when Gracie and Emily and their families came over, playing board games or sitting in the living room, listening to the radio.

And I saw Marvel Cunningham. She talked to me about scary things—things I didn't know or was afraid to think about.

One summer evening, we met at a café. I was in one of my disguises, a stylish large floppy hat that covered most of my face. I also wore the brightest red lipstick I owned, which actually meant it belonged to Gracie—and one of her dresses, a breezy flapper number made of gingham. Somewhere between sips of coffee, she mentioned something I'd heard about, but I played dumb Dora.

"You know about the one drop law, don't you?" Marvel asked.

I nodded and added a shrug, as if to say what does that have to do with me.

"It's the law in some of America's states." She lit a cigarette. "To qualify, you need one family member from yesterday or way back, whenever. But no matter where or when that pure white bloodline was interrupted, that one drop makes you a Negro."

"What does that have to do with me?" I responded, sounding appropriately insulted. "Are you talking about my father? If you are, don't. Those are the lies Lenny and his lawyers spouted."

"At some point, you may have to consider it. That's all I mean to say."

"You want to write a story about me. Something that hasn't been covered in the newspapers. Okay. But then, maybe I should want something from you."

"You need the press on your side, Alice," Marvel said. "Your lawyers are savvy. They've encouraged stories with newspapers and given off-the-record interviews that helped inform other articles. Stories about how sad you were about Lenny's accusations. Articles about the tears you shed rereading the love letters he wrote."

"That's right. Those articles make me out to be a weepy simpleton who doesn't know how to help herself unless a man like Lenny or my lawyer is around to take care of me."

"The story I write won't portray you as some babbling idiot. I promise you that."

I smiled thoughtfully. "I believe you." The way I saw Marvel, she didn't need a man, or at least not one who dared tell her how to live, love, or go after her career.

"Why, thank you. That's important," she said. "Trust."

She was the first Negro woman I'd ever shared a meal with, ever talked to about what it was like for a young Negro woman on her own in Harlem. Or how she felt, as a brown-skinned girl, about her opportunities in life—but that didn't mean I trusted her.

"I hate being hounded by reporters," I replied instead of commenting on what she'd said.

"You don't like the limelight? Having the attention of the city? Most reporters refer to you as beautiful, pretty and Leonard as the poor son of a bitch who fell for you." Marvel looked at me with a raised brow. "Are you sure you don't like some of what the newspapers write?"

"Perhaps I do. But how would you feel? Your life exposed as if you've spent it behind glass. It's one thing to write it, but to live it." I rubbed my forehead. A pain behind my eyes spreading like a spiderweb. "Have you ever felt like less?"

"How could you ask me such a thing?" Marvel frowned. "Let me tell you a few things about my life." She pushed her coffee cup aside and folded her elbows on the table. "I graduated from Brown University, top of my class, the first Negro to do so, and summa cum laude from law school. But no one hired me as a lawyer. I was a colored woman. That's all they saw. Good thing I could write and am organized as hell. If I couldn't make a difference in the courtroom, I would try to make a difference in the courtroom of public opinion. So, after a lot of doors slammed in my face, I decided to get into the newspaper game."

"That sounds impressive to me. You had a few doors close, but you had enough education to make other choices."

"Did you graduate from high school?"

I shrugged but thought about Emily's marriage, Daddy's reaction, and how my life changed. "I came close. But I had my family, and things happened there—so I couldn't do what I planned to do."

"What was it that you had in mind? Is it something you could still do—if you lose?"

Then Lenny crept into my mind, and my heart pounded.

Could it be that no matter what I did or who I was with, my life wouldn't be right if Lenny wasn't a part of it?

I pressed my lips together, searching for an answer. What dream had I ever had? Selling women's clothing at Saks? That idea suddenly seemed childish. "I don't know. I don't know what I'd do."

On another afternoon, I received a letter that had me screaming on the inside and struggling to keep from bursting into tears on the outside. The only person I knew who might help was Marvel Cunningham. I called. She was free and invited me to her place for an early dinner.

I hired Mr. Redding to drive me to her Sugar Hill apartment, and as she opened the door, I hurried by her, searching for a room with a sofa, the living room, and when I spotted it, I ran and plopped down, anxious to tell her what had happened.

But I couldn't be that rude. While sprinting from the front door to the living room sofa, I noticed I was in one of the most amazing apartments I'd ever seen. Not as wealthy as the Westchester County mansions I'd worked in—nonetheless, this place had the same kind of elegance, but it was a Negro's home—a Negro woman's home.

I had to pause to admire it.

Marvel lived in a building on the corner of 145th Street and Edgecombe Avenue—a five-story walkup that happened to be a few blocks from the 150-year-old brownstone her father owned.

"I need to calm down," I said. "How about if you give me a tour of your place?"

"You don't want to tell me what happened first?"

I shook my head.

"Okay, then. Let's go." Marvel grinned, and I was up from the sofa traipsing behind her.

It was a six-room flat overlooking Colonial Park with

every modern appliance and fixtures. It had a long-distance telephone, refrigeration, incinerators, parquet floors, a tiled bathroom with a shower, venetian blinds, and large windows that let in plenty of sunlight. Not that Marvel spent much time at home, she confessed.

She added casually, "It's a big apartment, but my fiancé lives with me, and we need all the space."

She explained that they'd set a date for New Year's Eve but decided to move into the apartment together while they waited.

"I had to sneak out of town and concoct stories to spend the night with Lenny. My daddy would never allow us to live together."

"It's 1925, Alice. Women can vote. Drink, smoke, and have lovers. I just choose to live with mine."

Then, an extremely handsome young Negro man bounded into the living room. "Alice, this is my fiancé, Trey."

"Hey, doll. Good to meet you." Trey carried a case that looked like he had a horn of some sort inside—and he caught me staring.

"Oh, it's a trumpet. I'm a musician. I play in a house band at Roseland Ballroom, a swinging joint on West Fifty-Seventh between Broadway and Seventh Avenue. Marvel should bring you by. It's ladies' night on Mondays."

He kissed her on the cheek and was out the door.

"I never thought you'd have a boyfriend."

"Why is that?"

"You're so independent," I said.

"A woman can be independent and have a good man at her side—and that's my Trey."

After that, I was hungry, and my problem could wait. When Marvel mentioned food, I was ready. We shared a hefty meal of roasted chicken, boiled potatoes, and asparagus with freshly baked bread.

"And you can cook, too?"

"Trey made the bread."

I thought she was joking but didn't ask—just in case.

After dinner, I sat on the sofa, admiring the art on the walls and the warmth from the fireplace. Then a sigh rose from my chest. I was ready to tell her what happened.

"Marvel, I've been receiving death threats," I told her.

She sat on a stool comfortably away from the burning fire.

"Did you hear me? I have been receiving death threats. The Ku Klux Klan is after me."

"Then take it for what it's worth. And consider it as a sign that you have arrived."

"If a white man in a white sheet walks up to my door in New Rochelle, they will get a chest full of buckshot. Daddy is not one to tolerate that kind of nonsense."

"Why are they making death threats against you? They are racist bastards and murderers, and I don't mean to make light of it, but why are they after you?" She pursed her lips. "What do these threats entail?"

I pat my chest, hoping to calm my racing heart. "Supposedly, I am in Florida right now. And if I am in Florida, the Klan is looking for me because they think I'm a Negro woman who married a white man—"

Marvel smacks her forehead. "And that's illegal in Florida and around twenty-eight other states. Damn."

"I want you to write an article about this."

She looked stunned. Before, I'd always said no, not yet, when she asked if she could write about some of the things I told her. But this story was one she had to write. "I am worried. My family is worried, too. What if these Klan people come after me in New Rochelle? They don't care that I'm not colored. They just care about what they read in the paper. And I want the New Rochelle and White Plains courthouse coppers to be on alert."

Marvel massaged her eyebrows and then her temples. "Alice, you know this story will only help you after the trial starts again."

"I don't care about court or Lenny. I want you to write it for my family's protection. If it's in the news, the court and the coppers will believe it's true. If I tell them, I don't know if they will believe me."

"You could be right. But you also want Lenny to know that this annulment trial puts you in physical danger."

I looked down at the floor, but only for an instant. "He should know what this is costing me. Not just losing the love of my life but also my safety and peace of mind." I sat up tall. "So, will you write it?"

"I'll not only write it. I'll make sure it gets bought and printed in the paper. You have my word."

"Thank you, Marvel."

"Thank you," she said. "Consider it done. Now, put the Ku Klux Klan out of your mind, and let's have some champagne."

The New York Times

July 11, 1942

RHINELANDER SUIT LOST BY EX-WIFE
Appellate Division Rejects a Claim by Alice Jones to
$3,600 Life Annuities
Agreement Held Illegal

. . . Philip Rhinelander was obliged under the terms of a
1930 property agreement to pay Alice Jones life annuities
of $3,600, suit was rejected yesterday by the Appellate
Division in Brooklyn.

CHAPTER 27

———— ◆ ————

ROBERTA

1942

February is as cold as ever. I barely make it out of the apartment, let alone onto the subway to New Rochelle to visit with Aunt Alice.

But I do, and now, I sit in the living room minding my tongue after learning she was right. Adelaide Rhinelander Thomas didn't give up. Aunt Alice won a decision, but Adelaide had gone right back in, her legal team harping on the same old story—the annuity was illegal.

Aunt Alice didn't even have a week to celebrate her victory before there was a knock on her door and a process server with an envelope in hand.

It is strange how the legal system works. There are so many inconsistencies: the corruption, the favors, the miracles, the lives saved and lost. It boggles the mind. Or my mind, that's for sure.

"I told you she wouldn't stop." Aunt Alice stands with her backside leaning against the kitchen counter, but neither of us is preparing water for coffee or tea. Sometimes, the Pelham Road kitchen is the best place to have hard conversations.

"You want to put together a jigsaw puzzle?" She opens a

lower cabinet and removes a box before I answer. Then she places it on the table where I'm sitting.

"I didn't know you liked puzzles," I say.

"I grew up with them. And I found this one the other day." She fingers the crinkled corners of the box top. "Do you want to put it together? It's called Stroheim's *Greed*."

I look at the image on the cover. "That's an old one, isn't it?"

"Yes. Based on a work of art by Eric Rohman with the same name," she says, and repeats, "*Greed*."

"I don't think I want to play."

"Do you want to take it home?"

"My mother loves puzzles, but it might be too ominous for her."

She nods. "I agree. You know your mother well. Emily doesn't like things that are twisted. I have another one I found. It's of Rudolph Valentino. She'll like that one. It's simple."

It is one of the oddest days we've spent together. Has she insulted my mother or just knows her too well? I'm not sure. But as I am leaving the house, I think I won't see Aunt Alice as much for a while, not just because of what she said that afternoon but because I am busy falling in love. I haven't mentioned it to her, but once I figure things out, they'll meet. And once Adelaide Thomas quits her lawsuits, win or lose, Aunt Alice will be better off.

She needs a forever break from the Rhinelanders. At least, that's what I believe.

The day is warm, but not for July, a light breeze carries a hint of cool air—and it's an exceptional Sunday afternoon, perfect for a walk to the beach.

These are the opening lines of my speech to Aunt Alice to convince her to join me on a short trek to the sandy shores of Glen Island Park. I figure some new scenery will help her talk about something other than less pleasant subjects like Adelaide.

However, the only enticement to grab her interest is the promise of cotton candy. "I'd wager you haven't had any since childhood."

"It has been a while," she says, adjusting the A-line skirt of her Kitty Foyle navy-blue dress with its contrasting light collar and cuffs. She looks lovely in the outfit.

"So, you'll go."

"I guess."

"That's swell. Then we can sit on the bench and stare at the ocean for a few minutes. How does that sound?"

"I said I'd go."

We are outside on the sidewalk within a few minutes, heading toward the park.

"So you knew Marvel Cunningham before she was employed as a reporter by the *Amsterdam News*?" I ask as we reach the end of the block.

"I did." Aunt Alice walks a few steps behind me. "Didn't I mention that to you before?"

"You said her name once. But nothing about having dinner at her house or meeting her husband."

"The musician? He was her fiancé back then," Alice corrects me. "Is she still married?"

"Yes, she is, but not to a musician. Her husband is a doctor, and they live in Washington, DC.

"You didn't keep in touch?"

"Oh, we kept in touch. Just not recently. The last time I saw her was in 1936, I believe." She stops walking. "You haven't said anything about the case."

"There is a Supreme Court decision that can help things go in your favor."

"That is if she doesn't try to fight the New York Supreme

Court." Aunt Alice continues walking but picks up the pace. "I don't want to talk about Adelaide. You wanted to come here. Let's enjoy it."

"You're right," I say.

We reach Glen Island Park, and I'm immediately reminded of how much I enjoyed visiting this park as a kid. It is New Rochelle's Coney Island, without the roller coasters but with a casino, museum, and Chinese pagoda. And then there is the shoreline with its beaches and fishing docks, and the sea smells, the sour whiff of fresh-caught striped bass, flounder, and fluke.

Momma and Papa would take me for a walk after Sunday dinner at my grandparents', and we'd stop by the candy shop in the park. My father had a sweet tooth, and so did I. Our eyes got so big when we studied the shelves and the jars of jelly beans, plain and jumbo, and containers of lollipops, hard candies, truffles, and other chocolates—and Dubble Bubble gum.

"There's the cotton candy vendor." I point. "Let's get that, and then we can go to the beach, find a bench in the shade, and watch the children play in the sand."

"Why are you sounding that way?"

"What way is that?"

"Oh, melancholy. Like you lost your last love, or could it be that you found one?"

I laugh. "I didn't think I was so obvious. But yes, I am seeing someone."

"If he's rich and white, beware."

My mouth drops open, and I reach for Aunt Alice's wrist, stopping her forward movement to see her expression. "Did you make a joke?"

"Are you laughing?"

"I want to, but I had to check first in case you weren't. I wouldn't want to hurt your feelings if it was only a slip of the tongue."

"You think I'm that fragile?"

I shrug.

"I can be, but it was a joke. But I think the moment has passed for outright laughter."

I chuckle. "How's that?"

"Fine. Now get the cotton candy."

We go to a bench near a red maple tree, which is greener in the summer sun than red. But it provides the shade we need to keep the heat and bright sun from beating down on our heads. We sit silently for a few minutes, enjoying the sticky, sweet cotton candy before it melts.

"You know I was listed in the *Social Register,*" Aunt Alice says out of the blue. "Imagine, I was among the four hundred most influential, important people in New York City. There I was, Mrs. Alice Beatrice Jones Rhinelander."

"I didn't know that."

"No longer listed, not now. Hell, not for years and years, of course. But back then, it stuck to the craws of the uppity in the Hudson Valley."

"When did this happen?" I ask between licking my fingertips.

"In 1925, during the hiatus before the jury trial began," she says. "I told the whole story to Marvel, and she ran with it."

I thought I'd gone through most of the articles from that period about the case, but some stories slipped by me.

"There were several articles. People had to know that Lenny spent a lot of time with my family. He called my parents Mum and Dad. He sat in our house, ate our food, and loved my mother's cooking. And after every meal, he'd come into the kitchen and help me with the dishes. Stand right next to me with a dishcloth in hand, drying the plates, pots, and pans I passed to him.

"I didn't want to be one of those four hundred, nor did he. Those women smoked and drank and lied. And the men took each other's wives. There wasn't a single wholesome thing in the life of the so-called four hundred. So far as I saw, there was no reason for me to be in that book."

I wait a moment for her to catch her breath. She says a lot quickly and with feeling. I know she's been hurt badly, and sometimes, that old pain is so alive inside her, I can taste her sadness in the air.

My reply is senseless. "I'll have to look that one up."

"Why? It's old news."

"Yeah, you're right. I read some articles my librarian friend Ethel Ray showed me the other day about the Klan."

"The Ku Klux Klan. Yeah. That ran in the *Amsterdam News* with Marvel's byline," she chuckles. "They issued death threats. Wrote me letters, letting me know to stay in New York or else."

"Weren't you scared?" I pop the last of my cotton candy in my mouth. I wish I'd gotten some extra napkins. Aunt Alice opens her purse and pulls out a handkerchief.

"I don't remember," she says, and frowns. "Clean yourself up."

I look at my sticky hands. "They aren't that bad." Then I look at her flawless hands. "You could teach a class. How do you eat cotton candy and not make a mess?" I say with a giggle.

"I learned long ago how to navigate between sweetness, kindness, and making a mess for mess's sake."

"I guess you did."

"You bet your bottom dollar I did."

CHAPTER 28

ALICE

1925

The only way I could get through the next few weeks was Marvel. She didn't think about things the way my mother or sisters did. She was more like Gracie, bold but calmer—I was excitable, and she'd help me think straight. I hoped. I had a lot to discuss with her—a lot to consider.

Mr. Jacobs, Lenny's lawyer, had notified Mr. Davis that the Rhinelander family would pay me a "handsome" sum. A settlement offer was on the table, Mr. Davis said. The gist was that I had to agree to the annulment, answer some questions—and permit my responses to be printed in a public statement.

"These questions, these goddamned questions, answering them will kill me." I pointed at the paper I'd brought and dropped it on Marvel's coffee table to read. "Look!"

She read aloud. "'At the time of our marriage, were you colored and of colored blood?' 'Before the marriage, did you represent to Lenny that you were white and not colored and had no colored blood?'"

I leaned forward and snatched the paper away from her. "This one. This one! Did I intend to deceive and defraud him and, thus, induce him into marrying me?" My throat suddenly was full of sand.

Instead of the chair on the opposite side of her desk, I sat on the sofa, with Marvel staring at me, the concern in her eyes unnerving.

She shot to her feet. "I think you need champagne." She left the room for a few minutes but returned with a bottle, two flutes, and a bucket of ice. After popping the cork, she handed me a full glass.

"I thought you never filled the glass to the rim when it's champagne."

"You need as much as I can pour, but the bubbles will die." She gestured at the glass. "Swallow and tell me the rest."

"Thank you." I took a sip and plunged ahead. "Did Lenny marry me with the full belief that I was white and without colored blood? Did I induce Lenny to enter into marriage?"

Marvel seemed more annoyed than angry. "It sounds like they think you are some sorceress who bedazzled that man into doing whatever you asked of him, whoever you asked."

My lips burned as if I'd kissed the sun. I gulped the champagne. Before I could put down my glass, Marvel poured me another.

"The critical questions, as they called them—I call humiliation. I call it condoning their lies. A big fat check won't change the fact that my husband has called me a liar in every newspaper in the country."

"At no time during our love affair, during our marriage, did I ever want to sue my husband about anything willingly. He knew me intimately, so for him to agree to have his lawyers treat me this way—our marriage has gone to hell in a handbasket.

"His father is orchestrating this mockery to save his deportment. It has nothing to do with his feelings for Lenny. He doesn't care about Lenny."

"Well, Lenny must care about his father, or why agree to this if, as you have said, he loves you as much as you love him?"

I put the glass on the coffee table and buried my face in my hands. Tears racked my body. And shame settled in the pit of my stomach. "I don't know what to do, Marvel. Sometimes, I believe I am as weak as Lenny." I raised my head, wiping tears from my eyes. "If I take the money and say these things are true, what becomes of me? I'll be a joke for the rest of my life. A foolish woman who went for something she could never have."

"Oh, Alice," she said, sympathy filling her gaze. "Some days, I think you will get on with your life. And other days, I think not. Why can't you stop loving him? I don't understand that kind of love. It doesn't leave any room for you."

"What's wrong with there being two of us? Not just me or him, but us. That's what I believe in—him and me." I curled up in the corner of the sofa in her beautiful apartment, her handsome fiancé out at his nightly gig, and here I was with my new best friend, a colored girl. Perhaps I didn't know what I wanted other than Lenny. And without him, I didn't know who I was. This obsession with Lenny stole everything I thought I could be. But how could I stop caring about him? No matter how mean, cruel, or ashamed he was about our love, would I ever let him go?

"You know, Alice. This would make a good article."

"The offer," I said, squeezing my eyes shut, trying to push the images from my mind. But I couldn't. I looked at Marvel. "Write it. But I won't take their money and agree to their list of lies." I sat forward, planted my feet on the floor, and looked directly into Marvel's dark eyes. "There has to be a way to get what I want and not have to give up who I am."

"Perhaps that's the problem, Alice. You don't want an annulment, but you don't want to be made out a liar. But . . . What if you turned the table so that he's the liar, which he already is? Make him the one who is fabricating stories about himself."

"I don't understand. How would I do that?"

"Come on, think." She filled her glass with champagne and emptied the bottle in mine. "He wants you to admit that you deceived him. What if he's the one who's deceiving everyone?"

I stared at her blankly. Nothing came to mind. "I'm sorry, I don't have any idea what you mean."

I shook my head, unable to see what she wanted me to do. But her gaze wouldn't waver from mine. And the moment it came to me, there were little beams of light, like the sparks from an electric wire, splitting apart and exploding like a meteor in the sky. "He says I lied; what if I say he's lying." I blinked. "Is that what you mean? That he has always known who and what I am?"

"And who are you, Alice Beatrice Jones?" She lifted the bottle of champagne. "There's one drop left. Do you want it?"

My breath caught in my throat. "One drop, that's all it takes."

"You want to stop what's happening in court. You don't want your marriage annulled. To win, you need to reverse the tables. And to do that," Marvel said, "all you have to say is—"

"I'm a Negro, and Lenny—he always knew."

I enjoyed watching Mr. Davis turn pale; today, I envisioned seeing him turn into a ghost.

"You suggested it a while back after your agent returned from England without proof or disproof of my father's heritage. So we'll go with this: I am Negro, and Lenny knew it. What do you think?"

Mr. Davis didn't disappoint me; he turned as white as my mother's bleached sheets. But he recovered quickly.

"It's an excellent strategy, Alice. Especially considering the settlement offer on the table. Turning it down without an alternative plan in place—would put our case at risk."

"So we agree, I will testify that I am Negro, and he knew

it. It's already on record that Lenny spent time with my father. Daddy's skin color is what gave credence to Lenny's lies. How can he back away from what he's already sworn to?"

"It's a different burden of proof if you declare yourself a Negro," my lawyer said, but I saw the smile in his eyes. "But now we can shout from the rooftops: Leonard 'Kip' Rhinelander knew from the day he met you that you were Negro. There was no fraud."

"And no grounds for an annulment," I added with a shiver snaking down my spine.

The fight was on. I put everything on the line, and the newspapers reported the story precisely as expected. RHINE- LANDER WIFE ADMITS NEGRO BLOOD.

Mr. Davis was thrilled. He claimed it was the story that Mr. Swinburne had sent an agent to England to get informa- tion on my father. Still, now that I was willing to say I was Negro—we could stop the annulment proceedings. We'd also take the Rhinelander family for that "handsome" sum they would have shared if I had caved.

Mr. Davis was a competitive lawyer, but only two things drove his goals: money and prestige.

He and his colleagues would become famous because the annulment proceedings had upped the salaciousness of the trial: If I was colored and admitted it—Rhinelander had to know. His claims of fraud were lies.

I wasn't even convinced we'd lose if we stuck with my original position, but I'd given up on Lenny. I couldn't trust his random proclamations of love and devotion or his pleas to trust him. I wanted my marriage, but I wanted it my way. Not his or his father's.

Meanwhile, I had a hell of a surprise in store—it turned out that being a Negro was my ace in the hole.

The tone of the newspaper stories shifted. I was no longer the witch, the sorceress, the trickster—it was Lenny. His case was wrapped around the fact that I hid my color from him, but now that I admitted it—and never lied to him about it—for he knew all along I was colored, why did he marry me?

The proceedings were a circus. And to add to our Barnum and Bailey sideshow was the day Mr. Jacobs called Al Jolson to the witness stand. He was asked about how it felt being Negro when he put on blackface makeup.

Three days later, my skin crawled when Lenny took the stand, and my lawyer, Mr. Davis, had at him.

Mr. Davis began: "I wonder if you loved her, but that's not my question." He glanced at the judge. "Did it amuse you to put your arm around her and kiss her?"

Lenny kept his expression blank. "Yes."

"You got a thrill from it?"

"Yes."

"So you were not so innocent, but you could put your arm around a girl, kiss her, and get a thrill?"

"No."

"You didn't know when you put your arm around her and kissed her that you would get a thrill?"

"No."

"Do you mean that? What induced you to put your arm around her?"

That's when I saw the flicker in Lenny's eyes. He paused long enough, not too long for anyone else to notice but me. At that moment, he didn't want to parrot what his father's lawyers had told him to say. I saw the rambunctious boy I'd met at the Orchard School. The young man who could make love to me all night long, tease me, and write me love letters that kept me reading and rereading them.

"Shall I repeat the question, Mr. Rhinelander?"

"No, sir. Human interest," said Lenny.

Mr. Davis then reached for the letters and commented about how he opposed dragging filth into the case.

Mr. Davis continued questioning Lenny. "Your treatment

of Alice Rhinelander in December 1921, was it in any way the actions of a gentleman?"

"Sir?"

"When you two checked into the Hotel Marie Antoinette as Mr. and Mrs. Smith, did you treat the then Ms. Jones as a gentleman treats a lady?"

"S-sir." Lenny seemed bewildered.

"Should I repeat the question?"

"No. Her actions were always ladylike up to that time."

"You had gone no further before your trip to Hotel Marie Antoinette than to put your arm around her and hold her hand?"

There was a buzz throughout the courtroom. I didn't know what to make of it, but no matter what Lenny said, no one would believe him.

I felt sorry for both Lenny and me. My lawyer had ripped away his manhood and made a whore out of me.

CHAPTER 29

Mr. Davis planned to read Lenny's letters in the courtroom, but he wanted me to pick the ones that were more amorous and open about our sexual relationship.

"I don't want to embarrass you in court. Lenny's lawyers will try and do that. But if you pick them, you'll know what's coming."

Mr. Davis looked pleased with himself. I was barely breathing.

I'd memorized Lenny's letters long ago and could've handed over the ones he wanted within minutes of emptying the shoebox of envelopes on the kitchen table. But if the intimate thoughts Lenny and I wrote to each other were to be read in court before a jury of twelve men, I wanted Mr. Davis to have to do more than hold out his hand.

By the end of the search, we had twenty-six love letters to be read in court. Most were written after the Hotel Marie Antoinette about our days and nights there. Those days when we made love and barely ate or slept. Those days felt divine until that knock on the door.

The courthouse buzzed with ardent *tsk-tsk-tsk* and my-oh-mys. Even if the sound wasn't made, I could feel the judgment like gnats climbing over the back of my neck. I never turned to see the expressions on the spectators' faces. The jury box reflected them adequately enough, I was sure.

I sat and listened, showing no emotion, just like Lenny on the witness stand, his nose glasses shielding his eyes, hiding any expressions he had. He looked stoic, unbothered, even when the questioning was insulting and, if answered, revealed more than anyone should have to about their sexual preferences in the bedroom with their wife.

Of course, the newspapers that supported the Rhinelander family referred to my letters as the fervid illiterate scribblings of a woman to whom Rhinelander was Prince Charming. Although, at times, the content was erotic, the reporter wrote, it was clear she was in love with him.

Thank you for believing that much.

Now that I was a confessed Negro, I didn't expect any kindness from the Rhinelander-favored press. So I didn't flinch when they called my love letters illiterate.

But for reasons that left me astonished, they enjoyed my poetry. It seemed my creative prose had a Negro rhythm. I didn't know poems had a different rhythm, one for coloreds and another for whites. So I sought some information, some intelligence, to give me a better understanding of my Negro poetry. I thought I was just writing about love.

According to the rags, my poems were so good they could've been the lyrics of a popular song, something one would hear on the radio or buy in a record shop. A backhanded compliment that essentially accused me of stealing. But I'd written every word myself, from my heart, for Lenny. But these people didn't know me, didn't care how much I hurt. Some hated me because I said I was Negro, which made me less than the daughter of an immigrant from England who cleaned houses in Westchester County and could only shop at Saks with her white, wealthy husband.

Kisses, dear, from you can cheer me when I'm blue,
Your gentle lips have always thrilled me throughout.
I need caressing, too.

There's the happiness I can't express,
And each kiss from you.
Kiss from you

I was having nightmares. They started when the whole mess began with the letters. Although they were just another way to capture the public's attention, the letters gave them another reason to fill the courtroom and witness my humiliation. It was a room of spies and savages hell-bent on digging every ounce of privacy out of my life. The sweet words that I'd read every night before falling asleep, the tears I'd shed as I held the letters to my breast, especially those two years without Lenny. And now, since the trial began, our words written with boundless love in our hearts and tears of despair were being read aloud.

Then, the dream shifted and went sideways through time. I was with my lawyers, and the news wasn't what I thought it would be.

"We want to win the case. Do you understand, Alice?"

"I don't think I do."

"You will no longer be able to save your marriage, but we will win in court."

Was that what I wanted? Was it? Was it? I yelled in the dream.

As I lay there, lonely and alone, I thought about Lenny. When was the last time we made love? It'd been so long. Had I forgotten how to make love with a man because I loved Lenny so deeply? Or had that young girl who met Lenny years ago become the spinster she always feared?

Kicking the sheets aside, I rose from the bed and planted my feet firmly on the floor, hands covering my face. I didn't want to cry. But sadness surrounded me like layers of wool, scratchy yet warm, mildewed, and rotting. Yet, I couldn't throw it away. Sentimentality was a monster that held me in place, hindering my ability to move on.

CHAPTER 30

I stood half dressed in front of twelve men, watching their eyes bulge and their backsides squirm in their seats, shifting from side to side, hoping to God that their manhood wouldn't reveal their imaginations. Leaving them the ill-mannered jackasses they were.

What was I willing to do?

That's what my lawyer should've asked me. But he didn't. He discussed how much I'd take off, whether I'd be completely naked or waist up or waist down. He hadn't even arranged for me to have a robe to wear after I stripped.

All that mattered was what the twelve-man jury saw what they needed to see to prove Leonard "Kip" Rhinelander was a fool not to recognize I was Negro from the hue of my naked skin and the curves of my nude body.

Lee Parsons Davis, Mr. Swinburne, and Prichard Anders, with assistance from their secretary Mrs. Sage (who was there to address any intimate topics that might arise, as if every moment wasn't meant to defile, humiliate, and expose me), discussed how and what was to be exposed on my body without asking me anything. The only instruction given: "Make sure your undergarments are decent," Mrs. Sage had advised.

What did she expect me to wear? A sheer teddy, a lace

brassiere, no pantaloons, or rolled-down stockings without a corset? I'd never worn a corset in my life.

I couldn't stop my mind from racing.

Take off your clothes. Show us your body. Show us the dark places on your skin. Your dark nipples. The black hairs of the triangle between your legs. We want to see what Leonard "Kip" Rhinelander saw. What's special about the Black sorceress who robbed him of his white dignity, his heart, his common sense, and his pride?

I scrubbed for hours that morning. After using a hairbrush with new bristles, my skin was bright pink and raw, but I was clean and as fragrant as a bouquet of fresh flowers.

I laid out several different undergarments. I had to thread a thin line between appropriateness and revealing, but the whole point was that Lenny had seen my naked body over and over and over again. He wasn't blind, so he had to notice my dark nipples, the dark circles around them, the line of sandy, black hair from my belly button, and the triangle curls between my legs. I'd caressed the curves of my backside and squeezed my buttocks as I lay on his body, riding in pleasure, pain, and love, but not today.

I strutted into the courtroom with my smooth fur coat with the big fox collar and cuffs, black gloves with pearls at the wrist, and a cloche hat on my head that showed the layers of dark curls framing my face. The long hair Lenny loved only got in my way, so I cut it to just below my ears. I now had a girlish bob hairstyle and a cascade of short curls.

That was my entrance attire. I don't remember much until Mr. Davis demanded that Justice Morschauser clear the court of all men not having business there so that I could disrobe.

"I propose that Mr. Rhinelander could not have had relations with her, thus knowing her well, and missed seeing her dark skin."

The justice allowed the humiliation to take place, but in

his chambers with lawyers from both tables, the defendant, and the plaintiff, to bear witness.

I undressed to the waist, exposing my torso, my face covered in tears, dripping from my chin, soaking my throat and chest.

Then it was over.

Mr. Davis led me from the chamber. His arm around my shoulder, and his hand holding mine. As we walked down a short hallway, he whispered. "I will not put you on the witness stand. I will not participate in further public humiliation of yourself by allowing Mr. Mills or Mr. Jacobs to cross-examine you."

I didn't have the strength to open my mouth to produce words. So I said nothing, hoping we'd soon reach a private room where I could pull myself together after the ordeal.

Mr. Davis opened the door to a room reserved for the lawyers of the defendant.

"Take your time. And, Mrs. Rhinelander, I apologize."

He left me alone then, but if he thought that apology mattered—if he thought his apology changed anything about how I felt at that moment, the anger at the humiliation, the rage, and the helplessness made a difference to me:

No, Mr. Davis. You wasted your breath.

I needed my mother after that day in court. I counted on her healing sympathy, her womanly understanding. I needed her to share my anger and humiliation.

When we reached Pelham Road, Daddy hurried into the living room, disappearing into the newspaper's sports section and his favorite radio shows. That left Mummy and me alone, which was what I wanted. Or so I thought.

I sat in the kitchen, stunned and wanting to weep louder and harder than I had all day.

"Wasn't it what you wanted?" Mummy's tone was casually abrupt as if we were discussing the weather.

Why was she acting this way? Didn't she see what had occurred? Wasn't she as disgusted as I? Apparently not.

"When was the last time you were naked when you didn't want to be, had to be looked at when you'd rather not be seen or had to keep quiet when you wanted to scream? So yeah, it wasn't my best day in court."

"I'm sorry it happened to you, Alice," Mummy continued. "But your lawyer was the one who had to prove Lenny lied. And that was what you wanted, what you asked for."

"Oh God. So you blame me for that spectacle today? That I asked for it?"

"Well, dear, when you told the world you were Negro, you might've considered the consequences."

"I cannot believe what I'm hearing." I couldn't stay seated. I leaped to my feet and fled the kitchen, seeking my coat, purse, and car keys. God, I wished I could drive. I had to get away from her.

"Where do you think you're going?" Mummy was on my heels, following me down the hallway and into my bedroom.

"Away from here. Out. Someplace, anyplace."

"Why? You can't go outside. Peek through those blinds. Twenty reporters are waiting for a glimpse of Rhinelander's wife, the Negro."

The way she said the word was an assault. She sounded like it was a curse that bruised her lips to speak it. "What is wrong with you?"

"I'll tell you what's wrong—you told the world a lie, just like Emily. My children have disowned their heritage that comes to them through me and my ancestors. Your English heritage. Your white heritage. It's as if I don't exist."

A gun was aimed at my head, and the pull of the trigger was seconds away.

"In the judge's chambers today, your humiliation was not on my mind, Mummy. Because you didn't understand that in America, one drop"—I raised a finger and waved it in her face—"One drop of Negro blood is all it takes to make me less of a human. A mulatto, like Daddy, is seen differently in England than in the United States. They may hate coloreds, but they don't lynch Negro men just because they can. They don't have Jim Crow laws designed to keep the Negro in their place. Why don't you understand this?"

"How dare you speak this way to me, Alice. And why do you suddenly know so much about the lives of the Negro in this country? What made you so interested when you'd never been interested before?"

"How dare you speak to me that way!" I exclaimed. "After what I went through in that courthouse, showing my body to prove the man I love is a liar and a coward. How do you think I feel right now? Who did I come into the house to talk to, to hug me, to tell me I'm going to be okay, that I'm going to survive this?"

Mummy's neck got stiffer. "Don't you dare accuse me of wrongdoing—this has been your pot to stir, not mine."

I seized her shoulders and squeezed them gently but firmly. "I fought for the man I have loved for years. Our love letters and intimate thoughts were shared in court—our deepest, most secret desires. I sat in a courtroom where our love letters were read like a grocery list. And then to prove I was right, to prove Lenny had always known I was Negro—although I only admitted it a few weeks ago, I was stripped naked." I shook her. "Naked. In a judge's chamber in front of men who didn't look at me like I was a defendant trying to win a court case, but like someone they wanted to—" My voice broke, and my hands fell to my sides. "To touch, examine, ogle."

I searched for a cigarette but could find only a rather long butt in the ashtray. I lit it. "When I confessed to my colored blood, I like to think of it as one of the few times in history when a colored girl, a brown girl, was the most powerful woman in the room because she stood up and said who she was. I was proud of myself until they made me take off my clothes."

"Alice, I don't want to hear this," Mummy said, tears in her voice.

"You don't want to hear it because you still believe that the Jones family is something we're not. We stopped being white the day you and Daddy stepped off the boat at Ellis Island."

CHAPTER 31

The weather was crisp. And my fur coat felt thin, my wool stockings clumsy. How could I show up in court looking like a pauper? Even the women in the back of the courtroom wore the latest fashions.

I could spot a pair of expensive silk stockings even while trying not to feel completely out of place and unfashionable. Wasn't I the main attraction to this courtroom circus? I should outshine all the other women in the room, I would think.

Then, I caught a glimpse of Marvel. She had promised me she'd be there, and there she was. Girls who looked like her were not allowed to be *Vogue* models. But if they were, she'd be the belle of the ball.

Thoughtlessly, I started to wave. But sensing my intention, she looked at me crossly. I had to remember our relationship was secret. No smiles could be shared between us publicly, not even a casual one.

"What are you staring at, Alice?" Gracie tugged my arm.

"Don't worry. I'm just looking at the people in court."

"You know what your lawyer said. We are to keep our eyes straight ahead. No looking at Lenny or the jurors also means no looking at the people behind us."

Gracie straightened her posture. "If we are being photographed, the best they will get is our profile. And remember, don't slouch."

"How about if I slipped under the table so no one could see me?"

Gracie nudged me, side-eyeing the table across from us where Lenny sat with his lawyers.

"Do you think he is in his right mind?"

I had a feeling I knew what was wrong with him. But I wasn't sure I wanted to tell Gracie. Watching him on the witness stand had been painful. Even if I still loved or hated him, the humiliation had been the work of a team of wild horses dragging him through the streets of New Rochelle.

LENNY RHINELANDER SAYS HE PURSUED ALICE
NOVEMBER 18, 1925

I'd never heard him stutter as much, even when he was eighteen and restricted to the Orchard School. I'd never noticed his quivering upper lip, twitchy eyelid, or constantly damp brow.

It was as if his body had lost all its strength. He was so much heavier, too. The seams of his shirt and suits were stretched to the edges, and I imagined if you hit him with a pen, he'd burst like a balloon because nothing was inside him.

It was clear Leonard "Kip" Rhinelander was waging war against himself. He couldn't sit still. Something was eating at his spine, worrying his shoulder blades and causing his nose to twitch. The man wasn't just uncomfortable on the witness stand in the Westchester courthouse, where he was forced to sit twenty feet from the woman he'd made love with and told how much he loved her a million times.

He was dying in front of me.

And dear God, forgive me. It warmed my heart to watch him suffer.

*   *   *

On December 5, Justice Morschauser's court in White Plains convened at 10:00 a.m., and during those proceedings, I was declared the victor. My husband was still my husband. My marriage was not annulled. Lenny and his family had to live with the fact that the *Social Register* entry, which included my name next to my husband's name, wasn't going to change. It confirmed to the world that a Rhinelander had married a Negro.

Victory should've soothed the aches in my bones. It should have stopped me from crying myself to sleep every night for a month.

I walked from the courtroom with my family surrounding me. They gave me the public support that helped prove we were decent, upstanding people, no matter how Lenny and his lawyers had tried to make me out to be a gold-digging whore.

"Aren't you the cocky one?" Gracie was at my side.

"What gave me the victory?" I started counting off the reasons on my fingers. "It's quite easy. The questions had yes or no answers. The judge asked the jury: 'At the time of the marriage, was the defendant colored and of colored blood?'"

I nudged Emily in the arm. "Yes or no," I said, but she didn't respond. "Well, the answer is yes."

"Are you going to go through each one, Alice?" Emily sounded exasperated and looked so, too.

"'Did the defendant, by silence, conceal from the plaintiff that she was of colored blood?' I'll make this one easy on you. No. She did not."

"Damn it, Alice." Daddy glared at me and then walked in the opposite direction of where we were headed. Our automobiles were parked in the rear of the building, where guards protected us from crazed reporters and onlookers.

"Daddy, please," Emily called after him.

"Let him go," I spat. "If he doesn't want to play, that is fine. You are still in the mood to enjoy my tirade, right?"

Gracie sighed. "Sure, Alice. If this is what you need."

"Now, the next question is tricky. 'Did the defendant practice such concealment or make such representations with the intent thereby to induce the plaintiff to marry her?' And again, a resounding no.

"And we aren't done."

"I'm going to find your father, Alice. Excuse me." Mummy left with a spring in her step. She also needed to get away from me, and that was fine. I needed to rant and rave.

I turned to my sisters and Robert. "We aren't done yet. There are two more key questions to go. Ready? 'If the plaintiff had known the defendant was of colored blood, would he have married her?'"

Waiting in the hallway, outside the exit to the parking lot, my legs felt weak, and a catch was in my throat. "My dear Lenny, your answer was another yes and another nail in your rich white coffin."

Gracie held my hand. "There's just one more, right?"

I smiled at her, lips trembling, fighting tears I refused to shed. "Just one more. 'Did the plaintiff cohabit with the defendant after he had fully known that the defendant was of colored blood?'"

Gracie squeezed my hand. "It was the only question the jury didn't find an answer to, but we know. Don't we, Alice?"

"Yes. We do. Another yes from the fans in the bleachers."

I was tired and exhausted by everything, including Lenny. He hadn't even shown up in court to face the music. Instead, his lawyers, investigator Alvin Miland, and Leonard's bodyguard, Navarro, sat at his table.

The Jones family exited the courthouse through the back exit, and cars were lined up, waiting for us. Gracie went off with my parents in Daddy's taxicab. Footsie didn't like courthouses and so far hadn't shown up. Not wanting to be alone, I dismissed my limo and hopped into Robert's automobile (one of the limos from the Baylors' estate).

I think I was feeling something for Robert. He'd taken the

scrutiny of the photographers and the reporters for showing up boldly to support his wife's family. But I had no idea he hated the reasons behind the spotlight.

It was one of the last times I saw Robert and Emily together in public. They remained together for another five years. Then, their marriage ended. But it wasn't my fault. I needed my family in court throughout the ordeal. And after declaring myself Negro, Robert's presence in the courtroom was a reminder to the jury that Leonard "Kip" Rhinelander, a man listed in the *Social Register*'s four hundred, had sat at the same table, ate meals, drank hooch, and played cards with his brother-in-law, a colored man.

"Are we going to celebrate?" I asked as I settled into the car. I didn't want to return to New Rochelle that day, but I had nowhere else to go—no one to welcome me at their door other than family.

"Would you like to come over to our house?" Robert's voice carried no emotion.

It was a rhetorical question, not an option for me to consider or a heartfelt invitation. But that didn't stop me from answering.

They lived in Harlem, and maybe now that the world saw me as a Negro it was the place I should go to celebrate.

"Let's do that. I want to go somewhere where people won't stare at me, which might be Harlem. What do you think, Robert? I can pass for a Negro woman."

"Isn't that all this trial has been about?" Emily said.

"No, it hasn't been about that," Robert disagreed promptly. "It's been about passing for white."

If it was meant to be tongue-in-cheek, sarcastic irony, it came off as a bitter indictment. Until that moment, Robert and Emily had kept their thoughts to themselves. The day in court had pushed a button they couldn't ignore.

"You're right, Robert," Emily said. "It is more about passing than being Negro."

"Well, aren't we high and mighty," I said roughly.

"You do not have to be rude," she growled. "We have supported you every inch of the way. You have no right to talk to my husband that way, not in my presence."

"Then perhaps you should take me home. Since I swear, there's no other place for me to go."

A few weeks later, it was Christmas Eve, and everyone was home. Gracie, Footsie, Emily, Robert, and little Roberta, and Mummy and Daddy—we were all in the house. My favorite holiday, and this year, I demanded everyone in the family celebrate at Pelham Road.

We'd have no interruptions, I promised. No press, no Lenny, no tears streaming down my cheeks unless they were tears of love for my family.

Some of us had little to say—Emily and Robert doted on their child. While some of us chatted endlessly about their adventures, traveling from town to town, visiting juice joints, casinos, and the like—Gracie and Footsie, with no explanation about his job. I tried not to mention courthouses, lawyers, annulments, or marriage. After all, I had won.

The decree from Justice Morschauser was straightforward: Lenny's annulment suit was denied. He and I were still married. According to my lawyers, the next logical step for me was to seek legal separation and an increase in alimony.

I couldn't give them an answer. I was spent. After the holiday, I insisted. I will give you answers in the New Year. All I wanted was to enjoy Christmas with my family.

We decorated the tree the night before with tons of tinsel, ribbon, and holly, and hung homemade wreaths. Gifts were piled high and wide beneath the tree, all shapes and sizes, and smelled of chocolate, fruit cake, and mincemeat pies wrapped in brown paper and old newspaper.

It was easy to guess what the presents would be: slippers,

dressing gowns, Mummy's embroidered handkerchiefs, table-cloths, and napkins. I bought Mummy a set of J. R. Watkins spices since I had some extra money.

The lawyers had given me an envelope with a bunch of dollar bills. Without asking questions, I thanked them. I thought it might be a gift from Lenny, secretly passed along, except my lawyers would never touch a dime from a Rhinelander. So I quickly let go of that fantasy.

After dinner, my family was sprawled throughout the house, bellies full. The men nursed glasses of bootleg hooch Footsie supplied. The rest of us sipped the loose-leaf tea my mother had made. There was also a pot of eggnog and more pies and cakes that didn't last long enough to be wrapped and placed beneath the tree.

I hadn't seen the newspaper that day, thinking it had been used to wrap gifts. But Daddy had hidden a copy of the *Daily News* near his chair.

I thought about not picking it up. I didn't want to ruin the mood if there was some annoying statement about Lenny and me. I should've trusted my instincts, for there was an article, but it didn't mention me. It was only about Lenny.

RHINELANDER OUT AS FAMILY CALLS ROSTER
FOR DINNER

How could a family do such a thing to a family member? The nerve of them not to give him a seat for a meal on Christmas Day?

Lenny had tried to tell me how vindictive his father could be, but I didn't have enough imagination to come close to this kind of thing.

Meanness met cruelty in a back alley, and who won didn't matter. Both were inexcusable.

Lenny must've felt so sad. He loved Christmas. In that regard, he was just like me.

Later, I'd wonder what I was thinking. But at the time, it made sense.

That evening, I made a telephone call to Ross Chidester, Lenny's chauffeur. I could trust him to deliver a message to Lenny. Sure, he was the man who had betrayed us to Lenny's father and busted into our room at the Hotel Marie Antoinette with Leon Jacobs, the Rhinelander lawyer.

Still, he'd kept our secret after driving us around the city to a handful of Broadway shows, a fancy restaurant, and more than one nightclub. Most important, when Lenny and I wanted to neck, he drove us to Glen Island Park, stepped out of the car for a smoke, left the motor running, and didn't return until Lenny called his name.

So I called. No answer. Out of desperation, I left a message. Still, no response.

I never spoke to Lenny, and it was the worst Christmas of my life.

PART 5

MRS. ALICE J. RHINELANDER

The New York Times

October 2, 1942

MS. BECKER TO BE WED TODAY

Rhinelander Girl to Be Married to Dickson Smith

CHAPTER 32

ROBERTA

1942

It's been several months since I last saw her, but my schedule has finally eased up so that I can make the trip to New Rochelle. It's early evening, the day after Christmas, and I have good news.

She opens the door, and her appearance immediately strikes me. She let her hair grow long with big curls like Rita Hayworth. She's dyed it, too—also red like Ms. Hayworth. The look is stunning. But the smell of gin overshadows anything she might be wearing.

"Is this the new and improved Alice Jones?" I ask, striving for a pleasant tone instead of showing the depth of my concern. "You don't need an upgrade."

She chuckles as she sashays toward the living room in chunky three-inch heels. Her gray silk dress with a fitted bodice flatters her slender frame. The slightly flared skirt has a matching thin belt covered in the same fabric as the dress and strands of pearls, short but impressive—and I wager they are real.

Compulsively, I glance down at my wool coat and gloves, bought at the five and dime, and look away.

I remove my outer garments—coat, hat, scarf, and gloves,

and quickly place them on the rack in the foyer before turning to watch Aunt Alice stroll into the living room.

I follow her, hoping she'll appreciate my good news. Hopefully, she'll want to celebrate, but not with gin.

She stands near the window, her weight on her right hip, her shoulders tilted toward the sunlight. She holds a tumbler with ice and a clear liquid; I wager it is the gin I smelled when I walked into the house.

"I've missed you, Roberta."

I haven't made it any farther than the living room's entranceway. My surprise at her unexpected admission warms my heart. "Thank you."

An eyebrow arches, and her hand grips her waist; I feel like I've been caught stealing and she's about to check my pockets.

"Don't be alarmed. I might've meant I missed our conversations. No need to get all weepy-eyed because we haven't seen each other in a spell."

"Okay. Okay. I won't," I say, entering the room. "I can't stop thinking about what you went through."

"Let's not talk about my humiliation. The only reason I mentioned it to you was—" She inhales profoundly and glances at the ceiling. Her eyes soften. "I can't remember." She laughs.

I sit on the sofa. "Well, let me tell you what brought me here today. I have news you'll appreciate."

"Lenny's sister will not let a Supreme Court decision stop her."

I am disappointed. "Oh, you've already heard."

"My lawyers called this morning happy as a lone cock in a chicken coop." She sits in the lounge chair. "I miss him."

"Ma'am?"

"Lenny," she says softly.

"What about him?"

"I did everything I could to not think about him. But the letters—" She rubs her fingers over her eyebrows. "Lord Jesus.

He could write a love letter. Every evening, I'd go out to have the time of my life, and when I returned home, there they were—more letters from Lenny. I couldn't get away from that man, and I tried. Believe me. With my entire being, I had to stop loving him so damn much."

She'll catch me staring if I'm not careful, for I've gone from admiring her new Rita Hayworth look to worrying about her drinking.

The drapes are pulled away from the window where she's taken up residence. Sunlight streams into the room with most of it shining on her face. With her hand on the wall, staring out at Pelham Road, she seems angelic and tipsy at once. But mostly, I see sadness and heartache, blinding as sunlight and dark as the shadows on the floor.

"Some days, I don't know what to think about other than Lenny and the Rhinelanders."

It's as if she read my mind. Now, she is lost in the memories, and for her, reminiscing is unhealthy. Christmas must bring back her past tenfold with all its ugliness and pain.

I notice there are no decorations—no tree, no holiday cheer in sight, other than the gin and tonic in her hand.

I think of something to distract her, to change the subject, perhaps even something clever. "Has anyone ever said you have a Roman nose?"

She gives me a strange look, and I can't blame her. My question was arbitrary and meaningless. Casual conversation is an art I do not possess.

"No, I can't say they have," she says, giving me a side-eye.

I have started down this path and cannot abandon it yet. "You remind me of a photo of my mother when she was very young. She has the same nose."

"Oh, thank you for adding the part about her being young. Otherwise, I might have taken offense."

Oh, there she is, a sign that my aunt Alice is coming back from memory lane.

"What's your mother up to these days?"

It still jars me to have Aunt Alice mention my mother so easily. I kept my visits to Aunt Alice a secret from my mother for a year before they were discovered. Then, the ease of their reunion caused me to think that the problem between them all these years wasn't so much my parents' splitting up but something to do with me. And now that I am on board Aunt Alice's train, it's okay for them to call a truce.

"When did you speak to her last?" I ask.

"Last month, wasn't it? I called her on her birthday."

"Her birthday is next month."

"Oh, so last year." She sighs. "It feels like yesterday."

I lean forward and decide to take the plunge. "My mother won't talk about it, but I'd love to know why—?"

"Why what?" she interrupts but doesn't turn to face me, and I don't wish to converse with her back.

"Aunt Alice," I say, standing. "Will you look at me?"

"No. Because I don't want to talk about it."

"Are you a mind reader? How do you know what I'm about to ask?" I walk toward her but don't get too close. "My parents don't blame you. Neither one of them has ever mentioned what broke them up. But I've always known it had something to do with you. And since they won't talk about it, I asked Aunt Gracie. And she told me what happened."

Aunt Alice faces me. "And what did she say I did?"

I wet my lips. "You kicked Papa out of this house after he sat in court for months and months, supporting you and the rest of the family." Anger climbs into my stomach and bites at my insides. Always there, reminding me that something is missing, that I am not whole.

My fingers tremble. I clasp my hands together behind my back, hoping to stop the shakes from consuming me. "Then one day, you called him a name and told him he wasn't welcome at 763 Pelham Road ever again."

"Oomph. I'm surprised. Gracie didn't exaggerate. Frankly,

she didn't tell you the whole story. That's not like my Gracie." Aunt Alice walks over and sits on the sofa next to me. "I called your father a nigger and told him to take his nigger daughter and leave my house."

There is a sudden haziness in the room, like it's slowly filling with fog, and I can't see where to go. "How could you use that word in front of my father?"

"I said it to him and your mother and you—you were there, standing next to them . . ." Her voice trails off. "I thought you remembered."

My lips tremble, and I bite down, desperate to find a part of me I can control. "You are a horrible, hateful woman," I say through clenched teeth. "I can't believe I've spent all this time getting to know you and feeling sorry for you when every ugly, horrible thing that has happened to you—you deserved." I leap up from the sofa and back toward the door. "I hate you!"

"I know." Her calm, untethered voice stops me cold. I was on my way out, but there she sits, empty glass in her hand, eyes level, her Rita Hayworth hair shining.

"I hate myself some days, Roberta. It happens when everything you want or think you have turns to ash, and your life is paraded in front of millions of people, and your dignity stripped from you, one layer of clothing at a time. So yeah, I called you and your parents that awful name, but I also offered your mother a choice."

My feet are still glued to the floorboards. "What kind of choice are you talking about?"

"I told her that if she left with him, she was no longer my sister, and what did your mother do? She promptly put on her coat, pushed your little arms into your jacket, and left." Aunt Alice shrugs. "And as she hurried out of the house, holding her daughter and her husband's hands, she yelled something about never returning as long as I lived." Aunt Alice puts the glass on the coffee table. "I don't know what happened when they got home, or what was said. But soon after, they split up. Perhaps that night. I don't know."

She reaches for the gold cigarette case, removes a smoke, and lights up. Her hands are steady. Not a tremble in sight. "So, you may be right, Roberta. It was likely my fault that your parents broke up."

I don't miss the sound of sarcasm in her tone. It shouldn't surprise me, but it does. I grab my coat and hat.

"I came to deliver good news, and this is what I get?" I shove my arms into my sleeves and tie the Dutch beret strings beneath my chin. "I knew I had a good reason to hate you. Thank you for proving me right."

I walk out of Aunt Alice's house, believing that there is no way in hell I will ever again step inside 763 Pelham Road.

CHAPTER 33

ALICE

1926

Another year. Another day in court. Another cold March afternoon.

Another basket of fresh rumors.

Had Lenny and I gotten back together? Had we seen each other since the trial ended? Did we plan to run away to Europe and live our lives in peace?

Questions. Questions. Questions.

Even Marvel asked me about them. But I couldn't get angry at her. She had a right. Over the years, I'd provided her with plenty of "scoops" and exclusives, or whatever she called them. We collaborated. But on that day, she wouldn't receive any answers from me. I had a secret to keep.

I had received a message that was short and to the point—only two words: *Central Park.*

It was from Lenny. He wanted to meet me. I was exhilarated and anxious and angry. And somewhere in the firestorm of emotions I waded through, I was afraid. But of what? Seeing him again outside a courtroom? What he might say? What I might say? A hollowness in the pit of my stomach made everything around me cold with fear, for I didn't know what I'd say or how I'd feel. I just knew I had to meet with him.

I arrived early at the same spot where we'd met once before. The East Seventy-Second Street entrance—but Lenny was already there, waiting.

"I'm sorry." The first words out of his mouth sounded hollow. "I know that doesn't mean much to you coming from me now, but I never imagined it would turn so ugly." He looked down, removing his nose glasses. They'd fogged up. Pulling a handkerchief from his pocket, he wiped them off. That's when I realized he hadn't stuttered.

"You can't do what you've done and think *I'm sorry* will fix anything."

"I know. I know," he muttered before raising his head. "We should walk. Standing here in the entrance is a risk."

"Of course," I agreed. "We are the only husband and wife in New York City who should never be seen together."

"Please, Alice, I wanted us to meet and talk, and you agreed. So I hoped there was a chance for us to have a reasonable conversation."

I sighed. "Yes, I did agree. And I'm here." I glanced around. "So let's walk."

The afternoon air was chilled, but no snow was on the ground, and the wind blowing over the lake wasn't bitter or biting—just wind. Sadly, there wasn't a sign of spring flowers or even green buds. It was too soon or too late for plants or flowers to come back to life.

"What happened, Lenny?" I asked. "Did this charade go too far, and now we are still married but must be enemies without a chance in hell of fixing our marriage? Is that who we are?"

"I still love you, Alice." He squeezed my gloved hand and didn't let go. "But winning the annulment was the only way we could've stayed married. It was our only shot."

I stopped and glared at him. "We did win. We are still married."

"That is correct. We are married." At that moment, he let

go of my hand. "But a Rhinelander cannot be married to a Negro."

I looked up at the sky. A group of clouds had several images jumbled together like a jigsaw puzzle. To my left was a herd of wild horses racing across a river, and to my right, a caged lion and its cubs. In another, an elegant woman dressed in a beautiful fur-trimmed shawl sat on a satin bench with a perfect haircut and expensive jewelry. Sitting primly without a worry in her pretty little head. She was Mrs. Rhinelander. She was me.

I returned my gaze to Lenny. "I had to win, and it was the only way. You and your lawyers, that evil man, Jacobs, were winning. Didn't you see that? I had no choice."

"I didn't know how important it was."

"To whom? Your father or to you?"

"You admitted it before the world—you're a Negro. We can't fix that." His face was drawn, exhausted. "But why, Alice? Why did you do it?" His voice broke. He was hurt. His heart was aching. But at that moment, I felt a thrill ride down my spine. I was glad to hear the pain in his voice. Excited that something I'd done hurt him as badly as I'd been hurt, and ashamed.

"Why, Lenny? Because I was vilified in the press. I was humiliated from the very first story, which called me a fraud, a liar, deceitful, and conniving. I didn't think about how this kind of cruelty would affect me. You, your family, had me drawn and quartered publicly. I went through hell."

"You don't think th-this hasn't been hard on me, too? I've been called a fool in every corner of New York City and most of the nation."

I felt like I was choking. "Is this why you're fighting the decision, filing papers because if the court had let me win and the annulment disallowed—we would've been fine but not after I'd declared myself a Negro?"

My gaze was skyward again; the horses had turned to a

pack of wolves, and the woman on the satin bench had disappeared. "I had to take off my clothes in the judge's chambers so I could be examined like a slave on an auction block, waiting for my master to tell me to turn left or right."

"Oh, God. Alice. Don't talk about yourself like that."

"What do you mean? It's no different from what you and your family did by calling me a fraud and you acting like loving me was the biggest regret of your life." I covered my mouth, stifling a sob, but I couldn't cry. Couldn't show him any more weakness, "How dare you treat me that way."

"Honeybun, I love you. And you love me. I know you do, no matter what you say. But I must contest the judgment. I must. And win or lose, I don't think we'll be able to be together for a while. There's too much going on at home."

"Home?" I chuckled. "You're right. Your family is the only home you will ever know."

He closed his eyes, and when he opened them, there was the weakness I should've seen long ago. "I—I can't fight them, my love. Not now. J-just you wait for me. We'll figure out something. Please believe me. If there is a will, there is a way."

Weeks passed. Then a few months. But I was on a merry-go-round. As strong as I believed I could be, as much as I thought I could hang on, I kept slipping off the horse, letting go of the reins, and feeling sorry for myself. Why couldn't I get off? Why couldn't I just dismount, grab hold of that long metal rod, and swing away? Would I always be in the same spot, sitting in the same chair, staring at the wallpaper that hadn't changed since childhood? At least I had some money, my annuity, my alimony. I should have fought for more. But if I took too much, Lenny and I would never get past it.

Oh, God. Why did such a thought enter my mind? Why? Why couldn't I let go?

"You've got to get out of bed, Alice."

I couldn't believe it. No one but a mother would dare wake a grown daughter this way. I rolled over, snuggling beneath the blanket, burying my face in the pillow. Maybe she'd give up and leave me alone.

"Alice, I won't stand for this. Get out from beneath those covers. I insist."

"I can't." My voice was a whimper. "He's appealing the court's decision."

"You took the steps you needed and got what you wanted."

"Did I? We wanted to be together." I pushed the covers away and sat up. "He had wanted me to fight the annulment. He even said it—*I hope you win.* Remember, Mummy. It was in the newspapers. And we had a plan."

"Alice, what are you talking about? What plan?"

I slid down onto the mattress and pulled the sheet over my head. "Nothing. Nothing."

"Don't behave like a child. You're all grown up now, and when I make the trip to your room in the morning, you should be courteous enough to sit up in your bed and say good morning."

"Mummy, I was up late last night, so I am not planning on getting out of bed for several more hours." I turned the sheet slightly to look at the clock on the side table, and I was right. It wasn't even seven o'clock. But my pleadings didn't make my mother move an inch. I could see her walking shoes on her feet.

"How about just another thirty minutes, Mummy? Then we can talk about whatever you have on your mind." I yanked the sheet completely over my head. If that wasn't a big enough hint, what was it?

"I'm not going anywhere until I see your feet hit the floor."

I felt the mattress indent. She'd taken a seat. "You've been sulking in this bedroom for a month. I won't have it. So rise. Rise up now."

"Mummy, I've had a tough two years. Can't we pretend

I got out of bed?" As the words dribbled out of my mouth, I felt suddenly ill. My stomach twisted in anguish. "Two years, Mummy. That's a long time."

"We need a vacation. I have relatives to visit, and I want you to come with me."

"Relatives? All of your family is in England."

I had never seen my mother have such a sly look in her eye. She was very pleased with herself.

"What is it that you have up your sleeve?"

She beamed, and self-satisfaction looked good on her. "We are going to England. Our ship sails next month."

My hands covered my heart. It was pounding so hard and fast that I worried for a moment. "Are you serious?"

"Of course I am. We are sailing on the White Star Liner *Majestic*, leaving on a Saturday for England. And I promise you, we will have a wonderful trip."

The flutter of excitement in my stomach only intensified. "What will we do? I've never been . . . I've never been on a ship."

"We have a small cabin in the second-class section. We can only bring a small trunk and a few handbags. But that will be quite enough." She patted my head. "Your father won't be joining us, though. He can't be away from the taxicab business for that long. But it'll be wonderful. Just you and me. We have a chance to spend time together, and you'll meet my family, and they'll meet you. You have aunts, uncles, cousins, and a slew of people who will love you at first sight. It will also give you a chance to get away from the press. It is ridiculous that these people are still hounding you." She patted my hand. "Let's see how they survive without you for a while."

"You're right. I need to live again. I can't stay in this room, in this house, forever." I inched from beneath the sheet, not wanting to upturn my mother with too swift a movement.

"You are a good girl, Alice. We will have a wonderful vacation, but half the fun is in the planning. Don't you agree?"

"I wouldn't know, Mother. I've never made plans for such a trip."

"Well, now, you will. Your first transatlantic voyage."

She smoothed the hair off my face and wiped my cheeks. I guess I'd been crying and didn't even know it. She rose and moved gingerly toward the doorway before she stopped and spun around, but not too quickly.

"It's time you met our family in England. You do know that your roots don't just go one way."

"Yes, ma'am."

"I've made a pot of coffee. You get out of bed and join me. I'll fix you breakfast," she said.

"Yes, ma'am."

Finally, out of bed, I put on my robe one sleeve at a time, tied the sash snuggly around my waist, and took a deep breath. I would join my mother in the kitchen, and maybe she'd make me a big breakfast like she used to when I was a girl.

I had to stop being sad, or sad would be all there was of me.

Just in time for summer, I perked up. I was leaving for a boat ride to England and maybe Paris, too. It had been a dream I'd shared with Lenny—my first transatlantic voyage. I never thought I'd go without him. There were so many things I never thought I'd do without him.

ALICE RHINELANDER IS ON HER WAY TO EUROPE
DEPARTS SATURDAY, JULY 21, BOUND FOR ENGLAND

The story appeared in the *Amsterdam News* alongside a large photo of me lounging in my cabin on board the White Star Liner *Majestic*.

The cabin was one of two. Mummy, thinking ahead, changed our reservations to ensure I had privacy. The journey across the Atlantic would take ten days, barring weather.

And we'd already had interruptions, a stalker at the house on Pelham Road and some man claiming to be a sheik, enamored with exotic women like me, requested my company for dinner.

I declined.

Be strong. Be brave. Cherish your first cruise, your first transatlantic voyage to England. Moving forward, I was not colored or white; I was a British girl, and in England, it wouldn't make a difference how many drops of colored blood I had in my veins.

The cabin door opened.

"Alice, I purchased one of those Kodak Brownie Flash cameras." Mummy grinned. "When we disembark, we can take each other's pictures on the stern, bow, or deck." Happiness exploded from her glowing cheeks. "This is going to be a fantastic voyage, Alice. Don't you agree?"

I felt better some days. But I swore I wouldn't spoil this trip for my mother. I wouldn't allow my melancholy to dim her light. "I completely agree."

She sat on the edge of the cot. "What do you have there?"

I smiled, holding up my letter. "I was writing a telegram to send to Marvel at the *Amsterdam News*. A farewell note, a see-you-soon to the press."

She held out her hand. "Can I read it?"

I held on to my note. "It will be in the newspapers soon enough."

"You don't want to show it to me?"

I pressed my lips together, then decided. "Let me read it to you."

She nodded, settling her spine against the wall surrounding most of my narrow bed.

I licked my lips. "I'm a little bit nervous to read it aloud, but it might be the best thing to do."

"Okay, I am ready to listen."

I cleared my throat. "'At the hour of my departure to England, I am thrilled. Mummy and I have planned to spend a lot of time visiting her relatives in England. This is the primary objective of our visit abroad, as my mother has not seen her relatives or mother in fifteen years.

"'I hope that during our stay in England, we shall be rid of the attention of the press as I think I have given the representatives of newspapers a bountiful share of my time and patience. No further statements will be forthcoming from me other than an expression of thanks to the many friends who have wished me bon voyage.'"

She wiped her eyes.

"You're not crying, are you? It's not that bad," I said teasingly. "Seriously, what do you think, Mummy?"

I held my breath, staring into her eyes.

She bit down on her lips. "The only quibble I have is that we are visiting our relatives. My family is your family. Don't ever forget there is more to you than one thing."

CHAPTER 34

ALICE

1927–1928

Home from the other side of the Atlantic, and I was heartbroken. Rudolph Valentino had died, and I feared my youth and my dreams had gone with him.

England had been divine, but the news of Valentino's departure was too much for my fragile heart and mind.

We arrived home after midnight, and I fell into bed. But I was up the next morning at dawn. I dug through my steamer trunk, thinking I'd wear one of the suits I'd purchased in Paris, but eventually slipped on a simple black suit. I didn't need to be too fancy.

I sat in the kitchen, drinking coffee, waiting for a decent hour to telephone. At nine o'clock, I called her.

"Are you busy for lunch? I want to tell you about my trip."

"You have a story for me?" Marvel asked.

"We can't see each other just for a social visit?"

"When have we ever been social like that?"

I caught the teasing tone in her voice and laughed. "Now and then."

"Can we meet at my office?"

"You bet."

"I'm on the third floor."

* * *

I arrived at the building on Seventh Avenue around 11:30 a.m. As I exited the elevator, there was Marvel with arms opened wide and fingertips wiggling, demanding an embrace. I obliged her, but my gaze darted around the hallway, expecting a photographer to jump out from behind a potted plant or around a corner.

"I'm glad you are here. Your timing couldn't be better." She took hold of my wrist and led me toward the other end of the hall. "I want you to meet Holden Richards. He's the reporter who helped me out around here. An all-around good guy. You'll like him."

"Marvel." I stopped in my tracks. "Marvel."

"Yes, doll."

"Is that a good idea? It's over and all, but I wouldn't want anyone to think I was too friendly with any one newspaper."

Marvel's expression twisted into an *Are you kidding me?* face. "Don't play that innocent-little-girl routine with me, Alice. You are no longer a spring chickadee. Neither am I. You and I did some good work and had great chats, resulting in some damn fine news articles. And I want you to meet the man who pushed me to get to know you."

Once again, Marvel held my wrist, leading me toward the end of a short hall.

When I entered the office, I spotted him before we were introduced. I remembered him. He was the handsome colored man who'd joined their group late at Smalls Paradise the night I first saw Marvel.

"Mrs. Rhinelander, Holden Richards. It is a pleasure to meet you." Standing, he removed his black-rimmed spectacles and extended his hand.

I complied. "Yes, sir. I am pleased to meet you, too."

His smile was bright. "Are you sure about that, Mrs. Rhinelander? You look as if you'd rather be any place but here."

"It's just awkward. I spent so much time hating most of the press the past few years." I paused to grin at Marvel. "Except for Marvel—and call me Alice."

"And it's Holden." He released my hand, which I hadn't noticed he'd held on to.

"Have a seat, ladies." He grabbed a chair from an empty desk nearby, and I sat in front of him.

"Alice, your story is far more layered than another Negro girl passing, getting caught, and being called a liar."

"But, Mr. Richards—I mean Holden—the Rhinelander name is the crème de la crème of Fifth Avenue. Even though I won my case, it won't change my life."

"Not if you write a book."

Marvel, sitting next to me, squeezed my hand.

"It will sell, and Marvel can be your ghostwriter. I'll help with the publisher. I know a few."

I closed my eyes, but only for the briefest second. "I am stunned. Although somehow I must've known I'd find an answer to the question, what do I do next? It's why I wanted to meet with Marvel. She always has ideas. And now that everything is over."

"Is it over? Really, Alice?" Marvel said solemnly. "Aren't you going to sue him for more alimony?"

"I already get alimony."

"Having this book will close the story, but on your terms," Marvel said. "Your truth will be the last words on Rhinelander versus Rhinelander."

From Marvel and Holden Richards, I glanced from one eager face to another.

"And your story will touch upon so many important themes," Marvel said.

Holden nodded enthusiastically. "Not only racism and classism but also passing—"

"I'm not sure I am ready to relive the story of Lenny and me."

"We just sprang this on you," he said, his voice warm, almost soothing. "Think about it." He smiled. "Meanwhile, you two get on out of here. And have lunch on the newspaper."

I lie in bed wide awake, perspiration on my brow and my legs tucked into my chest. I'd been having nightmares. Everything kept playing in my mind. The Victrola wouldn't stop spinning its vinyl.

First, it was the letters. They'd appear with legs and arms and ink that wouldn't dry. My lawyers in the background repeated the same sorry slogans: We must capture the public's attention. We must fill the courtroom and amass a crowd of blue bloods to witness your humiliation—a courtroom of savages hell-bent on digging every ounce of privacy from your life.

Then, the dream shifts and goes sideways through time. I'm with my lawyers again, and the news isn't what I thought it would be.

"We must win. Do you understand, Alice?"

"I think I do."

"If your marriage is annulled, all is lost. You will have nothing, no Lenny, no money, no name, only shame."

Was that what I wanted? Was it? Was it? I yelled in the dream.

My cheeks were wet with tears and my hands balled into fists. I heard the telephone and wiped my face. The only calls that came this early were from my lawyers.

I cast the sheet aside and planted my feet firmly on the floor, hands covering my face. Sadness surrounded me like layers of wool, scratchy but warm, mildewed, too. But there was nothing I could throw away. Love held me in place and stole my ability to move forward, backward, or sideways.

My mother was at my bedroom door. "The telephone is for you, Alice."

*   *   *

In 1927, the court announced its decision in April. Lenny had lost his appeal. He would not be granted an annulment. The language was straightforward and brutal to the ears of any upstanding member of New York City's four hundred:

> Leonard "Kip" Rhinelander knew that Alice Beatrice Jones was colored before he married her.

No one had to read between the lines. He always knew.

No one pressed me for a reply. Was it finally over? The court battles. The newspaper reporters, hovering? Were they no longer interested in badgering me with questions? No one was interested when Lenny and I first met and fell in love. But more importantly, how would I have answered the question, was I Negro back then?

I knew the answer to that one. I would've yelled from the rooftops: *I'm white. I'm white. Look at me. Can't you see? I'm white!*

But no one asked.

Lenny's next legal move, in 1928, sliced me up and spit me out.

He packed his bags and moved to Reno, Nevada. He wanted a divorce. A goddamned divorce. Now, why did that surprise me? Why did it hurt so much? I only wanted a legal separation. That's all I'd asked for. Nothing more.

Divorce had never crossed my mind.

What was wrong with me?

Not so deep down, I believed we'd get back together in a few years, once we were no longer in the spotlight or after his old man, Rhinelander, died. No matter the ugliness or shame he'd caused me, I never thought about Lenny moving to Reno. Poor, sad, foolish girl—I never thought he'd divorce me.

New York Amsterdam News

December 26, 1942

SUPREME COURT'S DECISION AIDS MRS. RHINELANDER

Kip's Widow Expected to Reopen Income Case

The Appellate Division, State Supreme Court, renders invalid the agreement granting Alice Jones Rhinelander an annual income of $3,600 from the Philip Rhinelander estate on the grounds that the Nevada divorce obtained by her husband, the late Kip Rhinelander, in 1929 was illegal since decrees are not recognized in New York State.

CHAPTER 35

————•◆•————

ROBERTA

1942

Aunt Alice and I are in the kitchen, and she's chain-smoking, puffing on one cigarette after another and avoiding eye contact.

The latter, I don't mind.

"I refused to grant him a divorce. He could move to Reno or goddamned Timbuktu. What kind of fool did he take me for?" My aunt Alice takes a long draw from her Camel. "How dare he do that to me after all he'd put me through."

She's going on and on about Rhinelander's move to Reno back in 1928, but I'm thinking about that word. That damn word. It carries more than insult or disrespect. Even whispered, it rips at the heart, stifles the soul, and delivers pain, anger, and evil as plentiful as salt in a sea.

The devil's side of history never stays in the past. It holds too much power, this word. It's in the back of our minds, for we know someone is thinking it, someone is muttering it, someone will shout it out loud.

I had to pull strength from the depth of my soul to return to Pelham Road after my last visit—after learning the truth about what she thought of my family and me.

What brings me here is my mother. She claims that I owe

her a favor and an act of unparalleled kindness—a grand gesture. So, I have obeyed, although I can't understand why.

The relationship between sisters is a mystery. I am an only child, and forever, it's just been me and them, never an us. That is why my mother has made choices I've never considered. She's been an us longer than anything other than a daughter.

The Jones sisters . . .

And that day, they'd banded together even if it wasn't apparent to the others.

I had blocked that day from my mind.

I'd heard it. My father calls some of his Negro friends or a colored man he has a beef with by that name. But coming from Aunt Alice, it wasn't the same.

And everyone in that room knew it.

No wonder my father couldn't live with us anymore. My mother may have left with him, but she didn't choose him. If she had, they'd still be together.

I don't blame my mother for what she did.

I blame Aunt Alice.

"Are you going to talk to me?" she asks, cigarette dangling from her mouth. "I told you what happened. If you hate me for it, why did you come back?"

I shake my head. "My mother made me."

"You sound like a ten-year-old."

"That's the age I was when you—"

"It was a bad day." She snuffs out her cigarette in the ashtray on the kitchen table. "I thought there would be no other day worse than that."

"So you took it out on the people who had supported you through years and years of court battles, testimonies, and newspaper reporters hounding them."

She combs her fingers through loose curls. "I won't apologize. If that's what you're looking for me to do."

"I would never want you to."

"I learned long ago that apologies are useless."

"I'm not sure what you've learned."

"If you aren't going to civil, you should leave."

Aunt Alice brushes strands of hair from her face. Her long red hair seems dull today. The house is dark, and I wish she used the fireplace. But mostly, I wish I could leave or had never come. But my mother said go. What happened was too many years ago to remain angry about. I don't understand my mother. I genuinely don't. But I also, as much as I can, do what she asks me to do. And that's why I'm here, looking at my aunt and trying not to spit in her face.

"I still don't know what happened. I don't know why. Can you explain that to me? Why would you say such a thing and ask my mother to make such a choice?"

Aunt Alice sighs heavily. "What if I don't want to explain?"

"Then I won't be able to do this, be around you, even for my mother, and I believe you've grown fond of me during the past two years." I straighten my spine. "And you'd miss me."

"Okay, okay, I'll tell you. But it wasn't just one thing. It was a series of things, and I lost track of myself." She chuckles. "Frankly, I'd lost track of me long before and was still a little girl counting on my lucky stars to find me."

CHAPTER 36

———◆———

ALICE

1929

One morning, after Daddy left for work and Mummy was in her sewing room going through the monthly bills, I was in the kitchen waiting for Gracie.

I had invited her to Pelham Road, for we hadn't talked in a while. She'd been angry because Mummy hadn't asked her to join us on the trip to England, which wasn't my fault.

She wouldn't have gone anyway. Footsie would never have allowed it. Over the years, his pleasant demeanor—although often rough around the edges—had been toughened by his lifestyle. He was a hoodlum. We knew it. Gracie knew it. And as of late, his personality had grown more unseemly, meaning he was venting his frustrations on his wife.

The doorbell rang, and I opened it.

"Well, it's nice to see you again, Mrs. Rhinelander." Gracie strolled into the kitchen, tossing her rabbit coat over a chair and collapsing into a seat as if she'd had to run from her car. "I was surprised to hear from you. I figured you'd take off for another voyage after your tour of England. Perhaps you'd want to hike off to, I don't know, Los Angeles?"

"Now, why would Los Angeles come to mind?" I asked, genuinely curious.

"Well, I read in the newspaper that Lenny moved to Reno. Los Angeles is mighty close without being in the same town. That way, you two could have a, you know, rendezvous." She chuckled. "Didn't the papers say you all met in Paris while you were traveling? Just a continuation of the cat and mouse game you like to play."

"There is no cat or mouse, and we didn't meet in Paris or anywhere else. Rumors. Nothing but nasty rumors." I took a deep breath. I should've known my sister would have already read the story, digested it, and prepared a nasty remark as soon as she saw me. "You'll be impressed to learn that I am not interested in a rendezvous with Leonard 'Kip' Rhinelander. What I'm interested in is suing his father."

"Whatever for?"

"Alienation of affections."

"Fancy lawyer talk," she complained. "It sounds like a bold move, but it also sounds like you're trying to fix what's lost. It's long gone if you ask me." She reached in her purse and pulled out a pack of Marlboros.

"Give me one."

"One what? A cigarette? When did you start smoking?"

"I picked up the habit onboard. Smoking on a ship helps pass the time. It's also very glamorous." It was fun to poke the bear. Gracie didn't need to know I'd been smoking for a while.

She rolled her eyes but passed me the pack, and I took out a cigarette. Then she gave me a lighter.

"I give as good as I get," I said with a cringing smile.

She lit her cig and blew rings of smoke. "So why are you telling me all of this? You and your lawyers have it mapped out. There's nothing for your little sister to do."

I took a drag of my cigarette. "I intend to file papers and do all the legal things that need to be done to stop the divorce. However, it would help me if I knew something more about Lenny's father. And I was thinking you or, more precisely, your husband could help me out."

"Can you tell me what you have in mind? I don't know what my husband can do for you, especially with the likes of Commodore Rhinelander. The kind of business Footsie is involved in doesn't include the Hudson Valley crowd."

"He knows people. I thought he might know a detective. Like a private eye?"

"He might. But can't your lawyers do that? What are you looking for anyway?"

"I don't need my lawyers to know. I want to find something to help prove Lenny's father plotted against Lenny and me."

"I would think that wouldn't be hard."

"It is when you're accusing one of them."

"One of the *Social Register* crowd? Really, Alice? Why can't you let it go?"

"I'll let it go when Lenny does. He's the one moving to Reno to divorce me. So that's why."

"Okay, I'll ask Footsie who he knows. But don't count on it."

"That's fine. Just ask."

"The story never ends. There's always something new for me to deal with, fight over, and cry about. And I'm sick of it." I tried to keep my voice down. I was in Marvel's office at the *Amsterdam News*. But I was too upset. Too frazzled. Too many loose ends in my life.

"I don't want to write a book, Marvel. I'm sorry, I can't do it."

She had listened to me complain, cry, and whine for an hour, sitting patiently behind her desk, her brow wrinkled with concern as she gave me compassion-filled nods.

"Okay. Maybe it's the wrong time. Maybe we'll wait a year or so. Let you adjust and finish any unfinished business you have with him. Meanwhile, you should find something to do with yourself. Something besides sitting down with lawyers and thinking of ways to ruin the Rhinelanders. Revenge against people like them is pointless, Alice."

"I can't just lie down. I can't." I wished Marvel had a window in her office. Seeing the sky calmed me. "I might hire a private detective. Gracie's husband, Footsie, says he might be able to help me." I chewed my fingernail. "But if he takes too long, I'll have my lawyers file the papers in the New York Supreme Court next week. But I'm giving the story to the *Amsterdam News* today." I gave Marvel a meaningful look. "You'll beat all the dailies if it goes into tomorrow's edition. Imagine a weekly beating all the other papers to the latest Rhinelander news.

"Do you have a smoke," I said, pacing. "I need it."

She pushed the cigarette case on her desk at me. "Here."

"And when the commodore reads it, I hope he chokes on his filet mignon or whatever overpriced meal he's munching on."

"You are going to sue him?" Marvel asked, sounding skeptical. "Have you lost your mind?"

"No, I've found it. And I thought you'd understand if no one else did. You've told me for years, in one way or another, to stand up for myself. Stop allowing the Rhinelanders to intimidate, threaten, and steal the man I loved from me. And now, I've got a case and a way to get a lot of money."

"How much?"

"Half a million dollars."

"Jesus Christ."

I smiled, enjoying the look of shock on her face.

"He should pay for what he's done to us."

Marvel grimaced. "What's he done to you or you and Lenny? It doesn't sound like Lenny has anything to gain from this other than more hard nights at the family dinner table." She wiped a hand over her mouth. "I thought seeing your name in the newspaper every day was killing you. Now, what's going on? You miss the limelight. Want to see your name plastered in the headlines again?

"Don't you ever want a normal life, Alice? Something that isn't tied to Lenny Rhinelander?"

"You're the one who asked me to write a book about him. I would think you'd love this idea," I said, my voice shaking. I searched my purse for my pack of cigarettes but didn't see it. "Do you have another smoke?"

"I'm out, Alice."

"Damn." I stood and paced in front of her desk. "Philip Rhinelander owes me a marriage, a life . . . my husband. And since he's not likely to return any of those items anytime soon, I will take him for every goddamned penny I can."

"I have known you for four years, and this doesn't sound like you." Marvel gave me her best version of a motherly scowl. "You love Lenny. Won't this hurt him, too?"

"You're wrong. I loved Lenny. I'd be a fool to be in love with him now."

MRS. RHINELANDER SUES FATHER-IN-LAW
CHARGES IN COMPLAINT THAT HE ALIENATED
KIP'S AFFECTIONS
New York Amsterdam News

CHAPTER 37

━━━◆━━━

ALICE

1930

Vengeance is not something I thought I would relish. But I have been wrong about any number of things. So when the opportunity to retaliate for the humiliation and allegations and desertion presented itself, I could not turn another cheek. I had read the news in the evening edition of the newspaper. After my nerves settled, I spent the following day coming up with a plan, a counterstrike.

My lawyers had contacted me over the weekend, Sunday afternoon, requesting a Monday morning meeting. I rose early and had my coffee and a few cigarettes before leaving the house for Lee Parsons Davis Law Offices.

It was strange to walk through New Rochelle, heading toward the train station, and not be accosted by reporters, photographers, or nosy neighbors. But if my plan worked, there would be renewed interest in the trials of Mrs. Alice Jones Rhinelander.

When I arrived at the offices, I was led to a large conference room, one I was accustomed to being led to. The team was there. Every face, from Mr. Davis to Mrs. Sage, looked stern. But I had faith. My idea would erase those pained expressions. First, however, I had to hear what Mr. Davis had to say.

"We have news from Nevada, Alice," he began. "And it's not what you had hoped."

I sat with my legs crossed beneath the table, but my trembling knee kept striking its underbelly. I'd surely have a bruise, but the idle thought didn't change what was coming next—the news Mr. Davis had to share. I took a deep breath, steadied my gaze, and looked into his eyes without flinching. "Go on. Say it."

"Mr. Rhinelander was granted an uncontested divorce in Reno." He had spoken quickly, but it didn't dull the blade.

My body, having a mind of its own, jerked backward.

Mrs. Sage stood, moving her notebook aside. "Would you like a cup of coffee, perhaps a glass of water?"

I sat forward, clenching my fists, taking more deep breaths, and gathering my thoughts. "No. I'm fine. I'd read about his Nevada divorce in the Friday evening paper. Why would you think I wouldn't know by Monday morning."

"We didn't want to discuss it over the phone," said Mr. Davie. "And hoped you'd miss it."

They were cowards, but I'd never get them to admit that. "I want you to file a countersuit."

"You want to contest the divorce," Mrs. Sage said, sounding dumbfounded.

"No. I want to sue for more alimony. As much as we can get."

"Why sue him?" Mr. Davis asked. "He has no money."

I smiled. "And I believe he's been disinherited, too."

"How do you know that?" Mr. Davis cocked his head.

"A friend of a friend." I had promised Gracie I wouldn't mention her husband.

"Well then. The papers will be filed, I assure you. But we'll still go after Kip. Publicly, he's inherited two large estates. And even if your information is accurate, when we win, a Rhinelander will pay."

"Thank you." I rose. "Is there anything else?"

Mr. Davis and Mrs. Sage were on their feet, too.

"Alice, I do hope you'll come to accept this divorce as the best possible outcome. You're a young woman and can now put this period of your life behind you." Mr. Davis had a kindly smile on his face.

I smiled in reply, but it was not sincere. Not in the least.

If you pay attention to lawyers and the law, you'll eventually learn a few things. I thought about that for hours and hours after leaving Mr. Davis's offices as I walked through Manhattan and Harlem by the *New Amsterdam News* building, Smalls Paradise, Central Park, and even to the Hotel Marie Antoinette. From one end of town to the other, I walked. Divorced. An unmarried woman. The spinster I was at twenty-two I was again at thirty-one.

I returned home but didn't remember how I got there. Did I walk to New Rochelle? Did I take a train?

I do recall the air had a stench that followed me, draped over me, seeped beneath my skin, and all of me was rotting from the outside in.

Love had turned into a poison, a splintering of the soul. I was a divorced woman. How could he do that to me after I'd given him my body, trusted him with my heart, and changed the woman I had planned to be? The hell that I went through could've been accomplished a month after our marriage. Divorced. That bastard.

I entered the house on Pelham Road, full of hate, self-loathing, and a desire to strike out to harm and make someone pay for what had happened to me.

The lawyers had done something I hadn't expected them to do. They'd called my parents and told them I was *sitting in the cat bird's seat*. The divorce was final. I was free after all the turmoil, headlines, and hours in court. I had my life back.

Those were their words, not mine.

So I was surprised when I opened the door, dropped my

bags on the bench in the foyer, walked down the hall, and stepped into the living room to find a banner draped in front of the window. It read in bright red letters:

CONGRATULATIONS, ALICE,
ON YOUR DIVORCE!

In various spots in the room, joining in on the celebration, were Gracie and Footsie, Robert and Emily with little Roberta, and, of course, Daddy and Mummy.

A card table sat in the corner with a colorful tablecloth that reached the floor. On top was a tall cake, white icing and pink flowers, and several bottles of champagne and one apple cider—Emily didn't drink much, and then there was the child.

Everywhere else, there were balloons and streamers.

I stood frozen, unable to think, let alone move. Mummy was the first to come to me and grab me around the shoulders.

"Could you give me a hug and a kiss on the cheek, my darling girl?"

Father was close behind. He patted me on the back. "My angel."

Standing behind her mother, Roberta gave me a little wave and a smile. Her mother rested her head lightly on her husband's shoulder, and his arms were around her waist.

They both beamed friendly smiles but looked like Cheshire cats, with grins too wide and grotesque to count as happiness.

I blinked. I then blinked again. My eyes were playing tricks on me. I don't know why that image came to me.

Then I looked at Footsie, who had a similar grip on Gracie, but I swear there was a bruise under her eye that no one would mention.

"Oh darling, it's over," Gracie said. "I am so happy for you."

She didn't fool me. I knew she knew I wasn't a cheerful cherub about the divorce.

I closed my eyes, wishing I could turn around and leave because I feared the thoughts spinning around in my head.

I shook free of Gracie's embrace and beelined to the card table and the champagne. I picked up a glass and raised it high. The family quieted, waiting for me to make a speech I imagined—words of praise, appreciation, and love for their support over the years.

But my eyes again played a game with my senses. I didn't see family; I only saw skin colors—my tan-skinned father. If he had been white, I wouldn't be the mess I was; I wouldn't be the broken girl. I couldn't blame him entirely. The worst of it was dear Emily. My sister fell in love with the Negro. And when she married him, she couldn't leave bad enough alone. She went and changed her race to Negro.

"Why did you do it?" Everyone in the room stared at me, unsure who I was talking to or what I was asking. I had to remember that most of my anger and hate was in my head, and I hadn't spoken of it to any of them, but that day was the day I couldn't stop my mouth.

That day, I believed I could do whatever I wanted and say whatever was on my mind. So I asked again, and this time, I looked directly at my sister Emily.

"Why did you marry him? And if you were going to marry him, if you had to marry him, why did you declare yourself a Negro?" Spitting mad, I felt as if I foamed at the mouth with every word. "Do you know how much that hurt my case? Do you know that is what ended Lenny and me?"

Robert stepped forward. A blaze of anger and frustration filled his gaze, directed at me. But I was ready for him. I wouldn't back down. I wasn't going to apologize.

"Don't do this, Alice," he pleaded. "What happened between you and Kip Rhinelander wasn't anyone's fault. Had nothing to do with anyone in this room." He looked around the room, his gaze moving deliberately from my parents to my sister and her husband, and then to his wife and child. "We are the people we are, and proud of who we are. So don't try and blame anyone here for what has happened to you."

"Then who can I blame? Who?"

He shook his head and pressed his lips together. Robert had been holding back an opinion, I believed.

"Go on," I said. "Say what's on your mind."

"You could've walked away from that man, but you didn't. You chose to be the girl on the front page of every newspaper in New York over and over again. You fought, and you fought, and you kept fighting for what? It was over before it began. That man was never going to choose you over his family's money.

"So, it's over, and your family is here to celebrate your freedom. We're all exhausted."

"Go to hell, Robert. Go to hell and take your colored wife and baby with you."

"Don't talk to my wife that way."

"Robert. Alice." My father's voice cut through the room. "You two stop. We're here to celebrate. Not fight. There doesn't need to be another day of pain and hurt in this house ever again. We've had enough."

"Enough?" I whispered.

Then, the situation went from bad to worse in seconds. My body shook with anger and hate, and the word came out of my mouth because it had been waiting inside me for a long, long time.

CHAPTER 38

ALICE

1936

On February 20, 1936, at age thirty-two, Lenny Rhinelander died of lobar pneumonia at his father's home in Long Beach, New York. He was to be buried in the family vault in Woodlawn Cemetery in the Bronx.

I stood at the corner of Pelham Road, blinking at the brightness of the streetlamp burning a hole in my irises. It felt like matches had been dropped on my corneas. I'd been sequestered in the house for a few years, only leaving to bury my father in '33 and accompany my mother to her doctor appointments.

I pulled a handkerchief from my purse and blew my nose, but I couldn't stop blinking. The daylight bothered me, but the smell of gasoline from the automobiles rolling up and down the street—and the biting cold wind—was just as merciless.

When did I become so sensitive to the outdoors?

I lumbered toward the train station. I had to move. If I kept still, I'd never make it.

"Safe from the horrors of death for one more day," I muttered, reaching the train station platform. Once the train arrived, I removed my gloves from my coat pocket. It was so cold. That's all I thought about as the train traveled toward the Bronx. How cold it was. How cold Lenny must be. Lying in his tomb, slabs of marble surrounding him. The family and friends who despised him were the only ones allowed to give their respects.

When I reached Woodlawn and exited the train, a police officer was at his post outside the station. Located at the intersection of Bainbridge and Jerome Avenue, it was a fifteen-minute walk to the entrance of the cemetery.

As I made my way, the number of police officers increased. The number of cars in the street grew. There were people on the sidewalk. Were the police there to keep the crowds away from the funeral procession?

Or to keep me away?

I pulled my fur collar around my neck and tugged on my cloche hat, covering my eyes and hair. Although no one would probably recognize me. I looked different from the last photograph of me that appeared in a newspaper six years ago when the divorce was final, and then the settlement was reached, and I lost the right to use the Rhinelander name.

But today was not about sour grapes. I kept walking, keeping my head down, not creating a fuss. No matter how hard it was not to cry out. To not grieve and rage for my lost love.

I had planned my arrival well. The line of limousines had stopped, and the automobiles at the front of the line were driving toward the mausoleum.

The sunlight flickered as if waiting for the clouds to get in the way. But there were no clouds in the sky. I reached into my purse for my sunglasses. I wasn't accustomed to wearing them since I rarely stepped out of the house, but today was an exception.

With them on, the sun rays flickered less brightly.

Four men carried the casket. I didn't recognize them. It had been so long since I kept track of Lenny's relatives. I knew that his two brothers were dead. With his death, that left Adelaide and a brother named Kip.

Of the men holding Lenny's casket, I imagined one was related to Adelaide, a husband, son, or nephew. I didn't know. Frankly, I couldn't have picked her out of the crowd.

They were dressed well, with heavy coats and black leather gloves. Had any of them been with Lenny when he died? He had to have been so frightened. He didn't like dark places. He loved the sunshine and would have loved a day like this one with the sunlight. He wouldn't have enjoyed the cold, of course. In that, he was like me. Snow and cold made him feel naked, stark, and vulnerable, just like I felt at that moment.

I swallowed the sudden flare of nausea floating in my throat. There had been so much death around me lately. Daddy died in '33 after a long illness. I thought he was just tired.

Mummy wasn't well, but I hoped she'd pull through. Although, she was mighty lonely without Daddy.

New Rochelle was where my memories lived—the street corners, the parks, and the motion picture show. All the places Lenny and I had gone when we first met. The places we'd sneak off to when reporters hounded us like we were wild beasts.

I glanced at the casket again. They were heaving it onto a flatbed truck of some kind. The journey to Lenny's last resting place was about to begin.

Watching Lenny's procession, I realized I would never leave New Rochelle. I didn't need to be anywhere else but New York State.

I'd lived a lifetime in the past fifteen years. I couldn't imagine not being near him. My legs turned soft and miserable, and I reached for a nearby streetlamp pole.

Then, I felt a tug on my arm. "How did you get here without being seen?"

Marvel.

"How did you find me on this crowded street?"

"I looked for a woman who looked sadder than anyone else."

I grimaced with a smile. "It is a sad day."

Her hair hung loose in dark curls that clung to her cheeks. She looked out of place. Too pretty and too brown for a Rhinelander's funeral. "Are you going to the cemetery plot?"

When I learned of Lenny's death, I reached out to the Rhinelanders, requesting to attend the funeral. She'd risen to new heights at the *Amsterdam News* over the years. She was a full-fledged editor and news journalist. She didn't cover the society gossip pages or stories like mine anymore. She wrote news and made headlines that mattered, but I needed her to help me get past the Rhinelander hate so I could say a last goodbye. So, she wrote the story.

RHINELANDER'S EX-WIFE WANTS TO ATTEND FUNERAL

"No, they refused my request. Thank you for the story, but the last thing they wanted there was me."

New York Amsterdam News

March 13, 1943

ALICE JONES WINS HIGH COURT BATTLE

ALICE WINS COURT BATTLE FOR HER $3,600

A year for life from the estate of Lenny's father. The court battle had been going on for three years, since shortly after Lenny's father's death.

CHAPTER 39

ROBERTA

1943

On New Year's Eve, I return to Pelham Road.

I am hustling across town to celebrate a victory with Aunt Alice. She has beat them. She has won.

We'll celebrate. She'll smoke a cigarette or ten and fix a cup of tea or a gin and tonic. She might even have a flask, now that I think of it. I'll remind her that Prohibition is long over with. But she'll be in a good mood, and I'm anxious to see her.

I received a telephone call from her this morning. She invited me to stop by.

"You likely have plans for the evening, but if you could pay me a visit, I'd appreciate it, dear."

Dear?

Oh, how could I pass up that invitation? She is in good spirits, and I am not about to disappoint her. "That sounds great. I'll see you around three o'clock."

When I arrive, I get right down to business. We'll socialize after.

"Here's what has happened, and I won't sugarcoat it, Aunt Alice."

"And when have you ever put sugar on anything you've slung my way, Roberta?"

I love it when Aunt Alice is in one of her aggressive moods. Finally, she is ready to fight back against the nonsense. And Adelaide Thomas is nothing but full of it.

"The Supreme Court decision made it possible for us to go back to court and fight the State Supreme Court's decision."

"Yes, I know that." Aunt Alice nods her head.

"You won," I say. "Adelaide and the commodore's other heirs have given up the ghost. You will begin receiving the checks for the rest of your life."

"Well, then, I'll have to live as long as possible, won't I?"

I laugh. "That sounds like a plan." I should leave the subject alone, but I have one more question. "Why did they fight it so vehemently?"

"It was the sapphire ring that Lenny gave me years ago. A family heirloom. It belonged to their mother. Who gave it to her, then Lenny gave it to me. But she gave it to him."

"If she wanted it back, why didn't she just ask for it?"

"She knew I'd never give it back. That's why." She shrugs and fills her glass before lighting up a smoke. "You know what I was thinking?"

"What's that?"

"Now that I'm a winner and have a hefty sum to live off of for the rest of my life, I should write a book."

"About you and Rhinelander?"

She flinches. "Oh God, no. There's been enough written about Lenny and me. I'll write about something else. Maybe I'll become a newswoman, like you and Marvel."

She laughs, and I get a tickle in my throat. "You want to go to lunch?"

"Okay. I wouldn't mind getting out of the house."

CHAPTER 40

———◆———

ALICE

1938

Two years after Lenny. Five years after Daddy. Mummy died on Wednesday, July 12, 1938. It wasn't easy losing them. They were my ports in the storm. They told me where I was and where I'd been: a daughter, a lover, a wife, and a headline. Three months after Mummy passed, I still grieved in the worst possible way. What did I have left but gin and tonic? Oh yes, I had my sisters.

The taxicab from Muriel's Café drove by the cemetery. I closed my eyes and felt the grief crawl through me. I should've instructed the driver to take another route to Pelham Road, but I knew what was buried beneath the dirt. Not only headstones and coffins but dreams, hopes, and lies.

I exited the cab, stumbled up the walkway, and entered the house.

Emily and Gracie were there, waiting for me.

"How much did you have to drink, Alice? A pint of vodka? You smell of booze."

"It wasn't vodka, Gracie," I replied, pleased I didn't slur. "You can't smell vodka. It doesn't have an odor."

"Alice . . ."

"It was gin and tonic, and I'm almost forty years old. I

don't need my sisters coming to my rescue every Saturday night."

"You're the only one left in the house, Alice. We worry about you," Gracie said.

Emily was quiet as usual. I sometimes thought she only showed up because Gracie begged her to. But since that nasty blowup a few years back, all my fault, and after she and Robert split, we'd had a conversation or two. "Don't worry." I looked at Emily. "I'll be fine."

My sisters moved in close then, each taking an elbow, and walked me to my bedroom, almost without my noticing. Perhaps I'd had more gin and tonic than I thought.

I started to disagree, but why bother? They guided me down the narrow hallway, passing judgment with each footfall. They didn't sound angry or put off by my odor or staggering feet. Still, I wished they'd leave me be so I could crawl into bed, pull the blanket over my head, and disappear.

"Did you drive by the cemetery?" Emily asked, her voice almost a whisper. "You shouldn't do that to yourself. None of them will return—not Daddy, Mummy, or Lenny."

I rested a hand on the wall to steady myself. "Can't I just go out on a Saturday night?"

"Of course you can," Gracie said, with an annoying *tsk-tsk* in her tone.

Emily entered the bedroom ahead of us but didn't flick the light switch. "Get her nightgown."

"Okay," Gracie replied. "You know we all miss Mummy and Daddy. And I know you still feel for Lenny but grieving over that man is a boatload of wasted time."

I thought about telling her how much I tried not to hear a word she had to say. And how often I rarely did. But her life wasn't a bouquet of roses either. She had filed for divorce from Footsie and lately, had been in the house with me more often than not. She even tried to help out around the house, but mostly, she turned on the radio to a bebop station or chastised me for staying out late on weeknights.

The next thing I knew, one of my sisters had removed my shoes, stockings, and dress. Another held my arms above my head, fingers wrapped around my wrists, and slipped a nightgown over my head and shoulders.

Not wanting to be completely helpless, I gave a slight wiggle. But before I could whine about being able to do it myself, I was in bed beneath a thick quilt. With the ceiling light off, only the small lamp on the nightstand beamed across the room.

"Do you remember being young? What do you miss the most?" I asked, not sure which of my sisters I wanted to answer me, but Emily chimed in first.

"I remember when I was a little girl, and Daddy and I would go to baseball games. I loved baseball. We'd talk on the train and sit up high with no one else. I couldn't see the men on the field well, but it didn't matter. Daddy told me everything that was happening on the baseball field. I miss that little girl."

"That's a nice story. You were always Daddy's favorite," Gracie said, standing in the bedroom doorway like Daddy used to do. "But to answer Alice's question. I'm still young, so I'm moving to Los Angeles. I think life will be better for me with sunshine year-round, and there's lots of work, I hear, for women like me out west."

"Who told you this?" Emily asked accusingly.

"I convinced myself. Why are you speaking to me like I'm a child? I have sense. Folks think I don't, but I know how to get by."

I rose on my elbows, blinked, and prayed my eyes would stay open. "It has to be a man you're running off to Los Angeles to be with. There's not enough sunshine for me to move to that town."

"Okay, fine," Gracie said. "How about you? How would you answer your question?"

"I just need to be where the beboppers are bobbing and the music is swinging hard and loud. I don't do it every night." Only as much as needed. "When I want to dance the night away and have a few gin and tonics."

Gracie sat in the chair next to my bed. She wasn't talking, but I could tell she was thinking.

"What?" I asked.

"Nothing."

I pressed my palms into the mattress and pushed myself onto my elbows. "You think a hardworking man can fix me, right?"

"I didn't say that."

"Maybe a post office worker or a car mechanic. Some churchgoing man who makes enough money to afford a two-bedroom apartment in a brownstone on One-hundred and Twenty-Fifth Street near Lenox Avenue."

Hope flashed across her eyes as if I was finally using my noggin.

"It's not going to happen," I said sharply.

"It would be lovely, dear," Emily said, the corners of her mouth hinting at a smile. "Some decent but affordable place, and then we could sell this old house."

"I'm not leaving New Rochelle."

Gracie laughed and moved to the foot of the bed, curling at my feet. "And I'm not staying. I'll be gone by Christmas."

Emily took her fingers and stroked Gracie's forehead like she used to do when we were little. "I hate that you're moving so far away."

The tears arrived like mythical creatures, protecting the gates of pain and sorrow. The three of us curled up in the bedroom we'd shared as children. We were weeping for lost lovers, husbands, parents, and lives.

"I must be sober now," I said, arms wrapped around them,

hugging my sisters with every ounce of strength I had left in my body. "Otherwise, I'd kick you both out of this bed."

We laughed—all three of us. It was a night for the ages, but we grew apart again. Or perhaps I couldn't stop being that girl who couldn't let go—not of Lenny, the house on Pelham Road, or the dreams I once had that would never come true.

EPILOGUE

◆

ROBERTA

1989

It was a struggle, but Aunt Alice pulled it off.

She finished her book thirty years ago, in 1959. When she was done, she threw a party on Pelham Road. Everyone was there: Marvel, Holden, Gracie from California (she'd moved there with her new husband), my mother, Emily, and my father, Robert. They remarried in 1947, right after I had my first child (I had four children, two boys and two girls). I married in 1946. My husband was a civil rights lawyer, Duncan Stovall, a fine man, the best husband I could ever hope for.

Back to the party, however. Neighbors came, too, and some of Aunt Alice's friends. And yes, she had friends. Other writers, with names like Langston, Jessie, and Nella. She joined a group called the Harlem Writers Guild in 1950 and the Negro Theater Ensemble, too. Although I know she never planned on becoming an actress. It was the writing that she loved.

However, you won't find her memoir in bookstores, libraries, or anywhere you might expect to see a copy of *The Trial of Mrs. Rhinelander*. That's what she called it, but she didn't publish it. She wrote it for herself, she said. She needed to remember all that happened. But mostly, she needed to heal, to cast the hurt and hate from her heart.

And she did that.

After that book was done and put under her bed, she went back to school and learned to type and take dictation. Then, she took cosmetology classes and got a job at Saks Fifth Avenue. When we first reacquainted ourselves in 1940, she'd told me about her dream of working in a department store.

I thought she'd forgotten about that dream.

In addition to Saks, she worked at Macy's and Lord & Taylor until she retired at seventy. She could've kept working. She was always a beauty and took care of herself. She still had a gin and tonic every day, but she stopped smoking in 1968.

My mother died in 1975, and my father died in 1980. Aunt Gracie wrote and said she'd try and make the funeral, but she was up there in age, too. Besides, it was a long trip from California, and she refused to fly. Aunt Alice and I would take care of things and do them as my mother wanted.

My family and Aunt Alice were close. She was a second grandmother to my children, and she loved my husband. She said he reminded her of someone.

I never asked who. I guess I didn't want to risk it.

On a blisteringly chilly day in late December, I walk through the cemetery on the path toward her grave. The wind howls over the Long Island Sound, throwing tiny sand pebbles against my heavy wool coat.

I stop by once a week since she passed. It had taken a year for her to meet her maker, and I decided to spend one more year checking in on her.

As I stroll toward her grave, I notice my reflection on a slab of shiny marble, a monument of some sort, and I pause. Who is that woman? She's not the same young girl, anxious to become the next Marvel Cunningham in the newspaper business. She can't be. But she is. I am seventy years old and have done everything I intended (check the list of reporters for the Associated Press).

Seventy. When did that happen? It makes me wonder what Aunt Alice thought on her last birthday.

In the 1920s, newspapers were gods, and Aunt Alice was God's most famous sinner—more demonized than Leopold and Loeb and more scandalous than the Scopes Monkey Trial.

Notoriety was like a noose around her throat. But her heart led her. Right or wrong, wisely, or not.

But now, Aunt Alice has what she dreamed of, fought for, changed for, and held on to no matter how difficult, how painful, or what else she had to give up to have it carved into her tombstone.

I lean forward, striving for a closer look at the headstone. It had arrived today. My Aunt Alice was a pistol. A bull in a china shop—tearing the world apart to get what she wanted.

Alice J. Rhinelander
July 19, 1899
September 13, 1989

She's giving Lenny Rhinelander a last little kick in the backside. "Way to go, Aunt Alice."

No matter what she was called or what she called herself—colored, Negro, white, rich or poor, Alice Jones or Mrs. Leonard "Kip" Rhinelander—none of that matters now.

Or am I wrong?

Perhaps I am.

For my aunt Alice, I truly believe every moment mattered.

AUTHOR'S NOTE

It has been a journey diving into the life and times of Alice Beatrice Jones or Mrs. Leonard "Kip" Rhinelander—one I have enjoyed tremendously. She was an intriguing woman who lived during a time when tolerance for differences, cultural, economic, or skin color, to name a few, weren't tolerated, weren't accepted, and in some states were illegal.

But one thing about the Rhinelander versus Rhinelander annulment hearings is that they were covered, discussed, and dissected in newspapers, law journals, student dissertations, essays, novels, and much more. And believe it or not, sometimes there's almost too much information to be researched—and there lies that rabbit hole novelists mention and warn others to avoid at all costs.

Whether I was successful or not, in terms of rabbit hole avoidance, my research was extensive and even included perusing some of the transcripts from the trial.

But there were also nonfiction books and essays in my stack, some of which included:

Property Rites: The Rhinelander Trial, Passing, and the Protection of Whiteness by Elizabeth M. Smith-Pryor

A Beautiful Lie: Exploring Rhinelander v. Rhinelander as a Formative Lesson on Race, Identity, Marriage, and Family by A. Onwuachi-Willig

Love on Trial: An American Scandal in Black and White by Heidi Ardizzone and Earl Lewis

This Rhinelander annulment proceedings were front-page news from the end of 1924 throughout 1925 and periodically until Leonard "Kip" Rhinelander died in 1936 and then after Commodore Philp Rhinelander died in 1940. And again, within months of his death when his daughter (Adelaide Rhinelander Thomas) went to court to stop paying Alice Jones the annuity.

I read more than five hundred newspaper articles from the following publications:

New York Times

New York Daily News

The Standard-Star (New Rochelle)

The New York Herald Tribune

The Philadelphia Inquirer

The Pittsburgh Post-Gazette

The Washington Post

and the

New York Amsterdam News

One of the pivotal archives I researched was the *Amsterdam News*, the largest Black-owned newspaper in Harlem in the 1920s (still a major newspaper today).

However, the *New Amsterdam News* staff in my novel, *The Trial of Mrs. Rhinelander*, are fictional. No Holden Richards or Marvel Cunningham has ever been employed at the newspaper. However, the character of Marvel was inspired by Marvel Jackson Cooke, a pioneering American journalist, writer, and civil rights activist. She was also the first woman to be hired as a reporter (in 1927) at the *Amsterdam News* in its then forty-year history.

However, Roberta Brooks was Alice Beatrice Jones's niece and the daughter of Emily and Robert Brooks. She was approximately twenty-two in 1940, but I could not find any information about her after a mention in one of the newspapers when she accompanied Alice to a social event.

So her story, as presented in the novel, is fiction. I'd also like to add that the address of 763 Pelham Road was published in numerous news articles. Additionally, so were the various lawyers for Alice Beatrice Jones and Leonard "Kip" Rhinelander. I did take some licenses with other names, such as Alice's nickname for her husband and her sister, Grace. I preferred Gracie.

Alice was born in 1899, but on her headstone the birth year is wrong. I corrected it in the novel.

Also, Smalls Paradise was a nightclub in Harlem that opened in 1925. I mention it as having opened as early as 1921.

ACKNOWLEDGMENTS

I am thrilled and thankful to have had the opportunity to write this novel about such a dynamic trial and the two people who embodied it, but mostly, I told the story of Alice Beatrice Jones. And for that chance, I would be remiss if I didn't begin by mentioning where the idea to write her story originated for me—that editor was Esi Sogah, my editor who was formerly at Kensington. She put the bug in my ear about the *Rhinelander* vs. *Rhinelander* case when I met with her in 2019.

But now, I must thank my current editor, Wendy McCurdy. Thank you so very much for your patience and guidance. This story took some doing, and you were there to help ensure it got done. Also, a big thank-you to Elizabeth Trout, editorial assistant. A special thank-you to Kensington's publicity and marketing team: Michelle Addo, my publicist, Vida Engstrand, and her entire marketing team. I'd also like to thank Felicia Murrell for her editorial support.

As I often say, it is no joke that it takes a village to get a book written, and I need an entire town of villages. So let me acknowledge those who have helped make this book happen by being there!

And they are Nina Crespo, my go-to brainstorming queen. They are always ready to help with an expert eye, Deborah Evans and her friend, Veronica Forand—also, Nalini Akolekar.

Also, my do-or-die women are Vanessa Riley and Nancy Johnson.

Finally, I'd like to thank my dearest friend, Sharon Shackelford Campbell, who passed away in November 2023. She is every best friend or most beloved sister in every novel I've written or will ever write. She was always the girl who loved better, forgave quickest, and never criticized, but she was always there.

Don't miss these other captivating historical fiction
novels from Denny S. Bryce . . .

WILD WOMEN AND THE BLUES

*In a stirring and impeccably researched novel of
Jazz Age Chicago in all its vibrant life, two stories
intertwine nearly a hundred years apart, as a chorus
girl and a film student deal with loss, forgiveness,
and love . . . in all its joy, sadness, and imperfections.*

1925: Chicago is the jazz capital of the world, and the Dreamland
Café is the ritziest black-and-tan club in town. Honoree Dalcour
is a sharecropper's daughter, willing to work hard and dance
every night on her way to the top. Dreamland offers a path to
the good life, socializing with celebrities like Louis Armstrong
and filmmaker Oscar Micheaux. But Chicago is also awash in
bootleg whiskey, gambling, and gangsters. And a young woman
driven by ambition might risk more than she can stand to lose.

2015: Film student Sawyer Hayes arrives at the bedside of
110-year-old Honoree Dalcour, still reeling from a devastating
loss that has taken him right to the brink. Sawyer has rested
all his hope on this frail but formidable woman, the only
living link to the legendary Oscar Micheaux. If he's right—if
she can fill in the blanks in his research, perhaps he can
complete his thesis and begin a new chapter in his life. But
the links Honoree makes are not ones he's expecting. . . .

Piece by piece, Honoree reveals her past and her secrets,
while Sawyer fights tooth and nail to keep his. It's a story of
courage and ambition, hot jazz and ˙illicit passions. And as
past meets present, for Honoree, it's a final chance to be truly
heard and seen before it's too late. No matter the cost. . . .

**Available from Kensington Publishing Corp.
wherever books are sold.**

IN THE FACE OF THE SUN

In this haunting novel, the author of *Wild Women and the Blues* weaves together two stories as they unfold decades apart, as a woman on the run from an abusive husband joins her intrepid aunt as they head across the country from Chicago to Los Angeles and confront a painful and shadowy past that has reverberated across generations.

1928, Los Angeles: The newly built Hotel Somerville is *the* hotspot for the city's glittering African American elite. It embodies prosperity and dreams of equality for all—especially Daisy Washington. An up-and-coming journalist, Daisy anonymously chronicles fierce activism and behind-the-scenes Hollywood scandals in order to save her family from poverty. But power in the City of Angels is also fueled by racism, greed, and betrayal. And even the most determined young woman can play too many secrets too far. . . .

1968, Chicago: For Frankie Saunders, fleeing across America is her only escape from an abusive husband. But her rescuer is her reckless, profane Aunt Daisy, still reeling from her own shattered past. Frankie doesn't want to know what her aunt is up to so long as Daisy can get her to LA—and safety. But Frankie finds there's no hiding from long-held secrets—or her own surprising strength.

Daisy will do whatever it takes to settle old scores and resolve the past—no matter the damage. And Frankie will come up against hard choices in the face of unexpected passion. Both must come to grips with what they need, what they've left behind—and all that lies ahead. . . .

**Available from Kensington Publishing Corp.
wherever books are sold.**

Visit our website at
KensingtonBooks.com
to sign up for our newsletters, read
more from your favorite authors, see
books by series, view reading group
guides, and more!

Become a Part of Our
Between the Chapters Book Club
Community and Join the Conversation

Submit your book review for a chance to win exclusive
Between the Chapters swag you can't get anywhere else!
https://www.kensingtonbooks.com/pages/review/